One Night In
Amsterdam

A Novel by

Nadia C. Kavanagh

ONE NIGHT IN AMSTERDAM

Try to be a rainbow in someone's cloud.

Maya Angelou

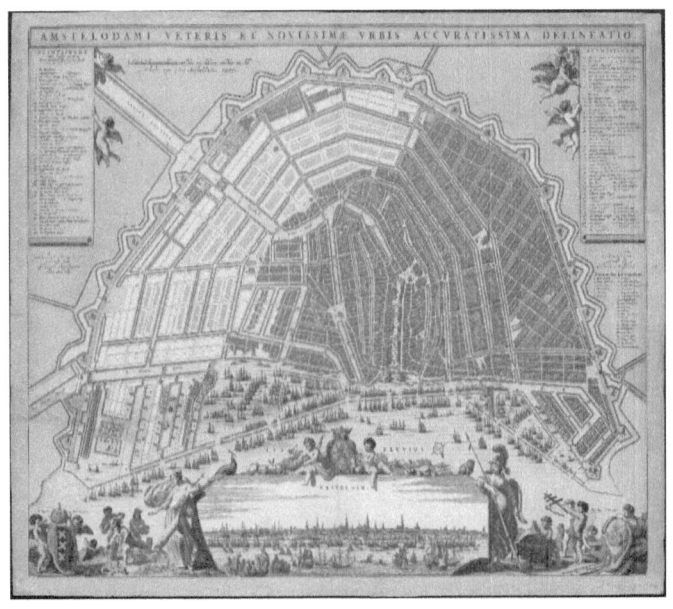

Amsterdam in 1662

TABLE OF CONTENTS

CHAPTER 1
EMMA

I glanced at the unusual sign our tour guide was pointing at for a second. The eccentric and kinky name 'Condomerie' etched in crooked capital letters was visible even far away. The triangle shaped, yellow sign hanging above the door swayed back and forth with the light breeze but I managed to read the words 'Het Gulden Vries' written underneath it. It was referring to the 'Golden Fleece of a winged Ram' in Greek mythology. Why in the world a condom store would reference Greek mythology on its sign, I had no idea but I didn't dare to ask.

Strangely, 'Condomerie' didn't look much different than other shops located in the highly touristic area of the city. In place of the succulent confectionaries embellishing the displays of a patisserie or mouthwatering truffles in a chocolaterie, the display behind the tall windows of 'Condomerie' were colorful condoms. They were all blown up like balloons in different sizes, strung out in multiple rows, and hung down with clothespins.

Sydney pulled my arm impatiently to cross the narrow, stone-paved street to check out the various designs up close. She was giggling and teasing me incessantly as I stood stubbornly. I threw a furious, disapproving look at Sydney and wondered again what I was doing in the most impudent area of the sin capital of the world, 'Amsterdam' with a group of brazen college kids.

"You need to check this out," Sydney uttered too enthusiastically.

'No!" I said and shook my head, glaring at her.

"Come on Ems… you promised. We were going to do this together," she tried to cajole me this time.

"Hell, no, Syd! I am not interested in a condom shop. That's not what I agreed." I said but she didn't care for my demur.

"Not just a condom shop Emma, it is Condomerie! Where else can you get customized condoms with different designs of the world?" she said, and crossed the street without waiting for me. "We are in Amsterdam. Loosen up a little, Miss Uptight!" She hollered across the street.

I ignored her and our loud group, hoping that they would stop bothering me as I checked my emails and messages. However, only a minute later, Sydney yelled again. "You've got to see this Emma.

There is a condom shaped like the Eiffel Tower, and another like the Statue of Liberty," she chuckled. "Oh my God, these are so hilarious."

To be honest, she made me curious when she mentioned the Statue of Liberty design. I wondered how the symbol of my city became a condom design but I wasn't going to let my curiosity surpass my rationality. I was soon to be a doctor. A year away from getting my residency. All I wanted was a relaxing vacation for a couple of days. Wandering around the Red Light District with Sydney and checking out condom designs did not fall under my definition of relaxation.

I was still mad at her for making me come to Amsterdam. I regretted telling her about my need for a vacation- it was supposed to be a short getaway to relax and recoup before my summer internship started at the clinic. My plan to go to Europe was meant for Bruges - the medieval picturesque city with pretty canals and houses that made the city look like a fairytale town. I wanted to visit the cathedrals and museums and of course indulge in most delicious chocolates and truffles in the world. As soon as I shared my plan, Sydney protested immediately, "Bruges… are you kidding me? How old are you? Fifty!" She said disapprovingly.

"Why do you say that?" I asked.

"Because, Bruges is a boring, old town. Only old people go there."

"I disagree. I've been to Bruges before. It happens to be a beautiful, quiet town, not boring at all."

"You said it… it is a quiet town! Again, it is for old people."

"Syd! I like quiet towns. They are relaxing and soothing. I also enjoy the canals and the architecture there."

"Well, if you want to see canals, great architecture and museums, I have another city in mind which is not so boring. I am sure you will love it there too."

A week after our short, instantaneous discussion, all thanks to my crazy cousin and best friend 'Sydney' and her fast planning, I found myself in Amsterdam. Shortly after our arrival, she convinced me to take a tour given by our eccentric, purple-haired tour guide.

We met in front of the national monument at Dam Square at noon with a group of college kids and since then Sydney was eagerly following our guide, while I was constantly falling behind. My lack of enthusiasm was palpable. Sydney, on the other hand, was having a blast. I could hear her boisterous laughs every time the purple-haired girl cracked another sex joke. According to our somewhat lunatic tour guide, we were getting the PG-13 version of the tour. She saved her unabridged, rated R version for the evening tour. Still, her brazen jokes were making me uncomfortable. I wanted to go back to my hotel and read the papers for the upcoming seminar. However, I knew there was no way to sneak out without getting noticed by Sydney. I decided to suck it up for a bit longer.

Before long, our tour guide, now holding a yellow umbrella in her hand, instructed our group to move along for the next stop. Of course, Sydney used the perfect opportunity to make me stop in front of the infamous store, and took a picture of me with the condoms in the background instantly.

"Say cheese!" she said with a priggish smile.

"Whatever, Sydney! You are acting like a ten year old." I grimaced, hoping the Red Light District part of the tour would soon be over but unfortunately, we had just started and had three more hours to go. Wishing the rest would be less embarrassing, I realized sadly that it was getting worse because our next stop was a BDSM store.

"Come on, Emma." She pulled me again to check out the store. "Ease up a little bit and let go. What's wrong with enjoying life a little?" She smiled mischievously, trying to soften me up. "You should try it, at least while we are in Amsterdam," she winked. It was her usual advice: Enjoy yourself! Get drunk! Have some fun with a hot guy! Have a one-night-stand! Oh, no! I didn't want to consider the possibility of that in a city like Amsterdam.

"I agreed to join you, didn't I? I am still by your side in the infamous 'De Wallen', and I have to say, I have not seen anything I've enjoyed so far, just so you know!"

I wanted to remind her about our agreement earlier before she got more out of control. I still wanted to visit Anne Frank's house and a few museums. Instead of enjoying famous masterpieces by Van Gogh or Rembrandt, I was in the Red Light District, passing in front of glass doors where sexy ladies dressed in provocative lingerie waved and blew kisses.

After a couple more blocks, our group stopped at an 800 year old church 'Oude Kerk', standing tall and impressive, and I was utterly surprised. Usually in normal cities, religious places are not located next to brothels or cannabis coffee shops, but apparently

Amsterdam wasn't a city like any other. Brothels and churches are located side by side in this unique city. Our tour guide explained how the church and clergy conveniently got rich, thanks to the sinners who felt bad for visiting brothels after returning from their long overseas journeys. I understood that everything in Amsterdam was about money, even religion. Back in the day, feeling guilty for their sins, sailors hoped that their generous contributions to the church and paid confessionals would grant them forgiveness. I felt sorry for those poor souls with guilty consciences, robbed of their money! Sex! Sin! Religion! It was certainly a lucrative business in Amsterdam.

Our tour guide continued to talk enthusiastically as we passed more glass doors rented by prostitutes who were considered independent business owners and paid a good amount of taxes. How great, I thought! The city of Amsterdam found a way to legalize everything people did anyway and made good money. Dutch people were awkward but definitely smart.

Next, at an open area surrounded by glass doors, our purple-haired guide started to explain the basic services the prostitutes provided and the base rate for a private fifteen minutes behind the doors, as if she was talking about a fifteen minute pedicure service. Thanks to her detailed explanations, I learned more about the sex trade in Amsterdam than I ever wanted to know. As she started talking about kinky details, I decided that I could not stand it anymore. I left the group and walked towards the church's courtyard to sit by a tree and wait for Sydney.

I was sitting idly and getting bored. I noticed multiple rooms with closed curtains and lit red lights. It meant the girls were busy performing the oldest profession in the world. I didn't want to think about the things going on behind those curtains but a part of me was curious – our guide told us that some of these girls made 30,000 Euros a month, averaging up to 300 Euros an hour. I was staring blankly at the window and calculating how many hours she had to work to make that kind of money in my mind when a tall guy with stylish jet black hair, broad shoulders and well-built physique came out of the door. He was ruggedly handsome, dressed in complete black: trousers, shirt, and shoes. He looked like he was in his twenties, however the Armani logo on his shirt told me he wasn't a college student backpacking across Europe. He was different. He oozed confidence, money and something else that I didn't want to think about.

When he caught me staring at him, he took his Raybans off, narrowed his sky blue eyes and studied me for a long minute. His eyes pulled me in for some unknown reason. I was having hard time breaking eye contact with him. He walked slowly towards the church and suddenly stopped. His gaze was unfettered and feral. His eyes trailed down my body and up again to my face. He approached me further and then abruptly sat next to me.

"Do I know you from somewhere?" He asked nonchalantly as if he hadn't just come out of a brothel. He moved my backpack aside and scooted over. He crossed his arms and looked deeply into my eyes. The contours of his muscles and a part of his tattoo were visible underneath his shirt.

I felt compelled under his gaze and couldn't utter a word. My face was on fire. I blushed inevitably and felt frustrated about his effect on me. "I don't think I know or want to know anyone coming out of that door," I said harshly, pointing at the now open glass door and the blonde girl waving in her next customer. I wanted him to go away and leave me alone so I could go back to feeling normal again.

He followed my gaze slowly and smiled warmly, showing no intentions of leaving. "You don't mince words, do you? Are you always this frank?" He asked, raising his eyebrow.

His proximity made me feel edgy, my breathing got faster. I sipped my water and took a deep breath. "Yes, generally I am!" I replied without looking at his piercing blue eyes.

"If these rooms bother you that much, what are you doing in the Red Light District?"

"I didn't say they bother me."

"You have a look on your face tells me that they do."

"I think you are saying that because you got caught."

"I don't care if I got caught. But I think you do. Why else would you be all red and upset?"

"Because, it is so damn hot." I replied tersely. I wasn't upset. I didn't like being around brothels, but that wasn't the reason of my disquietude. His closeness and boldness bothered me more than anything else, but of course I wasn't going to admit that to him. "I don't like the sex trade."

"Well, I don't like it either."

"Then, what the hell were you doing in there?" I asked. I was curious now.

He smiled beguilingly, "You wouldn't believe me, even if I told you."

"Why don't you give it a try?" I asked sarcastically.

"It looks ... you know how it looks, but I wasn't in there doing what you think." He paused, waiting to see my reaction.

"Go ahead! Share, by all means!"

"Okay. Well... you see that guy standing there, quite handsome..."

The guy he was pointing at was nothing compared to him. Yes, he would be considered good-looking by Sydney's standard: tall, blonde, well-built but he wasn't my type. To me, the handsome and charming one was him, staring intently at me and obviously, he knew it too.

"Yes, I see him." I said coyly, and agreed to play his game. At least for now.

"He is my best friend. We've known each other for ever and we do everything together. Unfortunately, sometimes he can be a bit too much. He parties like crazy and forces me to join him. Anyway, yesterday, he came back to the hotel and talked all night about this one girl behind that door. He insisted that I should meet her and experience her magic too."

"Uh-huh ... stop now! What makes you think I'll listen to your sexual fantasies?" I got up slowly and moved towards our group.

"No, no wait. It's not like that," he objected and followed me.

"Not like what ..."

"Well, yes, I admit I went in there to do you know what. Max convinced me to try it. We're in Amsterdam. You know... nothing is off limits. I got inside and everything looked so disgusting. I thought about all the other men in there before me, and suddenly I got grossed out. So, I didn't do it."

"How honorable of you!" I taunted him, fake clapping my hands. "What did you do in there for ten minutes then?" I asked.

"How do you know I was in there for ten minutes?" he smirked. "Were you watching me?"

I sighed deeply. I should have known this would be coming before I asked. He was too presumptuous. His conceit was not earning him any points with me. *But then why did I bother talking to this guy?*

"Of course not! Don't flatter yourself," I replied. "I didn't even notice you until you came over and sat next to me."

"Oh, then you weren't staring at me. You were looking at ..." He glanced around to find something interesting. He pointed at an old building, now turned into a cannabis coffee shop with 'Hi-life Coffee House' sign. "At that?"

"You know what…you are an arrogant son of a bitch! You are too presumptuous. Too full of yourself." I chided him. "I was bored and just looking around. I noticed that those doors were closed for a while. I assumed it was ten minutes, maybe it was less."

"Hey, I'm sorry. I was just teasing. I didn't mean to offend you," he responded with a modest grin. He sounded sincere. "I paid the girl up front, then I thought that if I am not getting what she offered, it wouldn't hurt to sit down and talk until my time is up."

"Really! You stayed because you didn't want your money to go to waste," I shook my head showing my obvious disbelief. "Then, what did you talk about?" I asked brusquely, glaring into his eyes and waiting for another smart-ass answer.   He fidgeted as if he was uncomfortable. Or somehow my snide remarks were finally getting to him.

"We talked about life in general. She has a son. She is doing what she is doing to make a living, like many others here. There is no need to be contemptuous or condescending towards them."

"I am not being condescending. There are other ways to make a living, but, anyways! So, what else did she tell you?" I questioned him further, then, I wondered inwardly… *Why was I still asking him questions? Did I not want this conversation to end?*

"She told me how much she made in general and what she did with her money. I work in investment business. I asked if she was investing her money wisely, so she could quit working before she got old."

"I could have told you that. Thanks to our tour guide over there, I learned more about Amsterdam's sex trade than I ever wanted to know."

"Ah-ha, is that why you are here? Taking a tour of the famous 'De Wallen'?" He asked. "I wondered what a girl like you was doing in the Red Light District." There was a hint of bewilderment in his voice.

"My crazy friend, who also happens to be my cousin, forced me to come to Amsterdam and take this tour with her. I couldn't say no."

"Actually it's great that you are here. Amsterdam is a beautiful city. You won't be disappointed."

"I'm not so sure about that. You don't know Sydney. God knows what other crazy things she's planned for us."

"I'd like to meet her." He said abruptly.

"Sydney? Why?" I asked.

"Because…" He paused. His intense eyes pierced through me. "I'd like to thank her for convincing you to come. Otherwise, how would I have met such an attractive and beautiful girl like you?" He grinned mischievously.

"Aside from being presumptuous, are you always this flirtatious?" I asked, but couldn't hide my smile.

"No I am not. I don't flirt. Usually, it's the other way around. Girls flirt with me. You are a very intriguing exception."

"I'm glad to be an exception." I shook my head still smiling and got up. "Well, it was nice talking to you, but my tour is leaving and I need to go now." I said curtly.

"Oh, come on. You cannot get rid of me that easily." He frowned and studied me for several long seconds while thinking. "I wonder if I could join your tour as well."

I hesitated to answer. Something about him made me perplexed. Part of me wanted him to leave but the other part wanted him to join us. He sounded like an interesting person and my gut told me that he was honest. He would be a better companion than the raucous college kids, that's for sure. "I don't see why not. It is a free tour. You've got to tip the guide at the end. I think the more the merrier for her." I finally answered.

"Awesome!" He exclaimed happily. I couldn't suppress my chuckle over his childish reaction. He was indeed sweet when he wasn't so arrogant.

"Since we are going to be together for a while, would you mind telling me your name?" He asked.

"I'm Emma." I said.

"It's really nice to meet you Emma. I am Dylan." He replied with a broad smile.

CHAPTER 2
DYLAN

I waved at Max, hollered and then whistled through my fingers, yet he still didn't hear me. He was only up for a couple of hours but he was already rolling his third cigarette of the day. It frustrated me that all he wanted from this trip was to party and get high. I was so mad at him that I thought about leaving his miserable ass there to let him figure out his way back to hotel alone. Then, out of the blue, I heard Mrs. Donavon's voice echoing in my head. "Take care of him Dylan. You are the only one he listens to. Don't let him do anything too stupid," she said. Well, that was some wishful thinking Mrs. Donavon had. I could only look after him so much. In the end, Max did whatever he wanted. Even I couldn't stop him.

Maximilian Donavon and I were inseparable friends... for what felt like forever. The only heir of the billion dollar corporation, Max was the richest man under thirty in Manhattan. His net worth was estimated to be more than one billion dollars, increasing more every day. How did it feel to be the best friend and the business partner of the wealthiest, bad-ass bachelor in Manhattan? It was cool, but it also sucked. He was the classic definition of a bad friend. He was errant and irresponsible. Like any typical spoiled rich kid with a lot of money, he didn't care much about anything, neither the rules nor the people around him. Despite his infamous notoriety, I knew Max was more than what people thought of him. He had a tough childhood and bad teenage years. I was the only one he trusted and didn't push out of his life. There had been times when I was tired of him but regardless of his problems and troubles, he was still my best friend. He stood up for me when I needed it the most. I trusted Max with my life and he trusted me. I knew I had to take care of him.

"Will you wait here for me a minute?" I asked Emma. "I need to go and get Max." I explained. Emma's eyebrows went up and her face turned into a frown. Obviously she didn't like the idea of Max joining us too. Maybe I shouldn't have told her about him earlier but it was impossible to resist her judging eyes. They made me obliged to tell her the truth, at least some of it.

Honestly, I was exasperated and furious with Max for making me smoke that cigarette and go in there after him. He enticed me to do some reckless stuff before, but this last one was too much. Whatever weed he rolled this morning for us made me delusional. I was totally out of it when the girl unzipped my pants. Then suddenly, things became clear, and I felt nauseated. I stopped and told her I didn't want it. She didn't understand me at first and thought I wanted my money back. I assured her that she could keep the money. I just wanted to stay there, and do nothing. I wasn't feeling good. Either I was going to vomit on the street or shake it off in there. Luckily, she was nice and understanding. While I held my head between my hands to stop the world from spinning, she tried to help me. She gave me some water, wiped my face, and then we talked. I didn't know how long I stayed in that room. I was doing okay, until I got out of there and saw those two green eyes on me. They were intimidating. Judging. They spoke the unspoken words, accusing me furtively. I wanted to escape from her 'I knew what you did in there' looks. However, I stood there completely hypnotized as she continued glaring at me, her eyes gleaming wickedly. I felt as if the air was sucked out of my lungs. It was that intense.

I had to get Max but I didn't want to leave Emma out of my sight, even if it was for a few minutes. I had this uncanny feeling that she was hesitating about her decision. I didn't want her to change her mind while I was trying to find my idiot friend. In a hurry, I grabbed Emma's backpack off the ground and put it on my shoulder. I wasn't trying to act chivalrously. It was more for me than her. I just wanted to make sure she didn't leave without me. "It won't take long, I promise." I said and left in a hurry to find Max.

Since the instant our eyes met, I couldn't stop looking at her. I took in her immaculate beauty, the curves of her body, her auburn hair and her milky white skin. She was innocently attractive; making me question how someone could look so innocent and attractive at the same time, but she was. Her green sundress tied around her neck left her skin bare in the back and on the shoulders. It also deepened the color of her green eyes, framed by full, long eyelashes. While we were talking, sitting side by side, our arms so close, almost brushing against each other, I imagined myself touching her soft skin and tracing my fingers starting from her nape down to the small of her back. With every breeze, jasmine and vanilla scent effused the air. It was impossible not be affected by her beauty, elevated even more so by her heavenly scent. Although I felt intimated by her intense gaze, blocked by her long wavy hair every now and then, I wanted to swirl my fingers around a strand and tuck it behind her ear. *God, she was so beautiful.*

Emma was completely different than the girls I'd met before. Probably because she didn't know who I was but I had a feeling even if she knew, it wouldn't have changed her attitude. She was blunt. She spoke her mind and didn't hold back. I didn't mind that. Strangely, I didn't want her to speak like the girls I hooked up with before: the vapid ones who buttered me up all the time or the slutty ones who sucked up to me just to spend a night with the most eligible and famous bachelors of Manhattan: Dylan and Max. *Oh, how I hated those girls.* Emma, she was just the opposite. I enjoyed her frankness, especially no-bullshit answers and curt replies. Her disparate style was so unique that I was determined to get to know her more.

I found Max just around the corner, and of course he was about to go into another coffee shop to get more weed.

"Hey man, I signed us up for a tour. Come on, we're leaving!" I explained quickly.

"Tour? I am not going on a tour. It's hot out there. I'd like to stay inside," replied Max.

"Well, too bad, because I am going. You can either come with me and enjoy more than the cannabis shops and brothels, or stay here and get high until you puke your guts out. Your choice!" I scolded him. "But, so you know, I won't be here to save your ass if you are in trouble."

"What the hell, Dylan. What's gotten into you?" He asked. "You were perfectly fine this morning."

"Well, it was before you made me smoke that shit. Oh, by the way…never do that again. You understand me! It wasn't like what we smoked back home, it was something else. It made me sick and delusional. Now, you have two choices. Stay or come with me. What will it be Max?"

"Fine, I am coming."

"Hurry up then. They are waiting for us."

"They! Who are they?" He asked and paused, looking confused. "Since when are you carrying a backpack?"

"It's not mine. It's Emma's and she's waiting for us. Come on now."

"Oh, it all makes sense now. We're becoming boring tourists because my dear friend wants to bang a girl with a backpack."

"Just shut up Max, and let's go."

When we got closer to the church, I saw Emma anxiously waiting and talking to her friend. I wondered what they were talking so passionately about. I could see Emma's eyebrows furrowing and her body getting tense. She pursed her lips. I wanted to kiss those lips so badly. Her indignation and furious expression were somehow turning me on. *What the hell was wrong with me? Why was I fantasizing about this girl I just met?*

I picked up the pace when I saw that the group was about to leave. Max grunted but followed me. I was sure Emma was pissed at me since we were late.

"Here we are!" I said cheerfully when we reached them. "We are ready to go."

The tall blonde girl standing next to Emma smiled, "Oh, wow! So, you are the hot guy who took Emma's backpack and disappeared," she uttered and burst into a big laughter. Emma rolled her eyes and shook her head. *Was she blushing?*

After hearing the hot guy comment, I couldn't help but smile broadly. I figured out that Emma told her cousin, Sydney about me while I was gone looking for Max and I wondered if she told her that I was hot. Since Emma was avoiding making eye contact with me, I guessed that she did.

"Yes! That's me. Sorry about being late." I apologized quickly. "I'm Dylan, and this is my friend Max."

"Nice to meet you, Dylan and Max… I am Sydney," she said. Emma was still quiet. She was now studying Max intently. I was glad that I wasn't at the receiving end of those withering eyes.

"So, how do we do this?" I asked trying to break the cold air.

"We follow the purple-haired girl with the umbrella. She is hard to miss. If you can't see her, just follow the loud college kids," Sydney explained quickly.

I really didn't care where the tour guide was taking us. All I wanted was to spend more time with Emma. Wherever she wanted to go was fine with me. I followed the group next to Emma in the back. When we finally got out of 'de Wallen' and had left the red lights and the sinful rooms behind, I saw big relief in her eyes. We were now walking on the outer layers of the city, famous for its series of concentric and bisecting canals. Canals out here were wider and streets were cleaner. Within less than a mile, the entire atmosphere had changed. Paved streets were no longer full of cannabis shops or glass doors. Instead there were museums, art galleries and cafés where people just ordered coffee, not weed.

We stopped in front of the Royal Palace and our guide asked us to squeeze closer to hear her better. I actually didn't care for all the tourist crap she was about to share. I couldn't concentrate on anything anyway when Emma was standing in front me, so close, within my reach. With every breath, her alluring scent filled my nose. I wanted to grab her thin waist, wrap her in my arms and rest her head on my chest, though I didn't dare to try. I was concerned that I would scare her away without getting a chance to know her. Instead, I just watched Emma, as our guide continued to talk about the history of the Netherlands. I didn't give a damn about their recently crowned king, his beautiful queen and all that information about how the Orange family ruled Netherlands for years. While Emma attentively listened the stories about Dutch history, all I could think about was how to find a way to hold her in my arms, touch her soft skin and make it look like an accident. *God… When did I become so desperate?*

After five minutes of torture, I uncrossed my arms, tucked my hands in my pockets and fought every urge not to get closer to Emma… I finally gave up. I slowly raised my hand, and with the tip of my index finger, I slowly caressed her arm. At first, she cringed but she didn't move away. Encouraged by her lack of demur, I slowly clasped my hand to hers.

Suddenly, she turned her head back. I was waiting for her to reprimand me or make a smart-ass remark for my bold action, however she did neither. She looked at me sweetly and continued holding my hand. Then, she stepped back a little and rested her head on my shoulder. Her soft, silk hair smelled like jasmine and vanilla was right by my face. *Oh, my god, she smelt like heaven.* Her complacent reaction had completely taken me by surprise. Now I wanted our chatty tour guide to talk more, so we could stay like that a bit longer. I felt like a teenager who just stole a kiss from the hottest girl in school. Unfortunately, purple-hair girl raised her umbrella up in the air and told everyone that we were moving on the next spot.

"What do you think about Louis Bonaparte? I guess he wasn't as bad as his brother?" Emma asked as we walked. I was disappointed that she dropped my hand when we started walking… *'Goddamnit. Come to your senses'*, I scolded myself inwardly.

"What? Who is Louis Bonaparte?" I asked absentmindedly. I was startled by her question.

"Napoleon's brother. You know…the one who became the King of Holland. Didn't you listen?"

I wanted to admit to her that I didn't. I was busy imagining things while she leaned on my shoulder. Like kissing her senselessly, moving my lips from her ear to her neck. I daydreamed about claiming every inch of her delicate body with my lips. The thought of Emma in my arms and her heat passing to my skin were giving me goose bumps.

I pushed my wayward thoughts away. "Sorry, I guess I wasn't paying attention."

"Well, she explained that Dutch people didn't have last names until Louis Bonaparte forced them to have them sometime in 1800's."

"Having last names, I guess it is a move in the right direction. Good job, brother Bonaparte!" I shrugged.

"But wait till you hear the last names the Dutch picked to piss off the King."

"What? Something funny?"

"Oh, Yeah! Naaktgeboren for nakedborn, piest for pissed, and the best one is, of course, bigballs. Some of these last names even survived to this day. Can you image having the last name bigballs?"

"Seriously? That's damn funny."

"Dylan Bigballs…that could be a good name for you." She teased me.

"Well that wouldn't be a lie…" I chuckled and made a mental note…*Emma was funny and she liked jokes.* "Speaking of last names, what is yours?"

"I won't tell a guy I met …hmm," she checked her watch, "about an hour ago, my last name."

"Why not? It's not like I am asking for your social security number. I am not a criminal, I promise. I won't hack into your personal information."

"I think it's better if we stay as Emma and Dylan." She insisted.

I shook my head with an incredulous grin. I wondered if she was always this reserved, or was she doing this purposefully to make me more curious. "Fine! How about you tell me where you are from then."

"The States…" she grinned playfully.

"Obviously! But where from in the States?"

"Are you always this inquisitive, Dylan?

"Are you always this difficult, Emma?"

"Why can't we just be two Americans who met in Amsterdam and went on a tour together?" She asked nonchalantly.

"Alright, fine! No last names, no states! What else can't we talk about?"

"What we do or where we work …Although, I kinda know that you work in investments."

"I don't mind telling you where I work. I work at …"

"No-No-No! Don't tell me any of that. Let's not talk about our lives in the States or the things we do every day. Instead let's talk about things we like to do, things that we enjoy. "

"You are certainly one-of-a-kind Ms. Emma."

"I hope you mean that in a good way Mr. Dylan," she smirked.

I crossed my arms over my chest and smiled showing that I meant it in a very good way. She was definitely something else. I was drawn more to her mysterious charm every passing minute.

After walking a couple more blocks, we stopped at Torensluis, the Widest Bridge, across from the Narrowest House. I tried to concentrate and listen to the guide this time, in case Emma decided to quiz me later on Amsterdam trivia. Fortunately, the information about Amsterdam's canals, bridges and architectures wasn't as boring. Torensluis was the oldest remaining bridge in Amsterdam and also happened to be the widest. The tower's foundations remained intact and the entrance and the barred windows of the tower's dungeon were still visible.

Across from the bridge was the narrowest house in Amsterdam. I'd say in the world as well because it was pretty damn narrow indeed, just three feet wide. Our guide explained the back of the house was bigger but the property taxes in Amsterdam were based on the width of the house overlooking the canals, thus one smart architect built a house in between regular houses and saved a lot of money. I thought I was smart, sparing my investor's money from the government… Hell, no! This city was full of surprises.

We kept walking along streets full of bicycles and crossed a couple more bridges. Amsterdam, the Venice of the north, had more bridges and canals than Venice and they weren't stinky like Venetian canals. I was totally amazed by the beauty of the city.

We took a short break at the famous 'Iamsterdam' sign before heading to our last spot. I was getting hot and tired but I didn't want to stop or complain. Walking under the fervent sun in complete black wasn't a good idea. I certainly didn't dress for the occasion. *'How could I have known that I was going to chase a girl in the streets of Amsterdam when I left my hotel this morning?'* I thought.

Emma probably sensed my discomfort and turned towards me. "You look like you are about to faint, Dylan. I have an extra bottle in my backpack if you need some water." She pointed to the backpack that I was carrying for the last two hours.

"Yeah, that's a good idea." I was able to utter. I could feel the beads of sweat trailing down my neck.

She had an uncertain, ambivalent look in her eyes as if she was examining me for something. She touched my wrist with two fingers and put her index finger over my lips. She shushed me abruptly, waited a bit and checked my heart rate, which probably was off the roof because I was fighting myself not to kiss the tip of her finger, graze my tongue over it and then suck it senselessly. "Your heart rate is too fast, and you are panting. It might be dehydration or something else, I am not sure. Are you feeling okay?"

"I'm fine, thanks. I think it's the sun," I mumbled. I couldn't tell her the truth. My heart was throbbing fast because of her and I was panting because I was still under influence. How could you admit to a good girl like Emma, a girl whom I was so desperate impress that I smoked weed in the morning and got this terrible reaction? Of course, I didn't tell her that. "Water sounds good. I think I am just dehydrated." I said.

"Stay in the shade and drink lots of water." She ordered. "I am going to use the restroom."

I was pouring water on my face and drinking big gulps when she came back just a minute later. She had a funny look on her face.

"Well… I am embarrassed to ask." She said shyly. "But… do you happen to have any change with you? I didn't know they charged for the restroom. Gosh, only in Europe!"

I tried to contain my chuckle. She looked extra cute frustrated. I searched my pocket and pulled out a hand full of change. "Sure, take what you need."

She took a Euro from the pile and smiled. "Thanks. I owe you one."

Our last stop was just across from Anne Frank's house. I studied Emma's face going from still to frown as she listened to the well-known, dolorous story of Anne, and how she wrote her diary. Anne's feelings about her life in hiding and the life outside while listening to the bells of the nearby church during Nazi occupation were more than heartbreaking. I saw streaks of tears on Emma's cheeks as the guide talked. I didn't like seeing Emma like that. She was too quiet and pensive. I wanted to hear sarcastic comments with her mordant wit.

"Come on Emma, it's all in the past. Let's not get all gloomy. Leave all the grief here, and let's go have some beer." Sydney said.

"But I want to go the Anne Frank Museum. You agreed, don't you remember?" she insisted.

"Ems! You're just going to cry more and ruin your day. Why do you want to torture yourself?"

"Life is not always just about having fun, Sydney." She sounded so damn serious. "You need to face the not-so-fun side of life sometimes as well."

"You are impossible to argue with. Why do you always have to turn everything into brutal reality? Can't you just let it go? Just this once? "

"Because you choose to ignore them, doesn't mean the horrible things didn't happen," Emma reprimanded her sternly. "And no, I can't let it go. I prefer to live in reality, not in a dream state like you. What happened to Anne still happens in our world today. Look at ethnic cleansing in Western China, Rwanda, or Syria."

"Oh, God Ems! Please don't start with your 'we need to save the world from horrible dictators' speech. I cannot take it during vacation," Sydney said harshly. I was surprised by her sudden outburst. I wondered how two girls this different from each other were close friends. "Let's go have a drink first, then we'll decide what to do next. Okay?" She tried to soften her.

"The tour is over. I am pretty sure Max and Dylan have other plans," she uttered, insinuating that she didn't want anything else to do with us. The warm smile she had given me when she leaned her head on my shoulder somehow disappeared. I didn't understand the sudden change in her attitude. However, I was still not ready to let her go.

"Actually, we don't have any plans for the rest of the day. We would love to join you. Don't we Max?" I raised my eyebrows signaling Max to back me up.

"An ice cold beer after all that walking sounds great actually," Max agreed, sensing my need for his confirmation.

"I am not in the mood for beer." Emma rejected again.

"Didn't you say 'you owe me one'? How about you buy me a beer and we'll call it even." I teased her, but the look on her face was not promising. Either she didn't want to hang out with us or she was still frustrated with Sydney. I hoped it was the latter.

"Come on Emma! Just one beer." I insisted. I was begging a girl to have a drink with me. That was a first.

After considering it a long minute, she nodded tactfully. "Okay, fine! Just one beer and we are even."

I smiled and immediately started thinking about a plan to make her spend the rest of her day with me.

CHAPTER 3
EMMA

"Where are we going for a drink, then?" I asked impatiently. I just wanted to get this over with. One beer and that would be it. The thought of spending more time with Dylan bothered me, and not because it wasn't pleasant. On the contrary, I enjoyed being around him, maybe a little bit too much. He was kind, congenial and funny. The hours flew by as we walked the cobblestone streets of Amsterdam, talked about various things and laughed. Not just little chuckles here and there, they were big, eye-watering laughs. What started as a little joke turned into a funny discussion of the worst first name and last name combinations. He knew William Tickel, 'will tickle', and Richard Kocke 'dick cock', while I came up with Benjamin Dower, 'bend over'. Thanks to him, I had more fun in the last two hours than I have had in a long time. *Then, what was the problem?*

The problem was, the second his fingers touched my skin in front of the Royal Place, I felt a sudden jolt up my spine, as if a surge had gone through my body. Every nerve, every cell in my body was aware of him. My heart was beating so fast that I was worried he'd hear it. I thought about retrieving my hand and scolding him for inappropriate intimacy at first. My logic was telling me that I shouldn't let a guy I just met get this close to me. Falling for his devilish charm was so unlike me. *Then, why did I let him touch me?* I confessed to myself grudgingly that I was attracted to this arrogant, self-absorbed, but regally handsome guy with a wicked smile. I enjoyed his soft fingers caressing my skin. I savored inhaling his manly scent, leaning on his broad shoulders, drowning in the depth of his eyes where circles of gray surrounded fascinating blue. I hated cigarettes but the mixture of musk, sweat, and tobacco coming from his masculine body that pervaded the air between us was dizzying. It made me take a couple of deep breaths.

After a long, exhausting debate in my head, I assured myself that there was nothing wrong with being attracted to a handsome guy and some innocent flirting. Nonetheless, it was only for a few hours and we were both going our different ways after the tour. I was doing just fine... until Dylan wanted to join us after the tour.

"I checked *tripadvisor*, and there should be a decent pub around the block," Sydney advised happily and tucked her phone with the resplendent cover into her designer backpack. I smiled thinking how everything Sydney owned, even a cell phone, was a fashion statement.

"Alright then, let's go." I mumbled.

We followed Sydney and Max, Dylan was walking leisurely by my side - our hands were close, but not touching. There was that unspoken attraction where we were both aware of each other, but we didn't act on it.

"I'll get the beer," Dylan announced when we entered the pub.

"Wasn't I supposed to buy? You know… to pay my debt."

He narrowed his eyes and grinned slowly, "I've decided to hold on to that a bit longer. It might come in handy again." He said playfully, and walked to the bar to get the drinks without giving me a chance to object.

A minute later, he sat four pint glasses on the table. "I didn't know what you liked, but since we are in the Netherlands, I decided to go with the local beer. Hope you like Grolsch. It is a pale lager."

I shrugged, "I don't even know the difference between ale and lager," I admitted shyly.

"That is some crucial information you are missing out on Emma," he teased.

"Since I am not much of a drinker, I never cared to know, but I have a feeling that you are about to enlighten me."

"Most definitely," he replied with a devilish grin again. "Ales are fermented warm at the top of the tank while lagers are fermented cold in the bottom of the tank. Ales can be brewed quickly, however lagers' brew cycles can be months. I like lagers more. They taste smoother and crisper."

"All yellow beer tastes the same to me but I can understand why some people prefer lagers. Thanks for the info," I said courteously. I didn't want to diminish his petulant enthusiasm for explaining the whole brewing process. "Now that we are clear on beer trivia… Sydney, have you made up your mind yet?"

"Do I have to?"

"Yes!" I snapped.

"Fine! I will join and visit all the boring museums with you, but I have one condition."

"And what is that?"

"I cannot take any more of this sober, uptight Emma. You are full of too much brutal reality. And since you moved out of my apartment, I guess I forgot how big a pain in the ass you could be. I'll go with you, but you need to loosen up a little bit."

"I am who I am, Syd! You can't expect me to act different just because you want me to."

"You can be a bit more relaxed and easy going, Ems. I know how we can make it happen. We are in the perfect place to do it."

"Oh, no! I know what you are thinking and I am not doing it." I shook my head vigorously as Dylan looked at me suspiciously, probably trying to figure out what we were talking about.

"Here is my offer. I am totally against the Anne Frank Museum. I can't do it. Call me shallow or ignorant. I don't care. I can't deal with that kind of sadness during vacation. It's horrifying. However…" She paused to see how I was taking her usual carefree attitude. "If you agree to do four tequila shots in two minutes, I will go to the Rijksmuseum with you. If you cannot do the shots, I vote for Casa Rosso. I've heard that Lady Gaga had been there and it is such a fun place. They have nine different live performances every day and I'd like to see them all."

"You are threatening to take me to a live sex show if I don't drink up. Am I hearing this right?"

"Yes, you heard me right. If you do your shots, I will tolerate the art museum, because at least, when you are tipsy, you won't try to lecture us."

I fumed with anger. If Dylan and Max weren't there, I would have kicked her ass. "Fine, I'll do it!" I exclaimed laconically.

Dylan studied me carefully a long minute. I saw his lips curving up a little, as if he was trying to keep himself from smiling. "Emma, are you sure about this?"

"If this shuts her up and makes her agree to do something more intellectual, something that I also enjoy, yes I am pretty sure." I glared at her. "Sydney?"

"Yes, I will shut up." She smirked and pretended to whisper. "I'm doing you guys a huge favor. Drunk Emma is funny and awesome."

"Whatever!" I snorted, totally annoyed with Sydney.

"Alright, I'll bring the shots. I'll also check if they have anything for you to snack on," Dylan said and sauntered towards the bar. My eyes slipped to his taut muscles beneath his shirt and his lean hips encased in his designer pants as he passed, and our bodies brushed against each other for a fleeting second. A sudden pang of delight suffused my body. *"What was happening to me? Get a grip on yourself Emma,"* I scolded myself inwardly.

I watched him stealthily as he talked to the bartender. Whatever he said to him, in a surreptitious manner, the bartender smirked and then nodded. After what seemed like a long discussion, he brought a small bowl of peanuts and four skinny but tall shot glasses. "Alright, your shots are ready to go," he said. His gaze was dubious for some reason that I couldn't figure out.

I put a couple of peanuts in my mouth and said, "I am ready, let's do it."

I reluctantly reached for the first shot glass and swallowed the whole thing immediately. Awkwardly the tequila didn't taste as strong as I remembered. Instead of burning my throat, it tickled but went down smoothly. Without waiting for long, I took the second one, this one tasted even less like tequila. At that instant, I noticed Dylan's intent gaze on me. He raised his eyebrows, and winked. It was subtle as if he was up to something and didn't want anybody else to notice it. He put his index finger on his lip and smiled.

We listened to Sydney prattle about our college days, her crazy parties and drunken nights as she sipped her beer, anxiously waiting to see the tequila's inevitable effect on me. Since I rarely joined her parties and drink nights, - med students didn't have the luxury to party every weekend like her sorority friends, she knew I was going to be tipsy soon.

I took my third shot hesitatingly; however this time, I realized immediately that I was drinking plain water in a shot glass. Dylan's smile broadened with my confused look. He whispered in my ear softly. "Shush, just go with it. I poured water instead of tequila in your glasses."

"But, why?"

"I happen to like sober and uptight Emma!" He whispered in my ear. "And also… I would prefer to go to a museum more than a sex show."

"Thank you," I whispered back, my lips slightly brushed his neck, and he flinched. Seeing how he responded to my imperceptible touch, made me grin blithely.

After my third shot, and looking completely unaffected, Sydney, of course figured out something was up with me and the shots. I was just about to reach for the last one when she snatched it away and took a swig. "This is just water. Emma!" She exclaimed immediately. "You are cheating!"

"It wasn't me! You saw it, Dylan brought the shots." I broke into a chuckle.

She eyed Dylan fixedly, trying to figure out what he was up to, but Dylan only shrugged. She sniggered. "Since you obviously want Emma to win this thing, even by means of cheating, I think it is only fair that you get punished by escorting her to the museum." Then, she turned towards me and continued. "Which means, Emma, I am out."

"But, Sydney! You promised." I tried to object.

Sydney pulled me aside and spoke quietly. "Ems, you have a gorgeous guy willing to go anywhere with you. Instead of diving headfirst into this opportunity, you are trying to drag me with you. What the hell is wrong with you?"

"I don't know. We were supposed to do this together. Wasn't that the plan? Spend some good time with your BFF?" I grinned.

"That was before you brought a hot guy, obviously very attracted to you, into our plan."

"You think he is attracted to me?" I asked shyly, biting my nails.

"Are you blind? He has been chasing you for the last two hours and he can't keep his eyes off you. Look at him now, he is still checking you out. Just go, and please do something with him other than just looking at paintings."

"You are incorrigible. You know that?"

"I am actually doing you a favor. You need some hot, naughty stories to tell your grandkids when you get old."

I rolled my eyes and sighed.

"Go, now. Have fun." She uttered loudly.

Dylan walked up to me with a beer in his hand. His eyes were on me, watching my every move. A soft smile lined his lips. "Sorry about my little game there. I hope I didn't get you in trouble with Sydney." He said shyly.

"No, not at all. Sydney wasn't so excited about visiting museums anyway, so she chose to bail. I guess she and Max made some plans already. Are you sure about joining me Dylan? You can go with them if you want to. Don't feel obligated to come with me," I rattled a bit, and then looked down at my hands, avoiding his eyes when I finished talking.

"Emma, are you still trying to ditch me?" He tilted my chin up with the tip of his finger. His unexpected touch made me shiver; I cringed unwittingly. I shook my head, said "No!" feeling frustrated with myself, especially about my so obvious reactions to his touch.

"Okay, then, let's go. What's your plan?"

"I can't decide between Rikjmuseum and Stedelijk. We don't have enough time to see both. We need to choose one. What do you think?"

"I'd choose Rikjmuseum."

"It is about two miles away. If you are not so tired, we can walk."

"I'll walk anywhere with you Emma, even if it is thousand miles away.'

I grinned shyly and shook my head. I had never met anyone like him. He was too outspoken about his thoughts and feelings. "Are you going to continue with all the flirting?"

"Yes, I plan to do so," he chuckled. "I enjoy seeing you blush."

"Well, then Mr. Flirt. Let's start."

We walked side by side along one of the prettiest canals of the city, 'Prinsengracht'. Dylan's presence was unsettling and comforting at the same time. He was easy to talk to. He didn't mind my bitter tongue or precipitous actions. It was easy to be myself around him. What was unsettling was my inescapable attraction to him. Each time our eyes met, I wanted to put my fingers through his tussled hair, touch his stubble and kiss his inviting lips. He was bringing out emotions that I didn't know existed in me.

I was trying to avert my thoughts when Dylan suddenly stopped, turned towards me and said. "I want to ask you something, Emma."

"Ok..." I mumbled curiously. It wasn't like one of his smug comments. He sounded very serious all of a sudden.

"How come a girl like you and Sydney are best friends."

"This is the second time you said a girl like me. What does that mean?"

"Come on Emma. You know what I mean. You are staid and solemn. You don't care much for useless activities. Sydney on the other hand is all about fun, partying, drinking, and enjoying the day. If I didn't know you were here together, I would have never guessed you were friends."

"Sydney usually comes off wrong. She has this easy girl image because of her relaxed attitude, but she is a good girl."

"That might be true but you are obviously very different, yet you said she is your best friend. I was curious."

I couldn't answer him right away. My relationship with Sydney was complicated. Telling him why we were very close meant opening up to him and sharing my personal life. *Did I really want to share the doleful days of my life with a person I barely knew?* I found myself admitting that I did.

After a long, pensive minute, I started to talk, "Sydney and I were best friends even before I moved in with her family. I was twelve years old when Aunt Helen, Sydney's mom, took us in after my mother died." I paused and took a deep breath, playing with my fingers.

"My mother was diagnosed with a malignant brain tumor the summer I turned eleven. It was a grade four glioma. She went through therapy to shrink the tumor as much as possible before surgery, but her surgery wasn't successful in the end." I explained quickly, trying hard to stay composed. My eyes welled with tears but I was determined not to let the tears flow. It was long ago. I had grown to live my life without my mother.

He held my hand and made me sit by the bench overlooking the canal. His eyes were full of unspoken emotions, but mostly sympathy and understanding. He caressed my wrist with his thumb, "I am so sorry, Emma. I didn't know," he said softly.

"It's alright Dylan. Sydney and I have a long, complicated history. She was my best friend during those difficult months when my mother died and my father left."

"Your father left? Why?"

"I suppose my father fell into a serious depression after my mother died. He couldn't handle her loss and the responsibility of taking care of two little children by himself. I guess he did what he thought was best for us: me and my brother, Steve. He asked Aunt Helen to take care of us."

"But that's too selfish. You lost your mother and father at the same time." Dylan stroked his finger gently against my palm as he gazed into my eyes. "You were just a kid. How did you manage to become this responsible, understanding person?"

"I had my brother, Aunt Helen, Uncle George and Sydney. They loved us so much. I grew up in a happy family, it wasn't as sad as you think. Also, my father didn't completely disappear; he might not have taken us to school or baseball games or movies but he visited us on birthdays… holiday. I guess he did the best he could."

"God, you are so forgiving!" He sighed heavily. "I hate my father and I can never forgive him."

"Why do you say that?" I asked in a quiet voice, wondering if he was going to confide in me, as I did with him.

His face turned rigid and eyes were unyielding. "Because he is a selfish bastard, that's why," he replied in a bristly tone. "He had an affair with his assistant while I was in college. A girl my age, typical mid-life crisis. He divorced my mother and married his stupid bimbo."

"Maybe he fell in love. They say, love is blind," I tried to quell him, although I sensed it was useless. It was obvious that he harbored deep unresolved issues and strong animosity against his father.

"That was not love. They got divorced two years ago. My father is not capable of love. He was just thinking with his dick. That's it."

"Dylan!"

"Fine, sorry. I am still mad at him. I don't think I can ever forgive him."

"I prefer to think, things happen in life for a reason. You either find a way to cope with it or let the sadness, grief or anger consume you. I chose to deal with the hand I was given. "

"How did you do that?

"I refused to be this lost, sad girl. I didn't let my anger burn me. I had to be strong for myself and my brother. I studied hard and chose to become a doctor. If my mother had been diagnosed earlier, they might have saved her. I wanted to learn about the tumor which took my mother and I made it my life's goal to fight it. "

"You are a doctor!" He uttered in disbelief. "I was suspicious when you checked my pulse earlier, but you had this no-work-talk-rule, so I couldn't ask.

"Almost a doctor. I still have a year before I graduate," I answered quickly. I didn't want to talk about the details of my life. I wanted to ignore the clinical rotations and the thesis dissertation waiting for me upon my return. Just this once, I wanted to enjoy my day without thinking about my obligations.

"Hey, enough talking," I exclaimed to change the subject. "If we don't get going, we won't make it in time."

"Rijks is too big to see everything in a few hours but hopefully we'll get to see some of the masterpieces."

"How do you know that?"

"I have been there before," he replied, smiling widely.

I looked up to him in bewilderment. "You are full of surprises Dylan. I didn't think you would visit museums without duress."

"You just wait. I plan to surprise you even more." He said nonchalantly and tugged my hand.

CHAPTER 4
EMMA

After the short walk, we arrived at the impressive brick building situated right next to another canal, built by the famous Dutch architect, Pierre Cuypers. Located in the Museum Square, Rijksmuseum stood stately and beautiful. The famous museum has dazzled art and history lovers since it was built in 1885; however, after ten years of meticulous renovation and restoration effort, it was more impressive and eye-catching than ever.

Since it was late in the afternoon, there wasn't much of a crowd trying to get tickets. After waiting a couple of minutes in line, we were in the museum surrounded by tall glass walls, allowing us to view the interior courtyard. I admired the brilliant design created by the great architect as I walked by the imposing columns under the big archways surrounding the vast space. I felt lost in the beauty of this magnificent building while Dylan's warm and strong fingers grazed my hand. His soft touches were making my heart race.

"I know it's such a beautiful building to admire but we don't have much time. I would love you to see 'The Gallery of Honour' and Rembrandt's masterpiece: 'The Night Watch' before the museum closes." Dylan commented and led me to the Entrance Hall. I was bewildered but also impressed by his ardor to tour the museum with me. He seemed to enjoy this as much as I did. *Who was this man?* The arrogant, cocky person I met in Red Light District or the sweet and kind person who was holding my hand and showing me around the museum... *Could they be the same person?* With every passing minute with him, I was getting more confused about him, myself and my feelings.

When we reached the Entrance Hall, I was stunned by its grandeur. It was more glamorous than I had imagined. Its floors were decorated with inlaid mosaics, the walls were covered with painted tableaux and windows were tall, made of stained glass. Spanning high above us was a vaulted ceiling embellished with lavish and colorful decorations.

"The highlight of the museum's display is, of course, 'The Night Watch', but there are also many other great paintings from the Dutch Golden Age on display here." Dylan explained enthusiastically. "Aside from the most famous artists like Rembrandt, Vermeer, Steen and Van Gogh, you will get to see masterpieces from artists like Verspronck, Ceasar van Everdingen and my favorite, Jan Asselijn.

"Are you teasing me or testing me Dylan?" I asked shyly. He was talking about artists that I could not even pronounce their names.

"Why do you say that?"

"Because I haven't heard of any of those names before. Of course I know about Rembrandt and Van Gogh, but the rest, I have no idea," I replied candidly. I liked art, enjoyed looking at beautiful paintings but I was ashamed to admit, my knowledge was limited to the famous artists and their paintings. "I hope you're not making those names up. Any name with 'Van Something' sounds real to me," I teased him.

He turned me around to face him in front of an impressive marble sculpture. Trying to avoid his gleaming, fathomless eyes, I concentrated on the soft details of the child angel's beautiful face and his wing. I was reading the name tag: 'Seated Angel' by Falconet when Dylan mumbled in my ear, "I promise that I am not tricking you." But then he broke into a wry grin, and looked at me mischievously, making me suspicious again.

I shook my head and studied him up and down in disbelief, "For some reason, I don't believe you."

"If you think I am tricking you, how about a bet then?"

"A bet? What kind of a bet?"

"Pick any three painting on display around us and I will tell you who the artist is without looking at their tags."

I raised my eyebrows and trying to contemplate if he was serious. Did he really know that much about Dutch and Flemish artists to go for a bet? Was he bluffing? I didn't know much about Dutch painters but eyeing hundreds of paintings from different artists and era around us, I doubted his erudition on the subject either. He was a businessman in the financial world. How much could he know about art?

"Alright, I am in." I said, smiling down at his disarming countenance. "What is the bet for?"

"Hmm," he mumbled, squinting. "Now, the bet needs to be something significant to make it worthy. Don't you think?"

"What is worthy enough for you to bet? A thousand dollars?"

"No. I won't bet for money. It needs to be something worthier than that. How about this..." He sighed deeply as he raked a hand through his hair. "If I win, I get to have one kiss and we spend the rest of the day together. I will choose where we go."

I chuckled at his playfulness, "Oh come on! That's the wager? You cannot be serious." He was taking his flirting to the next level. It wasn't as guileless as before, but strangely, I found myself enjoying it.

"No, I am very serious."

"Okay. What do I get if I win?"

"Let me think... If you win, I will be your servant, slave or whatever you want me to be for the rest of the day. If you want a foot massage, you'll get it."

It seemed like either way, he was determined to spend the rest of the day with me. "Hmm, very tempting but I need to think." I crossed my arm in the front, smiling amiably. My thoughts drifted back to the moment he caressed my skin. I yearned for his touch again and wondered how his lips would feel on mine. *Did I want him to win this bet?*

"Alright, let's see if you are as good as you think," I put out my right hand for him to shake. He took my hand slowly and squeezed it gently, but instead of releasing it, he subtly grazed his thumb over the back of my hand. His touch sent shivers down my spine again.

"Let's start with this one." I pointed at a painting, picturing four kids around a table: A girl with a flute, a boy holding a dancing cat, another boy holding its tail and the last boy looked like he was holding a spoon.

"You started with an easy one Emma. It is the Dancing Lesson by Steen. Steen is one of the highlighted artists in Rijksmuseum."

"I didn't know that. Hmm... Let's move towards the far corner then. I will try to pick a harder one." I heaved a sigh checking out the paintings around me. They were all very impressive. It was hard for me to pick one. After looking around for several minutes, I stopped by the painting of a beautiful lady with an exotic, broad-brimmed sun hat and suggestively exposed shoulder, carrying a basket full of fruits. I covered the tag with my hand and arched my brows. "This one!" I said.

"Most portraits are difficult to identify, since there are so many of them over different eras. However this one is very significant due to her very exposed shoulder, an erotic message to the viewers. It is Van Everdingen."

"You are really good!" I giggled, utterly surprised. "I better pick the last one carefully."

I walked back and forth in the long corridor and stopped in front of a painting of a swan. It struck me right away. White swan painted in fine details looked scared or rather threatened. It was protecting its nest and eggs from a dog. "How about this one?" I asked.

"Oh… this is a very famous painting as well." Dylan said while studying the painting. "It was interpreted as a political allegory: the white swan was thought to symbolize the Dutch statesman protecting the country from its enemies." He explained. "But I think I forgot the name of the painter."

"Really…" My heart sunk suddenly. I hoped he didn't notice the chagrin in my voice. *God, I truly wanted him to win the bet.* "Think carefully, Dylan. You might become my slave for the rest of the day." I mumbled, trying to hide my nervousness.

"Hmm, let me concentrate. I think it's either Pieter Gijsels… or Jan Asseljin."

"Jan Asseljin …." I exclaimed happily, hearing the correct name on his second guess. "Looks like you won!"

"Well, my price was very worthy, so I had to win." He watched me carefully as I straightened my dress, tucked a stray strand of hair under my silk foulard.

"I guess we will be together for the rest of the day."

"You are forgetting the second part of the wager," he squinted and knitted his brows, insinuating the kiss.

I pecked a small chaste kiss on his cheek and lower my head shyly. He tilted my head up with his finger and gazed intently into my eyes. I could see the yellow hue dusted in the blue madness of his eyes. "That doesn't count," he objected immediately. "I will collect my wager properly when the time comes…" He winked. "But, come now. We have only fifteen minutes left. You should see 'The Milkmaid' and 'The Night Watch'. He pulled my hand, and I found myself in front of a colossal canvas, one of the most famous paintings in the world.

"There are a couple of reasons why this painting is very famous," he started explaining. "Firstly, obviously its size! Mona Lisa looks like a stamp next to this. Secondly, Rembrandt's effective use of light and shadow is very impressive, and thirdly, the perception of motion in the painting. You see these men…" He pointed to the men in front. "The way he painted, it carries the illusion of motion."

"It's definitely impressive. Why is it called 'The Night Watch'?" I asked.

"Good question," he said softly. "The painting used to be coated with a dark varnish giving the incorrect impression of a night scene." He explained and continued to impress me more with his vast knowledge as I stood speechless in front of Rembrandt's renowned masterpiece. "Popular interpretations suggest that there are several layers of meanings and many symbolisms in this extraordinary painting. It is a glowing symbol of democracy first of all, also it symbolizes Dutch as a united nation…"

I was trying to understand the symbolism in the painting and admiring the fine details of the girl in the yellow dress when finally the museum attendant told the crowd that it was time to leave. People slowly dwindled away, and we were the last ones to exit.

"Thank you Dylan. I enjoyed it a lot, more than you could imagine," I confessed. "So, what should we do next?" I asked when we were out the door, standing by the canal in the back of the museum.

"I have an idea!" He said with a huge grin, and pleading eyes.

"Okay, let's hear it. Since you are in charge for the rest of the day, I am anxious to hear your plan."

"I think no visit to Amsterdam would be complete without seeing a real windmill. I was thinking, maybe we could go check one out."

"It is a marvelous idea," I exclaimed joyfully. I wondered how being around Dylan made me this completely different person. I didn't do anything instantaneous. I planned my days, weeks, or months. I even had a five year plan. However, with Dylan, I was living in complete 'carpe diem' mode. He made me feel alive again.

"Are you sure there are still windmills in the city?" I asked. "I thought they were long gone. Destroyed or removed."

"There are a few around town actually. One of them is even open to the public. I called them when you were getting us something to drink and asked if they could stay open late for us."

"So, how do we get there?"

"I was thinking about renting a bike," he paused and his gaze dropped to my lips while he brushed my cheek softly with his knuckle. I thought he was going to kiss me at that instant. And I wanted him to kiss me, but instead, he swirled a strand of my hair around his finger and tucked behind my ear.

We walked to the bike shop across the canal. After a quick negotiation, Dylan came back with a red tandem bike and asked. "What do you think?"

"A tandem bike?"

"Yeah, why not?"

"Well, you are much taller than me, how are we going to manage?"

"Don't worry, we'll do fine!"

"If you say so... I have the map."

"Ok, then, let's ride." He uttered happily.

Dylan sat in the front seat and set our tempo. He carefully matched his long strong strides to my weak ones. Somehow, we managed to ride in complete unison. Every now and then he turned his head back to look at me, and each time my heart melted with the sight of his beguiling smile. Dylan riding in front of me was a beautiful but torturous sight. His attractive body was such a distraction that I couldn't pay attention to the alluring scenery we were passing by. With each breeze, I inhaled his intoxicating smell. His taut muscles and broad shoulders were in front of me, within my reach, but I didn't dare to touch. I couldn't. My attraction towards him was too dangerous. I felt like a little rowboat in treacherous waters.

In half an hour, we arrived at the tall stone mill. We parked our bike by the green building and went inside. We were greeted by the volunteers and the miller, working extra hours because of us. They looked like they didn't mind; they were very kind and friendly. I suspected Dylan paid them a handsome amount surreptitiously.

On our private tour by the miller, we got to see how the mill cap turned and how the vanes faced the wind. We saw the vanes rotating and stopping by adjusting the sails. Being inside a working windmill was a unique experience. It was amazing to see the power of the wind and how people used that power to pump and drain water or mill grains for centuries.

"I would have enjoyed living in medieval Holland." I said after leaving the mill. We stood by a tall willow tree in the green pasture.

"Why is that?" Dylan asked. He rested his shoulders on the tree, and then cast a side long glance at me.

"Because life was simpler back then. It's great to have all this technology which is supposed to make our lives easier, but it doesn't. We are wired non-stop. I think we have technology overload."

"And you don't like that?" He said with questioning eyes. His fingers circled the back of my hand softly.

"No, I don't. It's too much. People are so attached to their electronic devices that they can't go anywhere without them. It seems like people share their experiences all the time in social media, but many miss enjoying the moment while they are too busy sharing it with the rest of the world."

"I am not so crazy about social media either."

"I am not against it, but I think people exaggerate everything. Many use social media as a way to brag about themselves or their lives. It portrays a pink clouded image of life which is not true. I think technology has become our enemy because we don't use it properly. I don't know. Maybe I'm not making any sense... "

"No, you totally make sense."

"I hope I am not boring you, Dylan. Maybe I am just a dreary girl, full of oppressive reality like Sydney said. Maybe I should have had the real shots and eased up a little bit."

"No, not at all. I think you are perfect..."

I took a deep breath and rested my head on his shoulder. "You know what Dylan! I think today is perfect."

"Yes, it is... and I don't want it to end," Dylan whispered in my ear.

"Me, too. You, me, us! I don't know exactly what this is, but it reminds me..." I paused to look into his sky blue eyes. "It reminds me the movie 'Before Sunset'. Have you seen it?"

He wrapped his arms around my waist, his palms resting on the small of my back. "No, I haven't", he uttered softly. His eyes darted up to meet mine. They were fathomless blue, edged in a deeper hue. I felt I could lose myself in their depth.

"It's about Jesse and Celiné," I started telling slowly. "They meet on a train in Europe and start talking about random things. Soon they realize they enjoy each other's company. Jesse convinces Celiné to get off the train with him in Vienna. They spend a wonderful romantic evening together. They both know that they have this one magical night, and next day they need to return to their lives. When the night is over, they depart at the train station. Jesse goes back to America and Celiné takes the train to Paris."

"Why would Jesse want it to be one night? I think he would want Celiné to stay with him or go to America together."

"Well, that's not how the story ends…"

"But, why?"

"Maybe it is magical and wonderful because they know that it is just for one night. They decide to see each other at the same place, same time, following year."

"I don't think Jesse would like waiting that long to see her again."

"But he must!"

"So, does Jesse fall for Celiné?"

"Yes, I think he does."

"How about Celiné?" He asked again, his gaze hinted a different meaning. It was obvious that we were not talking about the movie any more.

"I think she does too…"

"But they still part their ways…"

I nodded slightly. Solemn expression in his eyes told me that he wasn't happy with my answer. He looked at me for a long minute without uttering a word, and then he finally said, "I don't like the ending. I think it should be rewritten." He tightened his grasp. I leaned on his chest; now completely buried in his strong body. I felt the ripples of his stomach muscles against my skin. He rested his chin on my head and inhaled deeply.

"God, you are so beautiful and smell like heaven." He whispered in my ear, his lips almost touching my neck.

Then, suddenly, gazing intently into my eyes, he brought his hands up to cup my face, and caressed my cheeks with his soft fingers. With his thumb, he traced the contour of my lips. His face just an inch away, I was able to feel the heat radiating from his skin. In exquisite anticipation, as he slowly lowered his face to mine, I closed my eyes and parted my lips. After what felt like an eternity, he brushed his perfect lips to edge of my mouth. My heart started to flutter when they pressed firmly on mine. His kiss was slow and tender at first, but then, I felt an unstoppable desire building up as his mouth covered mine passionately. When his tongue slowly entered and explored my mouth, my body was about to collapse in utter pleasure. If he wasn't holding me tightly, my legs would have given up, my knees would have buckled. I reached for his shoulders and dug my nails into his skin to keep myself steady. Completely overrun with sensation, I pulled him to myself hard and sucked his lips. My tongue eagerly searched for his, and when they met, they entwined with each other. He tasted sweet like a combination of mint and chocolate. My hands grazed over his sinewy arms and his big, strong body tensed under my touch. My breathing deepened as he softly moaned my name "Emma" into my mouth. His voice was suddenly husky. His lips lingered on my mouth a few more seconds, before he broke the connection and looked at me in utter bewilderment.

"Oh, Fuck! Emma!" He cried. "What the hell was that?" He was still panting.

CHAPTER 5
DYLAN

I had thought about kissing Emma since the moment I saw her sitting in front of the church and staring at me. Her plump, red lips were so tempting that when she rested her head on my chest, my lips found hers almost instinctively. It was supposed to be a soft, tender kiss. However, when she responded to me with an equal amount of passion, it took all the power in me to stop. I was so lost in the temptation that I was about to peel her dress away from her silky white skin, trail kisses down to her neck and explore every inch of her delicate body with my mouth on the spot. I wanted her so God damned bad that it hurt. Just thinking about her, imagining her soft skin under my body was giving me a hard on. God… I needed to find a way to stop this madness … this strong desire for someone I just met. It was all new to me. A moment of passion unlike anything I had experienced before, and I was sure that she felt it too. To kiss like that, she must be attracted to me as much as I was attracted to her.

My problem was… what I felt for Emma wasn't just sensual. It wasn't a simple salacious desire for a hot, sexy woman. I was completely dazzled by her. Not just her beauty but her charm, her wit, her sharp sense of humor and her sweet smile made her completely dazzling. Actually, I found everything about Emma fascinating. I could listen to her for hours if only she talked a bit more. Especially about herself. Her brevity was killing me. Emma was everything I wanted and more. Sexy, funny, beautiful, intelligent and smart. I was madly attracted to a woman who was about to become a doctor for God's sake. If she knew about my infamous reputation, she would run away from me, but still, I couldn't stop falling for her. *I was certainly in trouble.*

"I am sorry Dylan. I don't know what came over me." She uttered softly when I broke away from her. Her lips were still swollen. The thought that I was the reason they were swollen and puffy like that filled me with more desire.

"Are you kidding me Emma? You are apologizing for the best kiss of my life."

"It was?" Her pink little tongue grazed over her lower lip for a fleeting second. The sight of Emma biting her lips, twisting her silky hair with her finger was so sensual that I couldn't stop imagining things. Things that I wanted to do to her.

"Yes, it really was." I managed to answer after adjusting myself subtly.

"I can't understand myself around you. I am..." she paused. Her gaze was pensive. She was withdrawing from me which I didn't like. "I become this different person."

"You don't need to tell me ... look at me Emma." I placed her hand over my chest. "Do you feel that? You did that to me. I am out of breath just kissing you."

She looked at me softly, and then wrapped her slender arms around my neck resting her head on my chest. "I could stay like this forever..."

"Me too!" I agreed. After a long, comfortable silence while I held Emma in my arms, "we should have dinner," I said.

"I completely forgot about the time. You must be starving."

"I really am," I confirmed. "How about you?"

"Famished... I was scared you would hear my stomach grumble."

"Why didn't you say so?"

"It felt so good to be in your arms. I didn't want to ruin it."

"Oh, Emma. What am I going to do with you?"

"You can start with taking me to dinner." She replied earnestly. She was straight forward, didn't play the little games others girls played. She didn't feign. She didn't pretend. I loved that she was honest, especially when it made her blush. *Seriously, what was I going to do with this girl?*

"I am taking you to De Basiel. It is THE place to dine in Amsterdam. Great food, great location."

"Sounds great!" She giggled. Happy and smiling Emma was a beautiful sight. I wondered why she wasn't relaxed like that more often. "I assume we need to ride there and park our bike nearby. Wouldn't that be awkward?" She asked.

"We are in Amsterdam. People ride their bikes even wearing suits. We'll fit in just fine with Dutch people."

"You definitely fit in ... being well built and tall. I, on the other hand, feel like I am in Gulliver's travels and I've just arrived in the land of giants."

"Oh, come on Emma. You are fine. No, not fine, you are perfect. I enjoy how you fit in my arms." I said frankly. In her petite but curvy body, she definitely looked much more attractive and beautiful than the six foot tall, esthetically altered models I hooked up with back home.

While she busied herself with finding a bottle of water for our ride to the restaurant, "Excuse me, Emma. I need to make a call," I said, and left her alone with the breathtaking view of the cloudless blue sky over lush, green pastures and red-brick houses strewn in between farmlands.

I wanted to arrange our dinner reservations. Our dinner had to be great and memorable, and I had to find a way to know more about her. I certainly didn't want this to be a one-time casual affair in Europe. A great romantic dinner in an immaculate setting might just be the key to open up Emma.

I called Lodewijk, the chef and owner of De Basiel. He was an old friend and I knew he would prepare an impressive table for us. I caught myself smiling, imagining Emma's reaction. She was turning me into a hopeless romantic without even knowing it.

When we arrived at De Basiel, Lodewijk greeted us personally and took us to the table overlooking the canal, set on the cobblestone street. Tiny gardenias and tea candles decorated our black and silver dressed table. Tall wine glasses and a chilled bottle of Corton Charlemagne Chardonnay Vintage 1996 were placed on the table. Amsterdam's famous bridges and trees along the canals provided the perfect background.

I pulled out Emma's seat and helped her scoot back in. "What do you think?" I uttered softly in her ear. Her silky white neck looked even more gorgeous after she tied her hair up with her foulard.

"Wow... This place looks awesome!" She uttered enthusiastically.

"Live music will start shortly. A British artist, Chris Hill, plays acoustic guitar here every night. He has a great voice too. I've been to his guitar concerto in Dublin. He is here for the summer. He is really good. I think you'll like his music."

"I've liked everything you recommended so far," she confessed. She had that ambivalent, shy look on her face and her cheeks blushed each time our gazes met.

"Maybe you and I have similar taste. We would make a good couple." I added in a sly tone.

"Well, it seems that we like similar things..." She squirmed in her seat, completely ignoring my other remark. "At least in regards to art, which by the way I'd like to ask you," she said, and with her incisive mind and quick wit, managed to subtly turn the subject away from my comment.

"Alright, Emma! Ask away..."

"How is it that you know so much about art? I thought you were an investor. You probably have a business degree and all."

"Yes, I have a degree in economics and also an MBA. I have my own company in..."

"No, no, stop! We agreed, Dylan," she interrupted. "Still no work-talk!"

"Alright, fine! I can't believe you are still forcing this," I frowned, feeling a bit disappointed. I was hoping if I shared a bit about myself, she would feel obliged to share some too. I wanted to know everything about Emma, where she worked, where she studied, where she lived. However, so far she parted with no information other than her name and being a last year med student. That wasn't much.

"Without going into too much boring detail, I minored in art history in college." I said.

"You didn't strike me as an art lover when we first met."

"Well, now you know that you are wrong!" I replied with a slight grin. I knew my first impression on her wasn't much more favorable, and I was determined to change that, even if it meant talking about myself and sharing personal, unpleasant details that I usually avoided.

"I was always interested in art. I've done oil paintings as a hobby since high school. My mother supported my passion for art, however, despite her support I wasn't even allowed to paint at home. My father, of course, didn't send me to a prestigious prep school to become a penniless artist. He had engraved it into my brain since I was a kid that I had to go to an Ivy League College, get a business degree and follow his and my grandfather's footsteps. So, since I couldn't paint, I did the next best thing I could do. I studied art." I explained quickly. I was surprised how easily I shared things that I never talked to anyone else before.

She listened attentively without feigning interest; her green eyes were soft and caring. "You weren't allowed to paint. That's just crazy," she said finally. Her eyebrows arched. She looked even cuter when she was furious and also confused trying to comprehend my twisted family. "Who didn't allow you? And why?" She asked.

"The explanation to your question involves an unpleasant topic regarding my obstinate, intolerant, narrow-minded father."

"I get that you don't have a good relationship with your father."

"Yes, that's the polite way to put it." I said. Talking about my father was the last thing I wanted to do. He was out of my life for nearly six years now and I wanted to keep it that way.

"So, what did you do? Did you just give up painting for good?"

"Not exactly. While studying at Yale… Oh, sorry, that just slipped." I grinned after revealing another thing about my life. "I stealthily took art classes and art history. I had to do it behind my father's back, of course. He would have caused a big scene and stopped paying my tuition if he knew."

"That bad huh?"

"Yeah, pretty much. When I got my degree, he coerced me to work for him and threatened to cut all my financial support if I didn't. That was where I drew the line. I was fed up with his unceasing repression on my life while he was fucking twenty year old bimbos. I told him to stick his money up his ass and get the hell out of my life. After my 'not-so-smart' remark, we stopped talking to each other. Of course, he didn't just acknowledge my decision. He decided to teach me a lesson by blocking access to all my funds and making it impossible for me to find a job. Since none of the big financial companies dared to conflict with my father, they didn't hire me. I became an unemployed, broke, college graduate. That's when Max saved my miserable ass. He took a chance and invested in me and we started our company together. We have been working together ever since."

She listened patiently as I talked about my problematic relationship with my father. She didn't pry with nosy questions, or judge me. With an indulgent smile on her face, she looked at me understandingly. The deep, vibrant hues of her green eyes were glowing brightly under the evening sun. "Do you still paint?" She asked after a long, quiet minute.

"No, not anymore. I hardly have enough time," I answered.

"It seems to me, if painting was your passion, you would have spared the time. I think not having enough time is just an excuse."

She was totally right. It was strange how she saw through my perfunctory answer. We had known each other for just a few hours, but I felt like she understood me more than most people in my life ever had. Yes, I was busy all the time. In the last five years, our business expanded much more than I had imagined and I always struggled to catch up with work, however, now that we were bigger, we employed fifteen brilliant consultants and five account managers. I could have given my customers and portfolios to them to handle and had more time to myself. *So why didn't I? Why wasn't I the idealistic romantic artist I used to be?* I didn't even feel the need to ask all those questions to myself until now. Emma brought back the memories that I buried deep inside. While I was occupied with asset allocations, enhanced index-fund investments or hedge funds in volatile markets, the Dylan I fought so much to be, the wayward son who stood up to his father in scathing terms disappeared and was replaced with this rich, famous, harsh Wall Street mogul. Infamous party boy on the weekends, cruel, merciless businessman during the week. I hated the person I had become. *Why didn't I try to change? Was I waiting for Emma to be myself again?*

After a long apprehensive moment, "I think, I haven't found anything worth painting in a long time. Not much inspires me anymore," I admitted solemnly, and then added with a huge smile. "Somehow I feel like, that is about to change..."

"Dylan. You and your boundless flirtation!" She said jokingly.

"But it's true. You fascinate me. I would love to make a drawing of you. Your impeccable beauty, long auburn hair, limpid green eyes. Look at your hands, they are beautiful..." Then, I whispered slowly. *"I do not know what it is about you that closes and opens; only something in me understands, the voice of your eyes is deeper than all roses, nobody, not even the rain, has such small hands..."*

"Oh, my God, Dylan. Now you are quoting E.E Cummings... Are there any more surprises I should be aware of?"

"I don't know. You inspire me and words come out naturally," I confessed. "I am not trying to impress you by using some trite phrases. I hate clichés actually." My gazes slowly drifted to her lips. I wanted to kiss her again so badly.

"No, Dylan, you are far from a cliché. Everything about you is so intriguing."

I smiled happily. "Well then, let's have a toast. To us and to this magical night," I raised my glass and gazed deeply into her eyes. "Emma, please eat something. Maybe some beef Carpaccio first.

You said you were hungry. I don't want to draw an unconscious girl."

"I will. I just want to know if you are serious about making a drawing of me tonight."

"The night is young. There is still time for more surprises. " I winked, smiling playfully.

"I think I would really like that," she replied with a radiant smile.

The next three hours went too fast as we sat outside in the comforting summer breeze enjoying the alluring view of the canal. I had dinner dates where girls hardly touched their food but with Emma, we ate everything and even shared a chocolate soufflé. "Oh, how can anyone say no to chocolate?" she exclaimed happily when Lodewijk personally brought the dessert topped with his secret cream sauce.

Before we left De Basiel, I asked Chris to play one last song for us. Under the clear night sky dappled with bright stars and a full moon, I asked Emma to dance with me. We moved softly with the music while she rested her head on my shoulder, her hand clasped around my neck. I buried my face in her soft curls, and inhaled her jasmine-vanilla scent. I could have stayed like that forever but the music stopped, announcing the end of a magical evening. I had to let her leave my arms.

Why did the time seem to fly when I was with her? Neither the afternoon nor the evening was enough. I wanted to spend the entire night with her now. "Would you like a walk by the canal towards the Wertheimpark?" I asked, hoping she would say 'yes'.

"Sure," she agreed with a cute grin and held to the crook of my arm. We walked the cobblestone streets slowly. I could tell she was getting tired but neither she nor I wanted to say anything. We both didn't want the night to end.

"What a gorgeous view. I'd like to take a picture of you under the moonlight." I said and turned her to face me.

She shook her head, objecting. "I don't think any still picture can capture the true beauty of this night, Dylan. Let's just take mental pictures tonight. Things we enjoy appear much more beautiful in our memories than on a paper or computer screens."

"But, I want to remember you and our night together. Are you still insisting on not telling me anything else about yourself?"

Her eyes were furtive; she didn't want to answer me. Instead she squeezed my hand softly and leaned her head on my shoulder. I ran my fingers through her soft hair and caressed her cheek with the back of my hand. I didn't know what else to say. I hated that we were getting to the end of the night and she was this delicate dove, ready to fly away without leaving a trace.

"Emma, you look tired. We have been walking almost all day. I don't think you have the energy to ride back," I said. "Why don't we spend the rest of the night in my hotel? It is close." I asked hesitatingly.

"Are you trying to get me into your bed Dylan?" She asked tauntingly. God, I loved but also hated her bluntness.

I grinned, blushing unwittingly, "As much as I would love to do that, kiss every inch of your body, make you scream with pleasure. No, that's not my plan." I replied back. *I could play her game too.*

"Oh, God! Dylan! You are getting me all intrigued now."

"I should continue then, maybe you will surrender."

"Honestly, I don't think so. I don't want to be the bimbo you banged on a one-night-stand in Amsterdam."

"You know that you are not a bimbo, and believe me if I make love to you, I don't think one night would be enough. I would want more."

"Dylan, we agreed. It's just one night. We will both go our separate ways tomorrow."

"I didn't agree. You just didn't give me any other option. You don't even want to give me your number or tell me where you live or where you work."

"It's better this way. We will have this wonderful night to remember forever. It is perfect."

"I can't win this argument with you and I don't want to spend my precious hours left arguing. All I want is to hold you in my arms for the rest of the night and kiss you. I can't let you go just yet. I am not ready to say goodbye."

"Okay, fine!"

"Okay, fine for what?"

"Yes, I will come to your hotel and spend the night with you."

I lifted her up and spun her around in my arms. "This will be the best night of my life." I shouted happily. She did say 'yes'… didn't she? Or was I daydreaming?

CHAPTER 6
DYLAN

We arrived at The Grand Amsterdam Hotel close to midnight. Built in 1578, I found the building very old-fashioned when I checked in three days ago; however, wondering how Emma would enjoy its quaint and unique atmosphere, I was thankful to Mrs. Donnelly, my kind, fifty year old personal assistant for reserving this historic hotel for me. When we got in front of the impressive building illuminated with soft lights, Emma's eyes grew wide, and a slight grin inched on her face. She liked historic places: it was too obvious.

I was about to open the door to the lobby when her phone rang, "I need to take this," she said politely.

"Of course! As long as you promise to come back," I said wondering who was calling her at this hour. "If it is Sydney, please tell her you'll be with me all night. I am not letting you go."

"Don't worry. I'll be back. It's my aunt. She is probably just getting off work and wants to check on me."

"Alright, I'll be here waiting." I let her hand go and watched her step outside.

While she was talking on the phone, I beckoned to Albert, the hotel's kind, white haired, bespectacled concierge to come over. I explained that I wanted something special prepared for my guest. Fresh strawberries, champagne and jasmine flowers. And for the morning, I asked him to arrange a royal breakfast overlooking the garden terrace surrounded by historic walls.

"I want the best of everything Albert. Nothing should be less than perfect!" I demanded resolutely.

"Of course, Mr. Hamilton!" Albert nodded eagerly. "I will arrange everything personally. I can assure you that all will be setup perfect for your taste. Do you want your order for tonight right away?"

"Yes, please bring them immediately."

"And if I may sir, I'd like to add one more item to your list." He said.

"What is it, Albert?"

"I think crème Chantilly would go very well with the strawberries, sir."

"Excellent idea Albert." I smiled. "Please add that too."

"Sorry, but one last thing, sir. It might be too late to get fresh jasmines. If I cannot find them, is there any other flower that you'd like instead?"

"It has to be jasmine, Albert. Just find it …"

"I understand sir. Have a great night."

Just a few seconds after Albert left, Emma came back, holding her cell phone in her hand. Her face was ambiguous. "After I hung up with my aunt, Sydney called. She wants to talk to you for some reason." She said with a nervous expression.

I held the phone, perplexed. I didn't know what to say and had no idea why her crazy cousin wanted to talk to me in the middle of the night. I only hoped that it wasn't because of Max. If he did something to make Sydney mad, I was going to make him suffer big time tomorrow.

"Hi Sydney," I said. My voice cracked a little bit.

"Hi Dylan," she replied giggling. I was relieved to hear her bubbly voice.

"What's up?"

"I don't know how you convinced my uptight cousin to spend the night with you. It is very unlike her, to say the least. Please keep doing whatever you are doing. She sounds so happy and relaxed. Just make sure that she has an unforgettable night, alright. You know what I mean."

"Yes, Sydney. I understand. Thank you for your kind warning." I uttered in an impish tone. Feeling overwhelmed under Emma's repressive expression, I ended the call immediately and handed it back to Emma.

"What did she want?" She asked curiously.

"She just warned me about your snoring. I need to pinch your nose if you do." I replied with a broad smile.

"Jesus, Dylan. You are as impossible as her."

Without letting her interrogate me any further, "Let's go," I said. I took her hand and led her towards the elevator. The anticipation of spending the night with her and Sydney's implicit comment were making me nervous. I wrapped my arms around her waist as the elevator slowly ascended to the top floor. Alone with her in the elevator, I desperately wanted to kiss her but I didn't want to rush into anything. We had all night and I was determined to make every minute of it memorable for her.

We entered the imperial suite at the top floor and Emma uttered joyfully. "Oh, my God Dylan! What a beautiful room. You have a gorgeous view of the canal. Sydney and I are sharing a dinky little room with a view of some old building's roof. This is awesome."

I didn't care much about the room or the view. The only thing that mattered to me at that instant was that she was there with me.

"Oh, look at that," she added, peeking at the stationary paper on top of the desk. "The suite is named after Willem Van Oranje, an ancestor of the Dutch monarchy. It is a classic," she continued happily, checking out the rooms and its decoration. She was telling me all about the Netherland's coat of arms when we heard the knock on the door. She squinted and bit the corner of her lower lip curiously. I opened the door, and the wonderful smell of fresh jasmines surrounded the air immediately.

"As you have requested, sir!" Albert arranged the food and the flowers on the table. He opened the chilled Dom Perignon, and then poured it into two tall crystal glasses for us. When he was done, he asked in the most respectful manner. "Is there anything else I could do for you, sir?"

"No, Albert. Thanks for all your help."

Emma's lips curved into a gorgeous smile that almost reached her eyes. "You are unbelievable," she shook her head and mumbled, inhaling the jasmine branches full of little fragrant flowers.

"Do you always impress girls with irresistible indulgences like these?" She asked after she dipped a strawberry into the crème Chantilly and took a bite.

"No, I definitely do not. This is a first for me," I said. If only she knew how she was inspiring me to do things that I had never done before.

I raised my glass, uttered "à la tienne" and then took a sip, watching her intently enjoying the cold champagne. I couldn't keep my eyes off her.

"To you…as well," she replied.

The sight of cream dipped strawberries between her soft plumb lips, and the pleasing noises she let out as she sipped the cold champagne were too much. I was utterly lost in temptation by just watching her. My eyes implored her lips, her elegant neck and the valley between her breasts; I couldn't hold myself back anymore. I quickly closed the distance between us, took the glass out of her hand and set it on the table under her curious eyes. Then swiftly, I grabbed her waist and pulled her into an abrupt kiss. I intended to kiss her tenderly but when I saw the passion flickering in her eyes; it wasn't possible to rein in my emotions anymore. My kiss became more heated reflecting the fire in me and her lips were the only cure, the only way to put out that fire. No, I didn't forget what I told her earlier. I wanted to be the gentleman but I had to relinquish my promise soon. I loved holding her in my arms and caressing her gently, but now that she was in my arms, I wanted to taste her delicate skin with my lips starting from her neck, trailing down to her breast. I wanted more. More of Emma.

As if she heard my inner thoughts, she wrapped her arms around my neck. She parted her lips slightly, enough to allow me in. We were timid at first, but when my tongue touched hers, there was suddenly an explosion of passion and desire in both of us. Her chest rose and fell in cadence, her breathing deepened and she pulled me closer, her hands caressing my arms. Our bodies were now pressed firmly against each other. I took a sharp breath when Emma's hands slipped lower. Her fingers were trailing under the hem of my shirt. I wanted her to peel the shirt off me, and graze her hands over my body. Everywhere her slim fingers touched burned with desire. Her touch was magical, sending shivers down my spine. *My God... she had no idea what she was doing to me.*

I moved an inch away breaking the kiss for a second to take a deep breath. Kissing Emma was mind-blowing. I nestled my face under her ear, teasing her earlobes with my tongue as I cupped her cheekbones softly and then brushed her bare shoulders with the tip of my fingers. She trembled and moaned in my mouth, "Oh, Dylan!" Hearing her whispering my name in her smooth velvety voice was such a turn on. My name never sounded this sexy before.

My hands trailed down and rested on the small of her back. She threw her head backwards giving me access to her neck. I inhaled her intoxicating smell, placed soft kisses on her neck all the way down to that maddening valley between her breasts. My eyes closed, I savored the sweet aroma of her lips again, my hands grazed over her legs, climbing up slowly, inch by inch towards her hips, almost touching the thin fabric of her panties. I was burning up with desire with every passing second. She was the only thing that could quench my raging thirst.

Engulfed in delirious desire, I thought about lifting her up, laying her over the bed naked and adoring every inch of her body with my lips. I wanted to give her pleasure like she never had before. 'Only if she would let me…' I wondered inwardly. For the first time in my life, I was worrying about giving pleasure to a girl, instead of rushing to the end to get what I wanted and be done with it. Emma was too special, and I wanted to be special for her. There was a gleam in her eyes that I couldn't decipher. *Did she want me to continue? Did she have second thoughts about what we started?* I hesitated to take the next step but feeling her soft hands rambling over my chest, gave me the courage I needed. She wanted me as much as I wanted her.

I slowly untied her sundress at her neck. The silky dress gracefully crawled down to her feet. I was speechless at the sight of her impeccable beauty. In her strapless black lacy bra and matching panties, she looked like a goddess - curvy and voluptuous. Her rosy nipples partially hidden underneath the black lace budded from her milky white skin. Her eyes were closed and her lips were sealed tight as I caressed her delicate skin with my knuckles, skimming over her round, perfect breasts. I wanted to remove that barrier between my sweet fantasy and my mouth immediately.

I pulled up her silky hair, and lifted her arms above her head. I started kissing the soft skin around her arm pit and her breast, slowly trailing kisses down to her stomach. My hands found the clasp of her bra. I brushed my fingers over thin lace slowly. Her chest rose, and her breathing quickened. I suddenly stopped, making her open her eyes. Our gazes met instantly.

"Emma. This is your last chance to say 'no'. Do you want this?" I asked.

She nodded once, but it was not enough. I wanted to hear her saying it. "Say it!" I whispered into her ear.

"I want you to make love to me, Dylan." She whispered back.

Upon hearing her confirmation, all hell broke loose in me. I was completely taken by lust. I unclasped her bra and gazed into her tantalizing green eyes. They were enticing, inviting me to the place above the clouds where all worldly matters disappeared, only the sweet sensations, a blissful state of mind existed.

I slowly lowered my face and flicked my tongue across the two pinky rosebuds hardening instantly with my touch as she ran her fingers through my hair. I took one rosy nipple in my mouth and starting sucking eagerly while I circled the other one with my thumb. *How was it possible for someone to taste this sweet?* Emma's soft skin tasted like sweet peaches. I knew I was going to be addicted to that taste right away. I cupped her perfectly round breasts and caressed them gently as I moved down, kissing below her navel. I slowly dipped the tip of my tongue in her bellybutton and the heat of her skin transferred to my lips instantly.

I lowered my head further, blowing cool air over her sensitive skin and heard her moans of pleasure. I brushed my hand over her lacy panties and then slipped my index finger slowly under the thin fabric. I teased her gently and watched her squirm under my touch, my warm breath seeping through the thin fabric. Her legs were already wobbly; she grabbed my shoulders to be steady. "Oh, God…" She mumbled softly.

I hooked another finger under her panties and tugged it off. I kissed her silky white skin of her inner thighs while I grazed both my fingers over her hot and wet spot. I nuzzled my face over intimately, demanding her to spread herself to give me access. Abruptly she tensed and closed her legs. I looked at her eyes beseechingly as I caressed her thighs to make her relax.

"Relax, Emma. Just let me…" I whispered.

"I…I …" She stuttered. "I haven't had sex for a long time."

"Don't worry, leave everything to me," I assured her. Then, I lifted her up and carried her to the bed in my arms. Lying on the bed, her slim fingers over her belly and her silky hair cast over her breast, she looked like the Venus in Boticelli's famous painting.

"Spread your legs Emma, and don't be shy. Tell me what you want." I demanded.

Her eyes darted up and met mine. She pursed her lips, but did not utter a word. She moved her eyes away before complying with my order. She parted her legs, but only a little bit.

"Not enough," I said smilingly and then I kneeled between her legs, separating them further with my knees to give myself the complete access. I patted her gently with my fingers and watched her tremble in pleasure. I knew what she craved for, and I was determined to give it her. I slipped one finger inside of her, touched her gently, my thumb grazing over her curls. I bowed my head and took her nipple into my mouth, sucking and licking her senseless as I eased my fingers in and out. Her eyes closed, she was biting her lips, inhaling long deep breaths. She gave herself to me completely, pressing her hips upward, moving them to the rhythm of my fingers. I could see she was getting close but I wanted her to reach her climax slowly, so I slowed my strokes. Her breathing quickened, and her eyelids slammed shut as I twirled my tongue around her wetness and sucked her hard. Soon, her body stiffened, and then shuddered in pleasure. "Oh, God! Dylan!" She cried out when I touched her one last time with my finger.

She was completely drained after she came down from her climax. I held her in my arms as she continued to shiver, her heart throbbing fast. Her breathing slowly became steady again, and she managed to utter. "Thank you!"

"Why are you thanking me?

"Because, I received this incredible pleasure while you didn't get anything…"

"Believe me Emma. It was my pleasure too. Watching you climax is a beautiful view." I confessed, smiling blissfully.

Her cheeks blushed completely red. She sat on the bed, looked softly into my eyes, then reached for the buttons of my shirt. "Aren't you a bid overdressed?" She asked friskily, and started unbuttoning my shirt. She grazed her hands over my chest, threading her fingers through my chest hair. She smoothened the hair with her palm, and leaned in to kiss me.

When her lips touched and swirled around my nipples, I felt a jolt going up through my body and down my legs. Her hands trailed lightly around my abs, placing soft kisses, and she pulled down the zipper of my pants. Her hand caressing me over my pants was torture. Her eyes feral, she licked her lips and looked at me tantalizingly. Not a second too late, she freed me of my pants and boxers. Her slender fingers skillfully brushed against my hardness. And oh, so unexpectedly, she took me into her mouth. Continuing with her soft but claiming touch, she stroked me gently as she licked my tip and then sucked hard. Her soft wet lips were my undoing. I knew I wasn't going to last any longer if she continued her sweet torture, and I didn't want that to happen. "Oh, God, Emma! Please stop…"

"But … why?" She asked innocently, looking confused. "You didn't like it?"

"Hell no! I love it. But I wanted to be in you when I come. If you kept that up, I wasn't going to last long." I confessed, and "wait here a second," I added.

I opened the side drawer and pulled a condom out. I ripped it open quickly and was about to put it on myself when she said, "Let me do it!" She rolled to condom on me slowly as if she was daring me to be patient.

"God, Emma, you're killing me," I managed to say through my clenched teeth.

I kneeled between her legs. I stroked her with my fingers just to be sure she was still wet before I eased myself into her, slowly, one inch at a time. And Oh! My! God! She felt so good. She was so tight but also so wet. She wrapped her legs around me; her green eyes on me, watching me carefully.

"I'm going to move now, Emma. Tell me how you like it."

I started to move, stroked her gently, trying to assess her reaction and waiting for her to respond. She moaned, but shook her head, turning her eyes away from me like a shy girl. I was waiting for that blunt girl that didn't mind speaking her mind to declare what she liked in bed.

"Tell me Emma," I whispered in her ear. I circled her nipples with my thumb and my lips under her ear, sucking her lobe. "Slow or fast…" I asked, as I continued slowly.

"Goddamnit, Dylan! I want it hard and I want it fast!" She finally declared.

And with that, I slammed into her hard and she jolted with pleasure. She bit her lips and smiled at me enticingly. I drew back a little before I thrust my hips steadily inside her. She met my thrust with same excitement and with each thrust I was climbing the ladder of passion like never before. "Oh, God! This feels so good." I screamed.

"Oh, please Dylan. Faster!" She demanded. The intensity of her voice matched the intensity in her eyes. Her hands were on my back… on my shoulder. Everywhere… digging into my skin. Hard! Her fingers tightened on my hips and a delicious sensation passed through me.

I lifted her legs up to my shoulder to penetrate her deeper. With each stroke, she squirmed more in pleasure. I kissed her ankles as I kept going. Going in hard and fast but easing out slow. I could see she was getting close, so I had to hold up a bit longer. After couple more deep strokes, she almost gave in. Her hands clenched into my waist, and her fingers dug deep into my flesh as she climbed higher. I eased in and out, and soon enough she bit her lips, her eyes grew wide and she cried out with pleasure. And only a few seconds later,

"Oh. Fuck! Yes!" I screamed out loud and collapsed on to her as I found my release and shuddered with overwhelming sensation.

That was mind blowing sex. The best sex of my life, indeed...

CHAPTER 7
EMMA

My heart was throbbing fast, about to come out of its cage. Dylan caressed my cheeks with the tip of his fingers, buried his face between my hair and my neck, and gave me small kisses. I didn't remember feeling this great. Ever! *Did sex always feel this good? Or was it this amazing, mind blowing and wonderful all because of Dylan?*

Truth be told, I didn't have much to compare it to. I had had two serious relationships before; my high school sweetheart, Justin, and Kyle, my charismatic teaching assistant at Columbia, whom I dated for three years and I broke up with after I caught him cheating two years ago. I broke off our engagement, moved out of our apartment in Manhattan and moved into my grandparent's old house in Brooklyn. It took over a year to put my heart back together after Kyle recklessly ripped it apart. *Why did I fall for an attending?* I still had to see him every day, either at the hospital or at the school which made me feel so uncomfortable. Sydney assured me many times that he was just an asshole and not all men were as despicable as him, but I didn't allow myself to be close to anyone after him. It was my choice. A wise decision that worked just fine for the last two years. But not today.

Today, I met Dylan and everything suddenly changed. He was a fascinating person with the soul of a romantic hidden under his rich and arrogant businessman look. I bet he didn't let many people see that side of him, the side that enthralled me so much that all my walls fell to the ground with one kiss. My defense mechanism became functionless. Even now, lying next to me, I couldn't stop staring into his deep blue eyes. His unwavering, intense gaze was making me drift far away from reality. Being in his big arms was so enticing but also very relaxing. *How was it possible to feel like I was in a safe haven and turbulent stormy seas at the same time?* I felt confused, scared, but happy.

"Penny for your thoughts." He said, breaking our comfortable silence.

"Oh, it's nothing…" I lied. I didn't want to share my mixed feelings.

"You look so beautiful." He said and twirled a strand of my hair around his finger. "You glow like a diamond. So precious."

I couldn't hide my blush. "Well, then... how about you prove your talent now, and draw me as you promised earlier. Let's see if you can capture my glow with your pencil."

"You mean you want me to draw you now, like this?"

"Yes." I smirked and squinted at him.

"You would like me to draw you nude." He repeated with a bewildered face, still not believing what I was asking for.

"Yes, Dylan," I replied with a big laugh. "You don't trust yourself that you could do it?"

"No! Not at all. I just..." He stuttered. "Let me think. I suppose I can try. Just remember I am a bit rusty and believe me, it won't be easy to draw you when you are so gracefully lying there, enticing me to do other things."

"I will look away and try not to entice you..." I smiled, and said playfully. "Now, tell me where you want me and what kind of pose."

He stifled a laugh, and was about to make a comment when I interrupted him. "Dylan, come on. No more joking. Are you going to do this or not? I'll give up on my offer if you are not going to be serious."

With my last comment his gaze changed, with the solemn expression on his face he gave me a chaste kiss, put on his boxer briefs quickly and got out of the bed. A minute later, he came back with a brown leather folder. He pulled out a clean white piece of paper, placed a pencil behind his ear and pushed the swivel leather chair in front of the bed. "Yes... I am ready," he said with a crooked smile. He placed the paper and the folder on the chair, scooted next to me, pushing the soft white linens aside.

"Hmm," he mumbled. "Let's tuck your right arm under your head and put the left on your belly without blocking your beautiful breasts. Then cross your legs, but bring your fine ass a bit forward." He ordered, helping me with my pose. His faint touches gave me chills each time, but I swallowed a deep breath and tried hard not to show my arousal. I wanted him to draw me, not do other things that he was so good at.

He studied me a long minute before his pencil moved slowly. His face was serious and his eyes were intense. His gaze moved back and forth between my body and the paper. He bit his chiseled lips every so often as he scrawled. His hand was moving on the paper eloquently as if it was dancing. I enjoyed watching him draw with a grave look on his face, as much as I enjoyed posing for him. I felt as if I was *Dora Maar* for a second. I wondered how she felt when she posed for Picasso for so many of his paintings. *How did it feel to be his lover and his model at the same time?* Did she feel as excited as I was feeling every time Dylan lowered his gaze to my breast, my navel and between my legs?

God, what has gotten into me? In less than twelve hours, I changed from a disgruntled and peevish girl into this hippie-like soul. The unusual feelings that Dylan resonated in me scared the hell out of me. 'Maybe I shouldn't have let any of it happen…It would have been better if I ignored him when he came out of that door and let him go his way.' I thought, but my heart told me to enjoy this one night and this wonderful man sitting across from me with the most handsome face.

I was lost in my thoughts when Dylan announced, "I think I am done."

"Really, you were quick. I thought it would take longer."

"It has been almost thirty minutes, Emma. I could not make it as a street artist with this speed."

"Oh, really? I didn't notice. Can I see it?" I asked.

He nodded and brought the paper with him to the bed and handed it to me.

"Wow! Unbelievable Dylan!" I exclaimed, the second I saw the drawing. "This is great. You are so talented. It is a shame that you're not painting or drawing. You are wasting your talent! Mr. Picasso."

"Ah-ha! To be called after the most talented artist of the last century. What an honor!" He bowed. "But I don't think it's my talent, my model was so inspiring that it couldn't have been less than spectacular." He teased me and then put his head next to mine, stretching his arms above his head. His eyes were on the ceiling. It seemed like he was in deep thoughts, drifting away, when suddenly he said. "Art is a lie that makes us realize the truth."

"Hmm…" I mumbled wondering. "What do you mean?"

"It is a quote from Picasso. He was a man of towering ego, almost a lunatic individualist but he was right about his assessment regarding art."

I looked at him quizzically, trying to understand what he meant.

"An artist does not necessarily create what he sees. It is a reflection of his view of life, shrouded with his emotions. In a way, it is not the reality that he puts on his canvas; what comes out of it is an illusion. Some might even call it a lie, same goes for me. It's my emotions that control what I scrawl on paper. If you think about it, I draw what I feel. Once the painting is done, I look back, and I see the truth."

I looked at his creation in my hand, trying to decipher what he implied. On the clean white paper, he accurately drew my body, my pose, linens half covering my legs, but soon I realized something was off. The girl in the picture was too perfect; she had an angel like stance. She was too serene, gracefully lying on the bed with a tranquil smile. Actually, the girl he drew was not me. It was a lie, but I wondered about the truth he was insinuating, that it revealed. I asked hesitatingly. "Then, what truth do you see when you look at this drawing?"

"That I am in love."

"What?" I cried out loud in shock, not believing my ears.

"I am in love with you Emma." Dylan repeated again.

"How can you be in love with someone you've met only twelve hours ago?"

"I don't think you need a grace period to fall in love. It just happens. It happened for me the moment I kissed you."

I couldn't say anything. How was I supposed to break him the news that I couldn't love him back? My life was difficult enough. I didn't have time for love. Love always hurt. It was inevitable and I couldn't risk getting hurt again. This was a one-day distraction, a fairy tale that was going to end in the morning. I looked at his penetrating eyes and saw my reflection in his irises. Instantly, I realized I couldn't tell him any of that. I didn't want to ruin the magic of our night. Instead, I put my head on his chest and brushed my fingers over his tattoos.

In comfortable silence in his arms, I studied the intricate design of his tattoo weaved around a very noticeable image. It was an image of a little girl and a boy, holding hands at the edge of a precipice by a lone tree in black ink. Striking words: 'always together, two free souls forever' were underneath it. "Your tattoo…What does it mean?" I asked curiously, touched by the dramatic scene, depicting the solitude of two people.

"It is Rachel and I; I got that tattoo years ago," he said. His gaze was pensive. There was an agony in his deep voice.

"Rachel?"

"My sister."

"Such a dramatic image." I whispered, wondering the afflictive situation that caused him to get him such a tattoo.

"Rachel ..." his voice cracked. "She used to be a gymnast. She fell from the cross bars during practice, six years ago, when she was twelve. She severed her spinal cord. She can't walk anymore. The days following her accident were so devastating. We thought she wasn't going to make it." He explained. His pain was visible in his eyes.

"I am sorry Dylan. I can only imagine how hard it must have been." I said.

"It was very difficult for her to accept her situation. I was terrified of losing her. It was the worst year of my life, the same year my father left. I don't care about what he did to me but I can never forgive him for abandoning Rachel like that."

There it was. The edginess and anguish in his voice whenever the subject of his father came up. I wished I had the power to eradicate his pain and make him feel lighter. I kissed him softly. His blue eyes were dark. They darted up and met mine.

"She pulled through. She is starting college this year." He said, sounding more relaxed.

"She is lucky to have a brother like you," I mumbled.

"You think so?"

"Yes, I certainly do." I said firmly, assuring him. Then, I snuggled his arm tighter, inhaling his manly scent. He played with my hair and sleep came almost instantly. I felt his soft lips, brushing mine. I vaguely heard him utter, "Goodnight Emma..." but I couldn't reply. I fell into sleep.

It was still dark, except for the moonlight seeping through the half closed curtains when I opened my eyes to the sound coming from my back-pack. My phone was vibrating in the front pocket. I wondered who was calling me at this hour. I chose to ignore it, not wanting to leave the warmth of Dylan's body surrounding me. He was sleeping peacefully. His lips were closed but I saw a glimmer of a smile on his face. *Was it possible for anyone to look happy when sleeping?* Dylan did. I touched the contours of his lips with my fingers, adoring his perfect face. I closed my eyes, hoping I could fall asleep again, however, when I heard my phone ring for the second time, I knew I couldn't. Wide awake now, I had to get my phone. I carefully untangled my legs first and my body without waking him up. I got out of the bed slowly and grinned when I spotted my panties and bra lying on the floor. My first time sleeping naked. I had never slept without changing into my pajamas before. Then again, I'd never slept with someone I had just met either. Dylan was my first for many things.

I put on my panties and clasped my bra quickly. Then, I opened the front pocket of my backpack and took the phone out. I saw that I had four missed calls in ten minutes, although I only heard the last two... While I was trying to apprehend why someone back home was calling me, I saw 'new voice mail' message popped up on the screen. 'You have one unheard message' said the mechanical voice.

"Emma, it is me. I don't have much time to talk. I am in trouble. I know you are in Amsterdam but I don't know who else to call... I had a bad accident. I hit a curb on the highway. I didn't hit anyone but I trashed my car. Police, ambulance, fire truck, every God-damn vehicle with a siren came to the scene and they pulled me out of the car. I was conscious but hurt pretty badly. They took me to the nearest hospital. Oh sis, I don't know how to tell you this. They checked me for things. You know... alcohol, drugs. I just had a couple of beers and a roll of weed. That's it. I wasn't doing anything major Ems. I swear... God, Ems! I've been arrested for DUI. They are not letting me go this time, not even with bail. As soon as I am released from the hospital, they will put me in jail. Please do something. Please ..."

I collapsed on the floor when I finished listening to his message. With one phone call, my brother managed to ruin my day again.

Steve always had issues, even during his childhood. I never blamed him for being a difficult child. He was only three years old when our mother died and father left. Not having parents around was a perfect excuse for him to act out and he exploited our love and sympathy to get away with everything. Aunt Helen and Uncle George were too understanding, regardless of his never ending problems. My father's approach to solve all of Steve's issues with money didn't help either. He was rebellious and wild, however, since he started college, he had gotten more out of control. He drank excessively. I found prescription drugs in his car, although he swore that they weren't his. After his first DUI, my father used all his leverage with the district attorney to drop the case, however this time, I wasn't sure if he would get away that easy. But jail time... was too much. There was no way Steve would survive in jail. I had to do something. I had to go back to New York and talk to Aunt Helen and my father. We had to get him into rehab, but first we had to save him from going to prison.

Devastated with the news, I forced myself to think straight. I was in Dylan's hotel room, standing half naked. I had to get to my hotel, talk to Sydney and return home.

I put on my dress and shoes and placed my backpack on my shoulder. I was about to leave the room when my eyes caught Dylan's drawing standing on the nightstand next to him. I turned back to look at him one last time. I lifted my hand debating with myself whether to touch his Adonis-like-body again when the drawing slid slowly off the night stand and landed in front of me. I grazed my fingers on the paper and his words and heartfelt confession rang in my head. *Why didn't I say something back?*

I stood by the window as the slivers of moonlight glinted above the dark blue waters of the canal. I replayed every minute of the day in my mind. My ambivalence between holding on to this magical day and facing the reality made me shiver. I knew I had to go, but I couldn't leave without saying goodbye. I turned the painting over and scribbled down what I couldn't say to his face. After a contemplative glance, I brushed his lips softly with my finger. And then, as the tears welled up in my eyes, I left the man who made me feel alive. I was probably never going to see him again.

CHAPTER 8
DYLAN

I woke up relaxed and happy for the first time in a long while. The absence of my usual mind-boggling disquietude was sheer bliss. A day with Emma changed me completely and I was impatient to start a new day with her. I had so many things in my mind that I wanted to do together: We still hadn't tried Dutch cheese, visited a tulip garden or taken a canal cruise. Doing everything or doing nothing ... it didn't matter. As long as I was with Emma.

I turned to my side to bring her into my arms again but found her side of the bed empty. I got out of the bed immediately and called her name multiple times but she didn't answer. I checked the bathroom, the study area, but she wasn't there. "Emma! Where are you?" I yelled out. Yet no one replied. Then, I noticed her backpack was not on the floor, nor her dress or her shoes. Only her silk foulard was left abandoned on the dresser. I started to panic.

Looking around the room, suddenly, I caught the glimpse of her drawing on the nightstand turned over. Rows of elegant handwriting in black ink were visible even from a distance. My heart squeezed and my stomach churned. I refused to believe this would be it. A cold goodbye note. She wouldn't do that. She wouldn't just leave without talking to me, without kissing me, without telling me how I could find her, how we would be together again. Not after all we shared. The thought of Emma leaving me while I was sleeping felt like a dagger stabbing my heart. It was madness.

I grabbed the paper and started reading immediately.

"Dylan, I am sorry. I am sorry that I have to go. I am sorry that I couldn't tell you how I felt, how great you made me feel. A day with you was enough to turn me into a completely different person, lively and joyful. It was as if I was reborn and living a different life. I enjoyed being that person for one day. It was like a dream. After listening to a dreary message on my phone, I had to wake up from this sweet dream and go back to reality. My uneasy life couldn't give me a break. Not even a day. Unfortunately, I have to go back home and continue my life as usual. You and the day we spent together will stay with me forever. Anytime I need a smile, I will think of you and our magical day in Amsterdam. I will remember you ... always. With all my love, yours Emma."

And that was it. No contact information, no phone number. Nothing to help me find her. Exasperated beyond control, I knocked the champagne glasses off the table, slammed them to the floor, and stared at the hundreds of broken pieces. "No! This can't be happening!" I yelled out in a terrible disbelief. I put on my jeans and a t-shirt quickly and went across the hallway. I started pounding on Max's door.

"Max, wake up!" I yelled. It was about seven o'clock in the morning. He was obviously dead asleep. After my loud banging and yelling at the door for couple minutes, he finally opened his door, dressed only in his boxer briefs.

"What the hell are you doing here at this God-damn hour?" He groused.

"Come on, get dressed. We need to go."

"What! No! God, no! My head hurts. I am not going anywhere! I am going back to sleep. What time is it anyway?"

"It is almost seven. And no, you are not going back to sleep. We need to find Emma. She is gone."

"Emma, the chick with the backpack."

"Yes! She left while I was sleeping. I have to find her."

"Did she stay with you last night? You banged her, didn't you? Oh yeah you did…" He smiled smugly, making me so mad that I was ready to punch his face. "She was all right, but too uptight and self-conscious for my taste. Sydney, on the other hand, was something else. She was hot and fun." He continued.

I silently counted to five to steady myself and calm down. "Max, cut the crap and listen. We were together last night, but when I woke up in the morning, she was gone. I don't know what to do. We need to find her immediately, alright!"

"Hey, chill out man. She is just another chick."

"No, she is not just another chick. She is THE girl. Please man, help me out. Did I ever beg you for anything before? I am begging you now."

"Alright! Fine!" He said and held up a placating hand with a solemn expression on his face. "But what can I do? I don't know anything about her."

"Did you take Sydney to her hotel after you guys hung out yesterday?"

"Yes, I did but nothing happened between us. I didn't fuck her if you are implying that. I promise."

"I am not implying anything. I am just saying if you have taken Sydney to her hotel, then you know where they are staying. We can go there and find Emma. Do you remember the hotel?"

"Not sure about the name of the hotel. If I see the building, I would recognize it."

"Okay, then, let's go!"

"We haven't even had breakfast."

"Since, when do you have breakfast?" I scolded him for being difficult again. "We will grab some coffee on the way. Come on now, hurry." I rushed him to dress up.

Max shook his head. He didn't understand what was going on, but he complied with my gruff orders anyway. I didn't have time to explain to him that I found the girl of my dreams and let her slip away. I was more upset with myself than I was with her. Why didn't I peek into her backpack or her purse? Why didn't I try to check her phone? I should have learned more about her, even if it meant sneaking around. It wasn't the time to be virtuous. I felt so stupid.

In less than a minute, we were outside the hotel with two dark coffees on our hand. Max took a cigarette for himself and passed the pack to me. I took one out and lit both his and mine. I took a long drag and asked, "So, which way is the hotel?"

"I remember it was by a canal."

"You gotta try harder than that buddy," I said annoyingly. 'Hotel by a canal' was not helpful information in a city full of canals.

"I think it was close to that funny 'Iamsterdam' sign."

"Okay, that's better. Now let's hurry. I hope they haven't checked out yet."

Unfortunately their hotel wasn't by the 'Iamsterdam' sign. We wandered around the narrow streets of Amsterdam for an hour without success. With every passing minute, I was getting more edgy and anxious. I was ready to take it all out on Max. "What the fuck, Max! How high were you? God damn it! How can you not remember?" I grumbled.

"I am doing you a favor here, man. If you don't mellow down soon, I am getting the hell out of here." He burst out angrily.

"Fine! Just think and try to remember," I asked calmly this time.

After walking hastily up and down every street around the museum, Max finally spotted the hotel. I rushed into the lobby and was disgusted by the smell instantly. The hotel was a dump. Why in God's name would two beautiful girls stay in a hotel like this, I had no idea.

A young guy, dressed like a hippie at the front desk greeted us with a very heavy accent. He had Bob-Marley-like long, greasy hair, braids sticking out everywhere. The stinking smell coming out of him was so strong that I had to hold my breath as I stood in front of him. Max didn't even bother coming inside. He was waiting by the door, lighting another cigarette.

I took a hundred Euro from my money clip and slid towards him. "I am looking for two girls, staying at this hotel. Emma and Sydney. I need their room number." I said and glowered at him, demanding an answer immediately. He took the money and cast a sideways look at me and then at my money clip. He checked the old fashioned log book without objecting. *God, what kind of a hotel was this? Didn't they register their guest names in a computer or something?*

"We don't have anybody with those names staying in the hotel." He mumbled.

"Two young girls around early twenties: Sydney, a blonde and Emma, auburn hair, green eyes. I am pretty sure you would remember them." I explained patiently. Two beautiful girls in a slovenly place like this would be as conspicuous as a Hollywood celebrity dining at a fast food joint.

"Oh, those two! They checked out this morning in a hurry." He said, and shrugged off.

"Would you please give me their information?" I asked and took another hundred from my stash and passed it to him.

"Sure," he said and gave me the guest book. "You can check it for yourself. Here are their names and the room they stayed in."

I checked the book carefully but there was nobody named Sydney and Emma in the book as he said earlier. Then, I studied the names that he pointed at. The names of the girls that checked out this morning were 'Elizabeth Bennet' and 'Elinor Dashwood'. I couldn't believe my eyes when I realized that they were the names of two famous Jane Austen characters. Reality dawned on me immediately. They didn't use their real names and the guy didn't care to question it. He didn't strike me as smart enough to figure out the names were fictional characters, but at least their credit card information should have told him that they weren't real.

"These are not their real names. Do you have their credit card information?" I asked solemnly.

He shook his head. "They paid cash for three days up front, but only stayed one night." He explained with an 'I don't give a damn' expression.

I was devastated, realizing that I had no way to track them down. No names, no credit card information, no phone numbers or address. *What the hell was I going to do, now?* Anxiety rushed through me. Fear of losing her forever left me in a bewildered state of trepidation. How would you find a ghost of a girl in city with millions of visitors? My logic told me it was impossible, but my heart was making me try.

"Let's go to the airport." I told Max when I got out of the hotel.

"Why?"

"Maybe we can find them at the airport. There cannot be many morning flights from Amsterdam to America."

"Come on, Dylan. We don't know their last names. We do not know where they are going. It is impossible to find them."

I was still not willing to accept the inevitable fact that I lost her. I was holding on to the tiniest possibility that I could still find them. "She said that her aunt just got off work when she called her around midnight. Considering the six hour difference, I think they may live in the East Coast. We can check out all the East Coast flights."

"We don't know if her aunt lives in the same city. We don't know if they are flying direct. They could catch a connection from London or Paris to go anywhere in America. Let it go Dylan. We cannot find them like this!"

"It sounds impossible, doesn't it?" I admitted grudgingly. "But I cannot let it go, Max. You don't get it."

"Yeah, I get it. She is your girl and all. You need to find her and be with her again. Right now, you are not thinking logically."

"I guess, you are right." I sat down on the bench with an unenthusiastic slouch. I rubbed my forehead with my fingers, trying to ease my headache. I searched my pocket for a pack, but couldn't find it. Max handed me a cigarette he just rolled.

"No, I don't want that shit." I rejected immediately.

"It would help you relax, even forget..."

He lit it for himself, took a drag and passed it to me. I shook my head again. I didn't want to relax or forget anything. I wanted to remember Emma, her beautiful face, her sexy curves, her wavy auburn hair and her deep green eyes. I wanted to remember how sweet she tasted. I gave Max a despondent look. He probably had not seen me this desperate in a very long time.

"How about this… Let's go back to the hotel and check out. Catch the first flight home." Max talked slowly.

It was either the weed making him more considerate or he pitied my desperate state. "I don't mind returning home a few days early. When we are back in New York, I will call Nolan. Maybe he can help us out," he said, sounding sincere.

"Nolan who?

"Nolan Whitaker."

"Isn't he your private investigator we used when we were tailing my dad years ago?"

"Yes, the one and only, and he is the best. Since he is a retired cop, he has great connections. He can track anyone. If you need someone to find Emma, he would be the one."

"Alright then... Let's head back home!" I agreed.

I was determined to find Emma. However long it took or whatever I had to do. I needed to make her part of my life, now that I knew how empty it was without her.

CHAPTER 9
DYLAN

The office intercom buzzed. "Mr. Hamilton, your two o'clock is here," announced Mrs. Donnelly on the speaker.

"Please, send him in." I said tersely. I was anxiously waiting for this meeting. Nolan Whitaker was a hard man to get ahold of. Since he was the best private investigator in the city, he was booked solid for two months. I had to get Max to arrange the meeting for me, and thank God, it worked. As soon as Nolan arrived in New York from whatever assignment he had in Florida, he agreed to meet me at my office.

"It is great to see you Nolan. I appreciate you seeing me on such short notice." I said and extended my hand.

He took my hand with a strong grip and gave me a firm handshake. He was well built and had at least two inches over me. Once a lieutenant in NYPD, Nolan Whitaker exuded confidence. No doubt about it. "No problem Dylan. I'd be happy to help." He drawled. "Max said it is quite important, but he didn't mention anything else. Is Richard bothering you again?"

"No, I haven't seen him for a long time, but thanks for all you did for me back then." I replied trying not to show my annoyance when I heard my father's name. "This time, I need your help for something completely different, but, I need you to sign a confidentially agreement before I can explain it to you." I added.

"Of course, Dylan. You know I honor the same level of confidentiality for every case I take on. It is part of the job." He said courteously and signed the non-disclosure my attorney prepared in a rush without even reading. "Now that we are done with formalities, how can I help you?" He asked respectfully.

"I need you to find someone for me."

"Sure. No big deal. We do that kind of thing all the time. Does someone owe you money? I can use some of my other resources if you need to get your money back."

"No, it is nothing like that. Let me explain," I paused and took the photo-copy of the drawing from my desk drawer. It was showing Emma's face only, enlarged into a full-size paper. "I need you do find this girl," I said and gave the copy to Nolan.

"Hmm, okay," Nolan uttered looking confused.

"Her name is Emma. She is a senior med student. I believe she has a brother named Steve, a cousin named Sydney, and her aunt's name is Helen."

"Alright. Good start. What else?"

"Unfortunately, this is it. This is all I know about this girl and I need your help to find her."

"You are kidding right."

"No, I am not. I don't know her last name, her school, or her phone number. I don't have any personal information on her other than what I have told you."

"But Dylan, it is impossible to find someone with this much information."

"Max told me you are the best with this kind of thing. You know, money is not a question. I just need you to find her."

"I understand Dylan, but you are not giving me much."

"I think you can start with checking the med schools in America and look at all their senior student list. Find any girl with first or middle name Emma. Then you can face-match to the picture I gave you."

"Do you have any idea how many med schools are there in United States?"

"I don't know, but I am sure you will find out."

"Some schools might not want to disclose their student list."

"I am sure you have resources to find a way around that problem." I lifted my brows, implying that I was aware of his computer guy who could hack into any database and find information.

"This could take a long time."

"It is okay. I am patient and I can wait. Just do whatever you need to do. I can even write you a blank check right now, if you need extra resources. I also have the foulard she left, if you need to get her DNA sample or something."

Nolan laughed. "Unless the girl you are looking for is a criminal, I don't think her DNA would help us. It wouldn't be in any system."

"Then, you can probably start your search with the med schools. Can't you?"

"I don't know," he murmured. "Let me think about this and get back to you. I don't like taking cases I cannot solve."

"Please Nolan. I ask your help as a friend. If you do this one big favor for me, I'll be in your debt forever, and you know I always pay my debt."

He held his intent gaze on me for a long minute, probably judging what to make of this unusual task. I was getting more nervous every passing second. I was praying inwardly that he wouldn't reject my offer when he finally uttered. "Okay!"

"You mean... you will help me find Emma."

"Yes, I'll take your case. Do you have any gut feeling where we should start our search?"

"No, not really," I said at first. "Oh, wait. She is a very smart girl. Maybe you should start with the top medical schools. Harvard, Stanford, Johns Hopkins..."

"Alright, Dylan. I will let you know as soon as I find something."

"Thank you," I replied joyfully, without hiding my excitement. Instead of a formal handshake, I gave him a big hug and a pat on his shoulder. Nolan shook his head and couldn't hide his smile. "She's gotta be one special girl," he mumbled with an insinuating expression.

My excitement was too obvious. "Yes, she is..." I smiled and replied tersely.

Five long and tortuous months passed after my first meeting with Nolan. Every week on Tuesday, we met in my office overlooking Hudson River, to go over his results and recent findings. Before long, I learned that there were over 140 accredited MD granting institutions in United States. Finding Emma in a pool of thousands of med students was like searching for a needle in a haystack. Every passing week, I was getting more despondent. I was losing hope, and my despair was making me gruff and edgy. Even my sister was getting wind of my irrepressible fury, and unfortunately, I didn't know what to do with myself or how to keep myself calm.

Besides Nolan, my partner, Max also helped me in the first couple months. I was like a modern day Romeo, trying to find his Juliet. My impossible search for Emma intrigued him so much that he even joined me on my trips when Nolan came up with a new lead. Our first trip together was to Boston to check out Emmanuelle Pierre. However, the girl turned out to be from France. She was not my Emma. Our second trip happened the week after Labor Day when we drove to Pennsylvania to check out Emma Bailey who turned out to be married with two kids. Definitely, not my Emma.

My worst day and my biggest disappointment, however, happened on the fourth month of our search. It all started with great news when Nolan found a girl named 'Emma Roselyn Conner', studying in UCLA. She was a senior med student. The vague picture of the girl that Nolan showed me matched my description of Emma. She had similar hair, curvy body but her face wasn't clear. Even the tiny bit of hope was enough to get me excited. I flew to California, the next day. I traveled six long hours on the plane and then I waited two hours outside of the medical building for her class to be over. My heart was pounding like a drum with the possibility of finding her at last. I smoked almost an entire pack waiting for my long anticipated union. I was down to my last cigarette when I saw her coming out of the building. She was talking to her friends. Her face was not visible. I yelled "Emma" and I rushed to the stairs to turn her around so I could see her face. She lifted her head slowly, and I stumbled on the stairs, almost fell when I realized with an obvious disappointment that she wasn't my Emma.

After a couple more unsuccessful attempts and fruitless travels, Max's enthusiasm dwindled. He couldn't comprehend why I was so obsessed with this girl whom I met five months ago and spent less than sixteen hours with. He did not understand why she was so special and why I had to find her. Before long, he started giving me advice on how to get over her.

It was one rainy Saturday evening when Max came to my apartment and caught me staring at her drawing again.

"You look terrible Dylan. Come to your senses! Snap out of this and let it go." He scolded me.

"I can't help it, Max. I am in love with a ghost."

"Maybe, it was not meant to be. Have you ever thought of it that way?"

"No, I don't want to think of it that way, and please stop bickering." I snickered back in annoyance. *Why couldn't he leave me alone?*

"I will stop bickering if you agree to come to a party with me."

"I am going to work on Mr. Hampstead's portfolio tonight. You can suit yourself and go to whatever party you want."

"You don't understand. Parties are not the same without my best buddy. I miss my wing man." He whined.

"Max, you can score any chick you want at any time. You definitely do not need me…Didn't you just bring two girls to the penthouse last night? I don't think you have any problems luring your admirers. Girls can't say –no– to Maximilian Donavon. Just go and leave me alone."

"Dylan, this stupid search is useless. It is eating your brain and you are turning into this incurable, dumbfounded, love struck idiot."

"Thanks for your kind words, man…I really wanna join you now."

"God damn it man! I am tired of your shitty attitude. I cannot stand it anymore. You either get your sorry ass out of this apartment, or I am done talking to you."

"I am not coming with you Max. You have a great night."

"Whatever… To hell with you and your stupid quest" He murmured.

"Great!" I replied back, but he didn't hear me. He was out of my living room in a fury. I heard him cursing more as he left the apartment.

Just as I expected, Max kept calling me all night, and I hit ignore each time. I was about to turn off my cell phone, when I remembered Rachel was supposed to call as soon as she got back from her trip. I was happy that she was living like a normal college student, not like a handicapped person, but on the other hand, every time she was out doing something unusual, I was worried like crazy. I wanted to hear that she was alright before I went to bed.

While waiting for Rachel's call, I headed to the kitchen to find something worth eating other than junk food, but all I found in the fridge was bottles of beer and a rotten apple. Since Rachel moved out to live in the dorms, my apartment didn't feel like home. It became a bachelor pad, especially worse now that Max was living with me. Looking at the empty shelves, I made a mental note to get Martha, my kind housekeeper, to buy some fresh groceries. Tired and exhausted, I picked up my cell phone to order Chinese. I saw Rachel's text that she arrived safely in NY, and then Max called again.

"God, Max! You are worse than your girls nagging incessantly after a one night stand. No means no…" I answered angrily.

"Get your lazy ass up here! Now! You don't wanna miss this!" Max yelled, ignoring all my comments. In the background, loud urban music reverberated.

"Stop yelling. I can hear you. I am still not in the mood to party."

"Can't hear you. It is so loud in here." He explained uselessly. "Dylan, this place is swarming with hot girls. You wouldn't believe it. It is the party of the year. I need my wing man."

"I am not interested in hot stupid girls. You already know that."

"Believe me these girls are not dumb bimbos. This is something different about this party...I am telling you." Then, there were more loud voices in the back ground. A happy birthday song chimed in my ear. I was bored of listening to the birthday party of a typical rich and spoiled Upper East Side girl.

"I am sure there is nothing I haven't seen before. I am still not interested." I said. I was ready to hang up, when Max interrupted me nervously.

"Hey, Dylan! Don't hang-up. Somebody just came in." He bawled. "They are all over her. I thought, she was a celebrity or something but she is not. This girl who just walked in, she looks like your girl."

"What girl?"

"Your girl. Emma. She looks like Emma."

"You saw Emma walk into a party in Manhattan?"

"Yeah man. About five foot four, light auburn hair, and gorgeous body! If it ain't her, then she has a twin in Manhattan.

"Don't fuck with me, Max." I shouted at the wireless headphones tucked in my ear. I was nervous and panting over the possibility that I might have found Emma. In New York, of all places. Still, I didn't want to get my hopes too high. I had this uneasy feeling that Max was playing a game with me to get me down there. I had to be sure. I couldn't handle another Emma look alike.

"Just walk over there and check her out. Does she have big green eyes and an infinity tattoo in her wrist?"

"Give me a sec. They are at the far corner. I cannot tell."

"Just hurry up, and check it out. Damn it!" I burst out impatiently.

"Damn you, Dylan. I am not your private investigator. Why don't you get your lazy ass up here and check for yourself! She is your girl, not mine." At that instant, I heard someone shouting out Emma's name in the back ground again and her familiar voice. My heart squeezed even more.

"Max, text me the address right away. Listen to me! Lay low, but do not let her out of your sight. I will be there as soon as possible!"

"Yes, sir!" Max answered mockingly.

I rushed into my bedroom to change as soon as I hung up the phone. Could it be possible that all this time while I was searching for her all over the United States, she was right here in New York, living within a few miles of me? I was so nervous that it took three times to correctly button my shirt. I wished I had the time to shower and dress up nicely, but I couldn't risk running late and missing her. If indeed she was my Emma, I had to get to that party quickly. I put on my old jeans, wet my hair and put my fingers through it a few times. I was out the door in less than five minutes and without even checking myself in the mirror, I hoped I looked decent enough.

As soon as I was out the building, I cursed myself. It was still raining, which meant there was no way to get a taxi quick enough. After a twenty minute wait and torturous forty minutes in traffic, I arrived at the night club close to eleven o'clock. I found Max, waiting for me nervously at the door.

"Finally! What took you so long?" Max yelled in a fury.

"It's Saturday night and raining. I couldn't get a taxi." I explained in a peremptory tone. "Anyways… where is Emma?" I asked curiously.

"They left… about twenty minutes ago."

"What do you mean they left? You just let her leave. Who was she with? Where did they go? Why did you let her leave?"

"Easy there, man. One question at a time. You told me to lay low. So I did! I watched her closely, hoping you'd make it here quick enough, but I saw her leaving with a guy."

"A guy... like a boyfriend?"

"I don't know, maybe. They looked close."

"God damn it! …" I cursed. "Now, what I am going to do?" I asked uselessly. I was frustrated and needed a drink right away. I walked to the bar, Max by my side.

"Just get me the same!" I said to the bartender, pointing to the drink at Max's hand.

"Macallan 18, on the rocks!" Max ordered for me.

I grabbed my Scotch and drank it gratefully right away. I hoped the burning sensation of Scotch in my throat would ease the ache in my heart. But it didn't. I was twenty minutes late and she was gone. I inhaled sharply, peering into Max's eyes, looking for some answers. Some help.

"Chill out, Dylan! I wasn't just waiting idly for you to get here. " He replied calmly, sensing my desperate situation. "I asked about her to some other girls in the party when I saw that she was leaving. I found out her last name for you and where she works. See, I am not as useless as you think." He laughed.

"Are you serious?" I exclaimed happily. "You are the best! So… tell me!"

"Not so quick. You have to promise me that when you find her, if she is with someone else, you'll give up on her. This obsession of yours needs to end. Happy or not."

I glared at him while he sipped his Scotch and smiled smugly, waiting for my response. The mere idea of Emma with someone else was enough to make me furious. I forced myself to keep my temper down in front of people who could possibly be her friends. "Max! Please!" I demanded unwaveringly.

"Fine," he knitted his brows and replied. "Her name is Emma Collins. She works at Harlem Hospital. She's there tonight, working in the ER. I'm not sure of her schedule for the rest of the week. That, you need to find out yourself. Are you happy now?"

I pulled him into a tight embrace and said. "Yes, I am!"

Max shook his head. "Get your hands off me, dude!" He chuckled. "Go, find her. Never forget who helped you …"

"Yeah…whatever!" I said and left the night club with a huge smile on my face. Finally, I was minutes away from seeing Emma. All I needed now, was a quick and affective plan.

CHAPTER 10
EMMA

I was about to change into my bleached scrubs when Amy entered the locker room. "Hi Emma," she greeted me happily, and smiled. A tiny dimple appeared in her left cheek. She was her usual, cheerful self. I didn't know how she kept her positive and joyful attitude all the time while I felt completely exhausted and mirthless.

Amy and I had been taking classes together for five years, however this was the first time we were in the same clinical rotation group. We both picked Harlem to do our four week emergency medicine rotation. It is one of the core, but also the most difficult rotations of the program. We were in our third week and I was so exhausted after our twelve hour long shifts. I was glad Amy was there with me. She was a good friend and a great study partner. She was also one of the best med students in Columbia. She was going to be a great doctor and probably get accepted to the Mayo Clinic for her residency.

Amy took off her rain sodden jacket, scarf and hat and then turned around, studying me a full minute, checking out my dress, my shoes and my hair before she changed into her scrubs. "You look different. Ems! Actually, you look great! I don't think I've ever seen you in a dress before. Look at you, all foxy." She complimented me.

"I had to attend a party." I replied.

"A party? How nice! What was the occasion?"

"My brother's birthday. Also, it was a celebration of completing his mandatory community service, as if it was something worth celebrating."

"You sound like you didn't want to be there."

"Honestly, I didn't. He doesn't deserve a party. You know he was charged with DUI for the second time this year. He is only eighteen. He shouldn't be drinking."

"He is just a kid Emma. He makes mistakes. We all make mistakes."

"Not like his mistakes. This one could have cost him his life or he could have killed someone."

"But he didn't... I think you are exaggerating."

"No I am not. He is always in so much trouble. After his accident, when the police reports got out, my father tried to keep it quiet, you know his usual way, handling everything with money, but it back fired this time. If my aunt didn't interfere, he was going to get a minimum of four weeks jail time, but he got away with community service only. I hope he learned from his mistake, but I know him well enough not to get my hopes up too high for him."

"Give him a break Emma, he has been through a lot this year. He lost his girlfriend. That's not something easy to deal with at his age." She said empathically.

"His girlfriend overdosed on drugs, Amy. Why doesn't he hang out with normal people and have a normal relationship? I don't care about all the drama in his life anymore. He brings it all on himself. If it happens again, I won't help him. I am done with cleaning up his messes."

"Okay, big sister! Calm down and lose that temper of yours right away. We have twelve long hours ahead of us. Our attendings are Dr. Marshall and Dr. Kim today. If you get Dr. Marshall, you are in for a rough night. He's not in a good mood, I'm telling you."

"Oh, tell me that you are kidding. I thought he was on vacation."

"Nuh-uh! It's the holiday season. All vacations are cancelled. Have you seen the emergency room? We are busy as hell."

"Or heaven. Don't you wish heaven would be busier than hell?" I replied with a smile.

"There you go...I like happy Emma better. Keep up that smile, and our shift will be over before you know it. Now let's go."

When we were out the door, I saw a swarm of grumpy people sulking, reading or chitchatting in the waiting area. Many coughs, sneezes and murmurs filled the room which was crowded to more than its capacity. I approached the head nurse, Mrs. Dorian. "Here we are," I said, already dreading showing up early.

"Great, you guys are here early. We need you to start immediately. The waiting room is full with not-so-happy patients." She spoke fast, moving around with a stack of yellow folders and registration forms piled up in her arms. "Emma, you are following Dr. Marshall. Amy, you are with Dr. Kim. And Emma, Dr. Marshall wants you to do the first assessments on all cases tonight. He will review your notes and then go in to see the patient after. We are trying to save time. We have over twenty patients waiting to be seen already. Let's go girls." She explained and hurried to the admittance counter as we followed her like little ducklings.

When I saw the tall stack of folders and admittance forms waiting to be processed, I exclaimed in shock. "Oh, my god! What happened? Is there a natural disaster that I don't know about?"

"Welcome to the holiday season in the ER, Emma. Wait till you see Christmas Day."

I shook my head in disbelief. "Okay. Who is first?"

"Four year old boy. Joshua Tanner. Unknown object lodged in his nose."

"Stuffed nose again!" I chuckled. "Didn't we have a girl who stuck a Barbie shoe up her nose two weeks ago? Why do kids like to stuff things in places where they don't belong? I wonder what this boy stuck in there."

"Ten dollars for peas." Nurse Dorian said smilingly. "Or french fries," the younger Nurse Johnson chimed in.

"I bet it is another toy. I'd go with a Lego piece," I said and took his folder.

I spent a few minutes checking both of his nostrils and assessing his general condition. Despite his constant crying, he was breathing fine with no aches around his sinuses. I noted that the object wasn't lodged in too far. It was visible from outside and could be extracted with tiny forceps. After my first assessment, I called in Dr. Marshall. Joshua's mother nervously listened to my comments and waited for the doctor to arrive. As soon as he was in the room, they asked him the same questions that I already answered, which I suspected would happen. A med student didn't give the same level of confidence to nervous parents as an attending doctor. "Only one more semester left and then I will be Dr. Collins, not the med student Emma, and things will be different." I thought inwardly.

Upon checking Joshua's nose, Dr. Marshall told them that I was going to remove the object under his supervision. I sensed their hesitation at first but, thank God, I was able to get it out in my first attempt. When I put the little round marble on the table, Joshua screamed happily and his parents finally took a deep breath with obvious relief. I smiled and sighed heavily for successfully handling my first patient of the night. One down...many more to go.

As soon as I was out of the room, I went back to get the charts for the next patient from Nurse Kelly. Kelly was our twenty four year old, cutest and youngest nurse in the ER. She had such a bubbly character and was the favorite among patients and doctors alike. I enjoyed working with all the nurses, but Kelly was exceptionally pleasant.

"Okay, I am ready for the next one." I said.

"Hi Emma." She said happily. "Here is the information on your next patient. He is in for difficulty breathing, severe cough and fever. Blood pressure is normal 110 over 65. Fever is a bit high but not too much, around 100."

"All right. Which room?" I asked.

"He is in room 104." Kelly answered and giggled, "Emma, watch out, he is a cutie. I lost my count while I was measuring his blood pressure. I had to do it twice."

"You and your cute patients! Thanks for the warning, though." I said and chuckled. "I think you need a boyfriend." I whispered.

"You, too!" She replied back, giggling again.

I took the registration form off her hand swiftly, raised my brows at her and started checking out the patient information immediately:

Last Name: Hamilton
First Name: Dylan
Gender: Male;
Address: 8857 5th Avenue, NYC, 10065
Age: 30
Height: 6ft 1in
Weight: 195 lb
Smoking: Yes
Drinking: Yes
Purpose of Visit Today: Trouble Breathing, Coughing and Fever
Existing Medication: None other than Protein Supplements and Vitamins
Medical History (check all that apply): No known problems
Allergies: None
Primary Care Physician: None

Other than the trouble in breathing part, which I knew that most patients tended to exaggerate, it looked like a straight forward case relating to the common cold or flu. General information about Dylan Hamilton was like any other patient. Everything but his name.... even after five months, I couldn't help but wonder every time I met someone named Dylan. Seeing his name and the description matching the man I couldn't forget, made me nervous. I pushed my wayward thoughts away and with his file in my hand, I knocked on the door, wondering why a 5th Avenue guy was visiting Harlem's ER, not Mt. Sinai and entered. A tall, dark haired man with a well-built body was standing in the middle of the room, facing away from the door. My heart started to race with the sight of his back. He was wearing a black shirt and jeans. *'Could it be even possible?'* I thought.

"Good Evening, Mr. Hamilton." I called his name nervously. I was about to say, "I am Emma, assisting Dr. Marshall" when he turned around. With the sight of his piercing blue eyes and disarming smile, I lost my already feeble balance and almost collapsed on the floor. I tried to recompose myself after the initial shock but my body didn't obey me and swayed as if I was dizzy. Completely speechless, I couldn't utter a word.

"Emma! Are you alright?" Dylan rushed towards me, holding me in his arms.

I straightened myself and took a step back, "Shouldn't I be the one asking you that question, Mr. Hamilton?"

"I guess you're right! Dr. Collins." He grinned.

"Why are you here, Dylan? What are you doing in the ER?"

"Really! Is that what you want to know after all these months? " He asked insinuatingly. "Do you have any idea what I've been through these last five months and all the things I have been doing to find you?" He said harshly. His eyes were wide and feral, demanding answers, I couldn't give.

"Dylan, I have many patients waiting with real emergencies that need to be seen right away. This is not the time or the place to discuss this. I have to go and I think you should leave."

"I am a patient too, Dr. Collins. Don't I deserve the same attention that little Joshua got?"

"Joshua was a real patient. You, on the other hand…"

"I am here to be seen by a doctor too."

"Okay, fine! Mr. Hamilton. Let's start." I replied in a fit of irritation. "You stated that you have been coughing and have trouble in breathing. Also some mild fever. When did your coughing and trouble in breathing start?"

"I think my trouble breathing started about five months ago and got worse every passing month. I've been coughing a lot more in the last few weeks, but my fever just started today."

"Why have you waited five months to see a doctor?" I asked, trying to soften the edginess in my tone.

"I've seen couple others in different hospitals and states but none of them could solve my problem. I have been trying to find the right doctor, and searching for her everywhere in the States." He answered again playfully.

I shook my head, feeling frustrated. I crossed my arms in annoyance and glared at him. I was in the middle of my rounds and didn't have time to play his little games. If Dr. Marshall found out I was here, wasting my time with a guy I'd been involved with months ago, I would be in trouble. It would be the end of my clinic here.

"Dylan, please, this is my work, and it is not a game. There are people who have been waiting in line for hours to be seen. The triage nurse probably got you in quickly because you stated difficulty in breathing. It looks like you are breathing just fine."

"I don't feel good, Emma. I am serious." He started coughing for real.

"Well, that cough doesn't sound good," I said. I was worried now. Maybe he wasn't faking after all. "You might have a chest infection. Alright, let me check you. Would you please unbutton your shirt and lay down. I need to listen to your chest." I ordered him.

"With pleasure!" He answered smugly. I bit back an angry response and gave him a warning look to behave himself.

Take deep breaths, in and out," I said, lifting his chin up and I felt his chest rise. I placed both my hands on his chest, feeling the palpation inside of his body. It was text book inspection. After the initial visual and hand assessment, I grabbed the stethoscope and listened to his heart beat as well as his breathing. He was about to say something when I silenced him. "Shush. Please turn around. I need to listen to your lungs from the back too."

He did as I told, without objecting. His back turned towards me, I was able to escape his penetrating glare. I had to act professional; I couldn't let him see how he affected me. If only he knew how I wanted to ruffle my hand through his chest hair and relive the magic of that night.

After listening to his lungs, his breathing and coughing for a few minutes, I finally broke the silence. "I hear some rattling sounds. It might be something serious like bronchitis or pneumonia. I am going to order a chest x-ray. Are you are coughing up phlegm… thick mucus, I mean?"

"No. I am not."

"Do you have any pain in your chest? And is it any worse when you breathe in or out?"

"Yes, I have pain in my chest. For over five months now. It hurts all the time."

"Dylan! Be serious." I rolled my eyes and scolded him gruffly.

"Emma!" He exclaimed, mimicking me. "I am serious."

"How much do you smoke?"

"About a pack a day."

"You know that smoking will kill you and you need to quit. Don't you?"

"Yeah. I know!" He replied without making eye contact. "It is not easy to quit when you have so many things on your mind."

"You should just do it."

He grabbed my arm and turned me around to face him. "One fight at a time, Emma. Maybe now that my biggest fight, the impossible search for Emma- the senior med student is over, I might consider quitting." He said without blinking.

Oh Dylan! Damn you and your bluntness! I blushed deeply and turned away. I had to calm down if I wanted to make it through the night. I couldn't let him see what his words and his touch did to me. I gestured towards the door, "Nurse Kelly will take you to radiology to get your chest x-ray." I said. "My attending Dr. Marshall will examine you after we get your x-ray results. He should be able to tell what's going on in your lungs."

"But I don't want Dr. Marshall examining me. I want you, Dr. Collins." He straightened up, sat on the bed and took my hands into his. His fingers were soft, caressing my palm softly and his eyes were warm and inviting again, just like I remembered.

"Dylan, please." I uttered, begging.

He raked his hand through his hair. "Don't, Emma. Don't fucking say 'please'! I have been trying to find you for months. You could at least hear me out." He sighed and shook his head.

"I will Dylan, but not now. Not in the middle of my rounds."

"Okay, fine. I'll wait. You will have a break at some point. Won't you?"

"It's a busy night. I don't know when. You should go home after Dr. Marshall examines you and writes your prescription."

"No. I won't go home. I – will – wait – for – you – here." He enunciated slowly.

"Fine, but don't wait in the ER. There are many sick people in there. Your coughing could get worse. We have a cafeteria around the corner. Wait for me there. I will come as soon as I have a break."

I left the room, panting. I was the one having difficulty breathing now. I dropped Dylan's paperwork and my notes on Dr. Marshall's desk, still shaking and went to check with Kelly for the next patient.

"You look like a ghost. What happened to you Emma?" She asked out of nowhere. "Was Mr. Hot Guy mean to you? Don't let these rich Manhattan playboys bother you. It's not worth it." She said.

"No, he was fine. I'm fine. Just tired," I mumbled, trying to evade her scrutinizing eyes. "I need you to get his chest x-ray while I check out the next patient. Find me when his results are ready. I will get Dr. Marshall to review them and my notes. He'll check him afterwards."

When Kelly came back with Dylan's x-ray results, without waiting for Dr. Marshall, I checked them myself first and was relieved to see he didn't have pneumonia or acute bronchitis. I wondered what the reason was for the rattling I heard in his chest. I called in Dr. Marshall and we got into the room together this time.

Dylan, to my surprise, acted completely different in front of Dr. Marshall. He didn't say anything or act to imply that we knew each other. He was a perfect gentleman.

"Mr. Hamilton. This is a teaching hospital, so we have students on clinical rotations here most of the time. Emma Collins is from Columbia University. I believe, she has already examined you and ordered a chest x-ray. Now let's see what your results show." Dr. Marshall explained and looked at his chest exam results. He listened to Dylan's lungs quickly afterwards, "There is faint rattling sound like Emma noticed, but your x-ray results look clean. As clean as it can be for a smoker." He said bluntly without trying to be nice. Dr. Marshall didn't like smokers. "The good news is that I do not see any sign of pneumonia or acute bronchitis. It might be the flu or your smoking. You should quit and see if you feel better. I'll write you a prescription for your coughing and fever just in case. Do you have a preferred pharmacy? We can fax it in for you. "

"No." He shook his head and kept his intense gaze on me without breaking his reticence while he patiently waited for Dr. Marshall to finish writing the prescription.

As soon as Dr. Marshall was out the room, Dylan grabbed my waist abruptly and locked me in a tight embrace. I didn't know what to say or what to do. It felt so good but also so scary to be in his arms again. I listened to his deep breathing, felt his chest rising up and down as he buried his face in my hair. His soft touch made my heart race again, and for that fleeting moment as he slowly raked his fingers through my hair and brushed my face with his finger, I was not a doctor in the ER dressed in scrubs. I was back in our hotel room in Amsterdam filled with jasmines, enjoying succulent treats. Feeling his lips resting on my neck, my body became a fire ready to ignite. I wanted to him to kiss me. I wanted to feel his strong body. I could have stayed in his arms, in that comfortable place where everything felt magical but I knew I had to stop this before it got out of control, and I had to do it immediately.

"I have to go." I whispered in his ears.

He didn't say anything back, but his solemn expression told me what he couldn't say in words. I could see in his dreamy eyes that Dylan Hamilton was back in my life. This time, there was no way I could run away from him.

CHAPTER 11
DYLAN

I was dreaming again. It was the same one I had every night for the last five months. Emma was in my arms, giving me soft kisses but before I could do something, she disappeared in the thick fog, as if she was a droplet of water, evaporating into the thin air. Feeling lost and abandoned, I didn't know what to do. I was aware that it was just a dream, but the same scene with the same vile ending threw me into nervous apprehension every time. Regardless of how I tried to grasp on to her, or freeze the image while she was still in my arms, it never worked. She always disappeared, turning a sweet dream into a nightmare.

So, there I was, having the same dream, wondering when she was going to slip away. However this time, something felt different. I heard a soft voice calling my name. Then, uncertain fingers stroked my hair. I kept my eyes closed, enjoying the relaxing, faint touch, and wondering how my dream felt so real. Then, I heard that sweet voice again. "Dylan, wake up!" The voice said.

I opened my eyes and couldn't believe Emma was there, standing in front me, gazing into my eyes. She was real - I wasn't dreaming. Still shaken, I moved towards her abruptly without giving her a chance to react. I cupped her face and pulled her into a deep kiss. Her lips were soft and sweet like ice-cream melting in my mouth. I couldn't get enough. I moved gently first with persuasive and eloquent touches, brushing her mouth. Her labored breathing was uneven. Her hands were in my hair, tugging it softly. I had a sweet satisfaction realizing that she responded almost as passionately as she did the last time we kissed. I was making her pant. Making her desire me. She inhaled deeply, parted her lips just a tiny bit and I slipped my tongue into her mouth. I was recklessly imploring for more when suddenly she broke away. I opened my eyes, feeling desperate from losing the touch of her lips. I pulled her to myself again but "Dylan," she whispered softly. "We need to stop. We are in a hospital."

"I had to make sure..." I mumbled, half consciously.

"What do you mean, you had to make sure?" She asked with a confused look on her face.

"Make sure that you were real."

"Dylan, I told you I'd see you in the cafeteria when I had a break. Don't you remember? I was able to get a break just a few minutes ago. I came right away and found you sleeping."

"What time is it?"

"About three thirty in the morning. Sorry, I couldn't come sooner!"

"No, it's okay. I was dreaming about you. It was the same dream. The one where you always disappear in the end." I pulled her close one more time, and placed just a soft kiss on her lips. "I just had to kiss you before you disappeared again. God! I missed you so much…" I whispered in her ear.

"How can you miss someone you've spent less than a day with months ago, Dylan?" She asked. Her innocent face and perplexed disposition made it obvious how clueless she was about what she meant to me.

"You have no idea, do you?" I asked and continued without waiting for her to speak. "You don't know what I have been going through these last few months."

She shook her head and turned her eyes away.

"Why did you leave me like that Emma?" I asked softly. "Why didn't you leave me a phone number, or an e-mail, or an address? Or anything? Anything that could help me to find you. I deserved more than a cold goodbye note."

"Dylan, it was one night. We agreed!" She replied back solemnly. Was she tired or did she just not care? It hurt so much seeing her living a normal, busy life while I was hopelessly lost in the affluence and emptiness surrounding me on the Upper East Side.

"You know I didn't agree to that." I shook my head, and objected immediately. "I even told you that I didn't want it to be one night. God damn it Emma. I told you how I felt about you. You knew, but you still left. I replayed every moment of that day in my mind millions of times. If I didn't have your drawing or your note, I would think my mind was playing a wicked game on me. I had the silk foulard you left and your drawing and my memories. The sweet taste of your lips, your skin, and your body… as if it happened yesterday. Still fresh! Still making me ache for what I lost. I knew I had to find you."

"Oh, Dylan, Stop! Please don't do this." She said solemnly. Her voice was cold. It cut through me like a sharp blade but her face and the soft hue of her green eyes… they contradicted the cold words slipping out of her mouth. I didn't want to believe that she was happy and content in her life while I was in complete turmoil.

"Don't do what Dr. Collins?" I spat aloud in an infuriated tone that I couldn't suppress. "Don't talk about how disappointing it was to realize that you were gone after such a wonderful night? You don't want to hear how I searched for you in the streets of Amsterdam for hours, and how I finally found your hotel, but found out that you used fake names and left no credit card information. You don't want to know that I hired a private investigator to find you, and how we searched every God-damn medical school in the States with a student named Emma."

"No, you didn't!" She uttered in disbelief.

"Oh, yes I did." I groused back. I couldn't hold the emotions I held within me for months. "I know that there are over 140 medical schools in United States and about 175 Emma's. I rode to Columbus, Boston and Baltimore, even flew to Los Angeles, to check some of them."

"But Dylan, why would you do that? Why didn't you just let it go?"

"How could you even say that, Emma! What I felt, I am sure you felt too. What we had was wonderful. Beautiful. Magical… but unlike you, I wanted that magic to continue. One day wasn't enough. I did everything I could to find you."

"So… your private investigator found me and told you where I worked?" She met my gaze in sad understanding.

"Believe it or not, it wasn't my PI who found you. It was Max. He was invited to a party downtown and said that he saw you there. At first I didn't believe him, but then I had to check it out, even if there was a slightest chance that it could be true. By the time I got there, you were gone."

"I had to work tonight. I left early."

"Max said you left with a guy, and you two looked close. Do you have a boyfriend Emma?" I checked her hand to be sure she was not wearing a ring. I didn't know what I would have done if she told me she was engaged or had a boyfriend. "Please don't beat around the bush… Fuck it! Just say it, if you do."

"God, Dylan, you are unbelievable. You can't barge into my life like this and demand answers! It was just one night. How dare you make Max spy on me? What gives you the right to pry into my private life?"

"Emma, just answer it. Damn it." I straightened myself up, leaning over the edge of the table. I stifled the urge to slam the table with my clenched fist and shoved my hands to my pants, instead. "The guy at the party… was he your boyfriend?" I asked after calming myself. I had no right to demand an answer, but I couldn't control instantaneous rage and jealousy. I was going crazy just thinking about the possibility of Emma being with someone else.

She swallowed hard and pursed her lips stubbornly. "No! He wasn't my boyfriend Dylan." She answered after a long, quiet minute. "Are you satisfied now?" She added looking upset, angry even.

"Who is he, then?" I asked, frustrated that I couldn't prevent my curiosity to show. "Tell me that you don't have a boyfriend Emma. Tell me that there isn't somebody…"

"I don't have anybody in my life Dylan. Anybody the way you mean." She replied. "God, don't you see my life. I work twelve hours in the clinic four days a week and then go to school. The guy who Max saw with me was my brother, Steve. He was the reason why I had to leave you that night in Amsterdam."

"But why?"

"Because… my brother is an idiot. He had an accident, crashed his car on the highway and got arrested for DUI. He is not even twenty years old and had his second DUI charge in a year. I had to come back and help save his miserable ass from going into jail."

"Sorry Emma. I didn't know." I paused, and sighed deeply. "But you should have told me instead of running away. I could have helped you, helped him! We could have solved all these problems together."

"No, Dylan, you can't help me, or help my brother, and we're not together. There is no us. Why don't you want to understand that?"

"You know the reason why!" I said in a stiff voice.

"Dylan! Please, don't!" She interrupted abruptly. She was biting the tip of her index finger nervously. A pair of unblinking wide eyes shifted to my hands. She unclasped them and held them between hers.

"Why Emma? Why don't you want to hear me?" I asked. My eyes and voice grew increasingly desperate. "All I ask from you is to give me a chance. That's all." I begged despairingly. My hands and body felt limp. I didn't have any strength or desire to stand up and show her that I was okay. The truth was obvious. I was debilitated without her. *Didn't she see that?*

It was the first time in my life that I felt this weak and hopeless. I nervously waited for her to say something while she stood in front of me, completely reticent. She put her hand on my arm, caressing gently and the other one, tangling my hair as if she was trying to calm me down before she broke the bad news. She didn't need to utter a word; her eyes reflected her confused emotions. Maybe she pitied me or felt sorry. I probably deserved to be pitied in such a desperate state. There wasn't a trace of the mighty, fearless Wall Street businessman in the person collapsed on the chair in front of her. The person looking at her beseechingly was scared like hell to be rejected.

I wondered inwardly what happened to famous Dylan Hamilton. Once a bad-ass bachelor, infamous party boy, enjoying a different girl every night, I never thought somebody could change me so drastically. *How did I become this man chasing one girl?* It just happened. Nothing was the same since I met Emma. After five long months of agonizing search, there she was, in front of me, and I was willing to bow and scrape, even beg for her to give me a chance, a chance to be with her one more time, while she stood austere, not touched at all.

I waited for her to break the silence as I confined her soft green eyes with my gaze. I wanted her to say 'yes'. But the longer she waited, I saw that she was getting more reluctant and I found myself utterly unable and impotent to do something. Not even during my dreadful fights with my father had I felt this powerless. During her lingering silence, it didn't matter that I was one of the most successful businessmen under thirty selected by Forbes Magazine or the part owner and the chief executive officer of Phliant Investments, one the nation's top twenty 'up and coming' companies. Neither the success of my company nor my personal achievements mattered while I was in front of this unpretentious woman, dressed in washed-out scrubs, with hair tucked into a pony tail and a pale, tired face. I owned almost everything that money could buy, but Emma...she owned me, and she wasn't even aware of it.

Finally, I couldn't stand the tense silence anymore. "Come on, Emma. Please say something. I am not asking for a lot. How about just dinner?"

"I'll be here till noon. Then, I will go home and sleep. I have to be back at the hospital by eleven tomorrow night."

"You still need to eat something."

"Yes, but I never have time for a sit-down dinner. I usually eat something on the go, or munch from a vending machine."

"I am fine with that. We can have our dinner on the go, we'll grab a hotdog or a sandwich. Or if you can spare an hour, I could bring a take-out dinner to you."

She thought a long second which seemed as long as an hour, and finally said. "You will not take 'no' for an answer, will you?"

"See, you already know me!" I grinned heartedly.

"Okay, fine Dylan, you win. Dinner… my house… 8:00pm. You asked for an hour, I am giving you two." She said, and her lips curved slightly, it was almost a smile. She took a pen from her pocket and jotted down her cell phone in my palm.

"Call me when you arrive. My doorbell is broken."

"Where do you live?"

"I live in Brooklyn."

"Brooklyn?"

"Yes, Mr. 5th Avenue. Do you mind getting out of Manhattan?

"No, not at all."

She wrote down her street name and number underneath her phone number and smiled playfully. "There you have it. All my information is in your hand now."

"Yeah, literally." I said.

"Now, you should go home and sleep. Also, don't forget to fill your prescription. Start taking them right away. I don't want to hear you coughing like that again."

"Ten-four, doctor! I'll see you tonight."

"Night, Dylan!" She grinned and sauntered back to the ER, waving me goodbye.

It was pitch black outside when I left the hospital. It was a moonless, cloudy night. My mind was still so occupied with the events of the day that I didn't want to take a cab back to my place right away. Any other night, I would have avoided the wet, muddy streets, but not tonight. Tonight, the fresh rain smell in the air drew me in. New York City didn't look gloomy or smothering, instead everywhere I looked, it sparkled. Resplendent icicles dangling on the roof tops, festive holiday decorations on the store windows and bright twinkling lights on trees turned the city into a winter wonderland. After spending many days in dejection, I just happened to notice the beautiful transformation of the Big Apple into the holiday season.

I walked idly on empty streets and thought about all that happened in the last few hours. When I got close to my apartment, I decided to take a stroll in Central Park instead of heading home. I lingered a bit in the park, watched the clouds move slowly, clearing the night sky. I didn't want to go back home and face Max and his mocking questions.

I regretted letting Max move in with me almost every day. His three story penthouse, only a block way, was under some serious construction and renovation. The rich bastard wanted to have a private indoor pool, as if it was something he was going to use. His instant desire had nothing to do with swimming, he just had to have one after he saw Marcus Lawrence, CEO of KPC investment's, new penthouse. So, right after we got back from Europe, the construction of his penthouse started, and instead of checking into a hotel and saving me all this grief, Max asked to stay with me. As his best friend, I couldn't say no. Thinking back, I know now why I didn't. I was so depressed and moody while searching for Emma that I thought having Max around would cheer me up a little. Unfortunately, as construction got delayed, his supposed-to-be-short stay got longer. After spending four months in the same apartment with the most selfish and arrogant man I knew, I was ready to kick him out.

I got back to my apartment just before dawn, hoping to find Max asleep. I wasn't ready to be interrogated about Emma.

When the elevator opened to the foyer of my living room, I heard voices in a language that I didn't understand coming from inside. "What the hell..." I mumbled, wondering if I had a break in, although I knew it wasn't possible. Russell, our old and faithful doorman, would never let anybody in without checking with the residents first, and only Max and I had elevator keys to the top floor.

The reality hit me quickly when I entered the room. In front of the tall bay windows overlooking the park, I saw Max with a tall blonde girl and a second one on the floor, getting herself ready to be next. His ass was half covered behind the white piano on the marble floor, however I could still see what was going on.

"What the fuck, Max!" I groused at him angrily.

He turned his head around just a little while he continued doing the blonde. "Hey, man…What's up! I wasn't expecting you to show up tonight."

"I see that! Obviously!" I said, totally abhorred and disgusted. I turned around and kept looking at the ceiling, waiting for him to stop while she kept moaning and speaking in a language that sounded like Russian.

"Max!" I shrieked to make him stop, but he was oblivious to my plea and he continued to slam into the girl hard, as though he was having a casual conversation. After a full minute of Max's silence, the girl's foreign chatter and various sex noises, Max moaned loudly. "Oh, fuck yes!"

"Are you done?" I yelled at him, completely frustrated. I was ready to punch him in the face and throw him out the door that minute.

"Yes!" He answered back, grinning annoyingly. He shoved the blonde to the side and put on his boxers. "Go to my room." He ordered to the blonde girl and the second girl followed her, completely confused.

Even for him, he was acting like a complete asshole. He was irrational, not himself. Something was off with him. Then I saw three lines of white powder on top of the glass coffee table, right next to my Van Gogh book, ready to be snorted. Immediately I understood that he was high on coke. "Can you explain to me now, what the hell is going on here?" I asked, pointing at the coffee table.

"I met the girls at Club V and we wanted to continue our party here- Larisa and her friend, Elena from Latvia. Where the hell is Latvia?"

"Max! Enough!" I yelled, frustrated with his nonsense talk.

"Stop yelling. You're so loud…" He said, and covered his ears with his hands. "My head is about to explode."

"Oh, God! You're totally out of it. How much coke did you snort?"

"Just one line. I prepared a line for you too and also brought you a girl. You know… in case things didn't go well with the doctor at the hospital, but she got bored waiting. I had to step in." He smirked.

"How thoughtful of you!" I flamed up. I wanted to wipe that smirk off his face with my fist but he was so delusional. I knew he wouldn't even remember getting punched.

"Anything for my best buddy!" He said.

"Shut up and listen now. One... you cannot fuck your girls in my living room. Two...you cannot do coke in my apartment. Period."

"I was in the living room because you gave me a bedroom with no view and I prefer the view from this window. I'm jealous that you have a better view of Central Park than mine. The coke was their idea... not mine!" He said nonchalantly and raised his hand up. There was no point arguing with him.

"You know what Max... I've had enough. Today is your last day here. I want you to move out and check into a hotel tonight!" I said resolutely.

"What! Why? ... We used to party like this all the time. What happened to you? Let me guess, things didn't work out with the doctor?"

"This has nothing to do with Emma."

"So, why then?"

"Because I don't like this... this fucking life anymore. I want more than sex with a random girl, getting high, throwing money at dumb chicks and parties. I am done. I want out! Sometimes, I feel like I am dying here. I want to sell everything... the business, the apartment, just go away and disappear. Maybe I should just do it."

"Okay, chill out man. You can't sell the business. I couldn't stand anybody else running Phliant. If it bothers you that much, I'll move out. "

"Yeah...That's a good start."

"Are you this pissed because of Emma?"

"No, just the opposite. She is giving me a chance and I don't wanna screw it up. She can't ever know about the life I had or all the shit we did. I want a new beginning. I want to win her heart and be with her."

"You are full of shit, but whatever...If that's what you want, I won't stay in your way."

"Good. Please do that." I said determinedly.

And with that, I started a new chapter in my life.

CHAPTER 12
DYLAN

Past Manhattan's vivid, eye-catching skyline, past the Brooklyn Bridge, through the quaint neighborhoods with many historical houses in Park Slope... I was in front of an old yellow house on Tenth Street at seven thirty. Even after I told Jeffrey, my kind, sixty year old driver to kill some time by driving around the block, we were still early. Given the fact that I had an infamous reputation for being late, arriving thirty minutes early for a date was unheard of for me. People are used to waiting for me since I am a busy guy. Every minute of my time is precious, so I have seen it as acceptable, and totally normal to make them wait. I wouldn't stand for it the other way around, except for Emma. Yesterday at the hospital was the first time I waited for someone for hours. Today I was trying to kill time again while taking a tour around the park, anxiously waiting for my watch to show eight o'clock.

"Let's go around the block one more time." I told Jeff after checking my watch. He was probably wondering what the hell was going on with me. I was overly stressed. The irritation and dithering in my voice probably showed it too.

At fifteen minutes to eight, Jeff parked the limousine in front of Emma's house. I waited another minute by the stairs, however, her neighbors' curious looks made me feel uneasy. I decided to just knock on her door. I climbed the stairs of her old fashioned Brooklyn house and noticed the hand written note by the doorbell. My grin got wider as I read her note.

"No luck with the bell. Still broken. Try knocking, but I probably I won't hear it. If you are here to sell me something (except for the girl scouts), leave me a note! Girl Scouts: Sign me up for three boxes of thin mints."

It was the cutest note one could put out for a broken door bell. That was my Emma. *How can you not like a woman like that?*

I dialed her number and leaned on the wall, staring at her delicate handwriting. After the third try, she finally answered her phone, "Hi, Emma. I am here. Outside your door." I said.

"Oh, really. You're early!" She answered, sounding surprised.

"Yeah, I know... We went around the block and then parked in front of your house. I was going to wait a bit longer but I think your neighbors are getting a bit suspicious of me. A guy, waiting outside with two big bags in the rain... I'm guessing it's not a usual scene for this neighborhood. I hope it's okay if we start our dinner early."

"Of course it is okay, Dylan. Why didn't you just call me earlier?"

"You said eight o'clock. I didn't want to bother you in case you were sleeping or resting. You had a long day yesterday."

"You are silly. I wasn't sleeping. I've been making us dinner. Soup, actually. It's not ready yet, I am still working on it. Hold on a sec... I am coming right down."

With that, I heard her footsteps approaching. She opened the door with a spoon in her hand and an apron around her waist. She looked lovely in her dark blue jeans and Columbia University t-shirt. Her auburn hair was tucked in a high pony tail, which made her neck stand out even more.

"No kidding. You really are cooking." I said when I got inside and smelled the aroma coming from the kitchen. I handed her the flower bouquet.

"Jasmines again!" She said suspiciously.

"What can I say? They've become my favorite flower."

"Oh, Dylan. You are not going to stop trying, I ..."

"So... what are you cooking?" I interrupted her, not letting her finish her sentence. I didn't want to hear her explain how she was not ready for a relationship. She was probably going to come up with a bunch of excuses to stay away from me, but I was ready to rescind them all.

"Nothing too fancy. Just some tomato bisque." She said and headed back to the kitchen and I followed her. In her tight t-shirt and jeans that cupped her body and defined her curves, she looked sexier than ever. I wanted to grab her tiny waist and kiss her right there, but I promised myself earlier that I'd take it easy and stay cool.

I shook off the randy feeling boiling inside me and said, "It smells really good Emma," instead. Then I added. "But you didn't need to cook. I planned on taking care of the food tonight, so you could just relax and enjoy." I gestured at the two big insulated bags I was still holding. I set them on the granite counter and watched her stir the pot on the stove.

"You are my guest, coming to my place for the first time. Of course, I'd prepare something. I also thought it would be nice to have a warm meal." She said smilingly and looked through the kitchen window. "It looks like it is freezing outside. I am already dreading the walk to the subway tonight."

"Yes, it is really cold. It got colder with the rain and the wind. Please don't worry about the walk to the subway. My driver, Jeff, is going to pick me up, so it would be my pleasure to give you a ride." I said and heaved a sigh, thinking how nice it would be to ride back to Manhattan with Emma, and how I would get to spend another hour with her, if she would agree.

"Let's have dinner first. We can talk about the ride later. Maybe I will be so boring... you won't want to stick around that long."

"You could never be boring. If you remember, we spent an entire day together before you ran away, and not a minute of it was boring."

"It was more like sixteen hours..." She corrected. "That was in Amsterdam when we were both on vacation. My life here, between Manhattan and Brooklyn, is pretty dull. So, consider this fair warning."

"You gave me two hours. I am planning to savor every minute of it."

"Fine!" She chuckled. "Let's see how the night goes. First, why don't you warm yourself in front of the fireplace while I set the table and do the final touches on the soup. Hope you like basil."

"Yes, I like basil, and Emma... I am okay. I don't need to warm up. I'd like to help."

"You are wet and cold. Not to mention that you were coughing pretty bad last night. I don't want you to get worse."

"Believe me, I am fine. You need to stop being Dr. Collins for the next two hours. Alright! "

"Fine!" She huffed and narrowed her eyes at me with a slight grin. "Would you like to try this for me?" She extended a spoon to me. Her other hand brushed my skin lightly as she held it under my chin so the soup would not spill, but that smallest contact was enough to awaken every nerve in my body. I swallowed the soup slowly while my eyes feasted on her hot, luscious body. Emma in a sundress was beautiful, however, Emma in tight jeans and a t-shirt was simply dangerous.

"So, what do you think? More salt or pepper?" She raised her brow and asked, then wiped the tiny drop of soup off my lower lip with her finger.

"Actually, it tastes perfect just the way it is." I said, feeling disoriented with her proximity and touch.

"I thought I could arrange a nice dinner for you by bringing take-out from Cucina di Fabio. I was planning to charm you with his delicious dishes." I admitted jokingly. "Though I don't think anything I brought can compete with your soup. I can just have this with bread and its heaven."

"Oh, thank you Dylan!" She smiled. "How did you manage to bring take out from Fabio's?" She asked completely bewildered. "I thought that Fabio didn't do take-outs. Even to dine at his restaurant, there is always a long waiting list."

"Let's just say that he owes me one, or a few million to be more correct."

"What do you mean?"

"I handle his investment accounts. While everybody got screwed and lost millions when the market crashed six years ago, my company made him a lot of money." I explained quickly, although my history with Fabio went further than that.

I remembered the early years at Phliant Investment, how Max and I used our personal contacts to get clients and start our new business. We agreed on less than normal commissions to win the accounts. Fabio Modigliani was one of the first clients we had. As a young, ambitious and bold economist right out of college, I spent countless days running risk analysis, investigating unpopular stocks, and unknown firms when I took his account. I made a few unusual and a bit risky decisions and turned his ten million into twenty in less than a year. Fabio Modigliani's account was our first big win and things got exciting from there on.

It was during the tough years in the stock market, when the real estate market crashed and billions of dollars were lost instantly, when even the big investment firms were struggling. Being the small, new company like we were, nobody gave us a chance to survive in the most volatile market of the last decade, but the people in the investment business didn't know that I had ambition, determination and patience unlike anyone else on Wall Street. I spent countless nights and long days, analyzing small companies with possible break through products. I studied stock exchange markets from Tokyo to Frankfurt, from Moscow to Sydney. It's easy to make money when everybody else is making money but the real challenge is to make money when nobody is. It requires talent, and I had that rare talent and intuition. Soon, we were making unusual investments. We were everywhere, investing in a new oil rig in Nigeria… a stem cell research company in Switzerland, marine and ship building industries in Korea. In less than two years, we turned three hundred million dollars in profit and we made our first billion in the third. The big sharks of Wall Street were surprised; they couldn't understand our unprecedented success. Both people and companies were getting in line for an appointment with us. A lot changed in seven years. From a penniless college graduate, I turned into a successful CEO of the most promising investment company in the United States.

"Impressive." She said concisely. "I didn't know your company was that good, however I'd be lying if I said I'd like to hear more about it. Not much about Wall Street interests me." She admitted honestly.

"But…" She chuckled, glaring at me mischievously like a little kid who was up to something. "I'd be more than happy to talk about food. Italian food is my favorite. So, what are we having?"

"Triple cheese lasagna, veal ossobuco with saffron rice, chicken saltimbocca and mushroom tortellini. I also got us some foccacia bread…There is also cannoli for dessert."

"Oh my god, Dylan. It was supposed to be a dinner for two. There is enough food here to feed an army."

"I might have over-ordered a little bit."

"Only a little bit!"

"Just be glad that I didn't bring the entire menu…" I teased her. "Maybe I did it on purpose. This way you'll have enough left-overs to keep you out of vending machines for a few days."

"Thoughtful and charming as always." She commented. "What do you say? Shall we start?"

"Yes, let's start." I answered.

We started with her delicious soup. Then I had a piece of the veal and some saffron rice. I loved Fabio's food, however tonight I couldn't eat much. Instead, I watched Emma trying every dish and listened to her various comments on the subtle, hidden ingredients. She looked happy and relaxed, and I was happy just seeing her happy.

"I thought this was supposed to be a dinner for two. I am the only one eating." She said as she poured me more cranberry juice. I wished we were drinking wine, it would have eased my tension, but she was going to work in a few hours, and that meant no alcohol.

"Somehow I don't feel like eating much tonight."

"Why? Is something wrong with your stomach? Are you feeling alright? Do you have heartburn or any other problem?" She started asking without a break.

"Easy Dr. Collins… you're diagnosing me again. Believe me, there is nothing wrong with me. I just don't have an appetite." I said without admitting the real reason. The reality was that my stomach was in knots. I was taking deep breaths in and out and trying damn hard not to show my nervousness.

"Okay, how about dessert then…Do you want to have a cup of coffee with it?"

"Yes, coffee and dessert sounds great."

We carried two cups of coffee and our cannolis to her living room. We sat on the sofa side by side, sipping our coffees quietly as we watched the flames dancing in the stone fireplace. The faint crackling sound of wood was soon lost in the soft music, playing in the background, O soave fanciulla from Puccini's La Boheme, followed with Mozarts' Magic Flute and Rossini's William Tell. The album was a compilation of various opera songs and each one was as touching and impressive as the previous.

I was lost in my thoughts, lost in the music. I couldn't believe that Emma liked opera. I knew immediately where I was going to take her next time. There had to be a next time. Two hours weren't enough. I had to find a way to convince her. Every minute I spent with her, with every little thing I learned about her, I was falling for her more and more. It was hopeless. I was head over heels in love.

"You are awfully quiet tonight." She muttered breaking the silence.

"Am I?"

"Yes. Actually you look a bit pensive too. Why?

"I don't know, maybe because… I am nervous. I am scared. I am excited. I am hesitant…" I wilted.

"Dylan…" She stepped in, but I didn't want to her to stop me after I finally summoned up my courage to talk.

"My mind is occupied with a lot of things, but especially with …" I paused to regain my thoughts. I couldn't just tell her everything on my mind. I knew that it would only scare her. "Well, let me just say that all I can think about right now is finding the perfect moment to kiss you again." I confessed and closed the gap between us abruptly and tugged her into my arms. I held her face in my hand

and gave her a long, scorching kiss. I kissed her hard and fervently, punishing her with my mouth for making me hopeless and defenseless. She didn't give into my kiss. Her lips weren't moving as they did when I kissed her the other times. I sensed her ambivalence between her never-easing mind, occupied with thoughts and feelings.

"I know you want to kiss me, so kiss me…" I told her finally and moved an inch away. A flicker of hesitation moved through her eyes as she drew her lips between her teeth. I wanted to suck her lips, to make her squirm with desire. I wanted her to want the sweet cohesion of our lips as much as I did.

While I ached inwardly, stopping myself from plunging into her mouth and claiming her lips, I waited patiently, gazing intently into her eyes. There came my sweet torture, the anticipation of holding her tightly in my arms and exploring her mouth as she stood austere, not moving an inch.

I couldn't wait any longer. I was supposed to give her time, let her set the pace of the evening, but I couldn't. Her beautiful face with her luscious lips an inch away, my feelings became unbridled. I leaned in, traced her cheek with my fingers and brushed her delectable lips with mine. I was slow and tender this time and she finally parted her lips and responded to me. She ran her hands through my hair and kissed me back. I wanted to touch her, feel her naked body under me. I inched her t-shirt up slightly and grazed my thumb over her belly, caressing her softly, but suddenly, she broke away.

"No, Dylan. I can't." She rejected with lifted brows and tightened lips.

"I'm sorry. I shouldn't have. It's my fault." I cursed myself for rushing and ruining things again.

"It's not you. I am not ready for this, for us. Dylan, I cannot give you what you want."

"How do you know what I want?"

"I'm just guessing …"

"And your guess is?"

"You want someone you can have a relationship with."

"Why can't you be that person?"

"Because my life is complicated. There is so much going on in my life that I don't have time for a relationship. Plus, I don't even know you. All I know is that you work on Wall Street and have a successful company."

"Come on Emma. You know more than that. I've told you things that I have not told anybody else in my life."

"Maybe, but that doesn't change the fact that I am not ready for a relationship."

"I understand that you are not ready. But don't just cut me off completely. I promise I will take it slow."

"Dylan, we passed the level 'slow' our first day in Amsterdam."

"Then, let's forget about Amsterdam. I am asking for a clean slate. Pretend we just met. I'll take you on a date, nothing else... scout's honor."

"Were you even a scout?" She folded her arms across her breasts and asked accusingly.

"Indeed, I was."

"Hmm." She shook her head and sighed. "Can I at least think about this a little bit? I have to leave in ten minutes to catch my train."

"I told you Emma, Jeff will be here any minute. Don't be stubborn. It's raining like crazy outside. Let me give you a ride."

She squinted at me and pursed her lips. "Alright, a ride it is..."

"How do you even bear the stench of the subway?"

"It's not that bad, and as they say, you are not a true New Yorker if you don't use the subway."

"Born and raised in Manhattan and I've never used it once."

"Here comes the arrogant guy I met in front of the brothel."

"You're not going to let that one go, are you?

"Nope. I think I can use it wherever and whenever it suits."

"Fine! Not liking the subway has nothing to do with arrogance. It's crowded. It stinks and I don't think it's safe, especially close to midnight."

"NYC subway after midnight being dangerous is a myth. I have been using it for over a year now and it is perfectly safe. There are other people like me taking the subway all the time. I always sit in the first car right behind the conductor and just in case, I always carry mace in my purse. It is totally fine."

"Can I ever win an argument with you?" I shook my head. Emma riding alone in a deserted subway in the middle of the night was a scary thought and her using her mace in case she got attacked was even scarier. "Why do you live in Brooklyn, anyway?" I asked, feeling apprehensive and concerned. "Wouldn't it be easier to live in Manhattan, closer to Columbia or the hospital?"

"It would, but I like it here. This was my mother's house and it belonged to my grandparents before her. It is a special place for me. The title of the house was transferred to me when I turned eighteen but I didn't move in until last year."

"Why last year?"

She shrugged, "I just wanted to get away from Manhattan for a while, that's all," she said briefly. Obviously she didn't want to talk much about why she had wanted to leave Manhattan, and I left it there. I've learned not to push Emma.

"Well, Jeff is here. Are you ready to go?"

She looked out the window and saw my black limousine and uttered incredulously. "You are going to take me to the hospital in a limo?"

"Yes, that was my plan."

"If the other nurses see me arrive in a limo, they will mock me for the rest of my time there. Nuh-uh... I am not going to the hospital in that."

"We'll drop you off a few yards away, at the corner of the newsstand, and you can walk to the hospital. Nobody will see you in the shameful state of getting out of a limo." I said sarcastically. "Come on Emma, stop making excuses... let's go."

She heaved a deep sigh and huffed. "Can I ever win an argument with you?" She said, mocking my prior comment.

"See. We make a perfect couple." I chuckled and replied. She was stubborn, but so was I, and I was determined to win her heart, even if it was the biggest and most important challenge of my life.

CHAPTER 13
EMMA

After a long twelve-hour shift at the hospital and another hour to get back to Brooklyn in a blizzard, all I wanted was to have some hot chamomile tea with honey and get into bed. However, when I saw Sydney's name blinking on my phone, I knew immediately that I wouldn't be able to put my head down for a while. I stared at my phone and opted to press decline. I had avoided talking to her for a couple of weeks and I was worried she would come over and interrogate me, face to face. At least on the phone it was a bit easier to evade her snoopy questions. So, I decided to bite the bullet and answer the phone.

"Hi, Syd." I said with a tired voice.

"Don't play the 'I am so tired, I can't talk to you right now' game with me." She snickered immediately. "You've been dodging my calls for three weeks. We have to talk."

"It's almost Christmas, Syd. The ER is packed and we are short-handed. I am working five days a week." I explained quickly, using work as a good excuse for not returning her calls.

"Stop making excuses… I don't care how sick New Yorkers are… They should eat healthier, maybe they would feel better."

"I'm glad to hear you are just as caring and charming as ever."

"You know very well that I am not calling you to hear about the ER or your patients. You can whine all you want to your doctor friends or nurses."

I was disgruntled with her typical tepid attitude. "If you do not want to hear about me, why are you calling me Sydney?"

"Of course I want to hear about you, just not the boring old hospital crap. We haven't talked since Steve's party. I saw Amy a week ago and she said some hot guy showed up at the hospital that night and he has been visiting you almost every day, sending messages and flowers. Spill it Ems! What's going on? Who is this guy? And more importantly, why haven't you told me?"

"Because there is nothing to tell. Nothing is going on."

"That's bullshit and you know it. Start! Now!"

"Oh, fine." I grumbled. "Yes, there is someone. He's a bit too persistent and also won't accept 'no' for an answer. You already know him."

"What do you mean I know him? Who is it?"

"It's Dylan from Amsterdam, and somehow he found me. I guess he was in New York all this time. He said he was searching for me all over the States for months. Max, his best friend if you remember, happened to be at Steve's party, and he told Dylan that he saw me. The rest is just like you heard from Amy. He's come to the ER a couple of times, the first time as a patient. We had dinner and he has been calling me almost every day since."

"You are kidding, right? The 'sex god Dylan' found you and has been trying to see you, and you are saying 'no' to him. Oh my god Emma! What's wrong with you and how could you not call me and tell me about this?"

"Stop calling him sex god."

"Your words, not mine."

"I am sooo regretting telling you about him and our night in Amsterdam. You are pure evil."

"I am not evil. I am so happy that I pushed you to go with him that day. Now tell me more. How is he? Is he still super sexy and handsome?"

"Yes, he is alright, but it doesn't matter. There is nothing between us."

"Why not?"

"Because… I am already struggling to catch up with my life as is. I don't need a boyfriend to add to my troubles."

"Ems, you have to get over this 'I hate relationships' syndrome. Kyle was a jerk. Dylan is awesome."

"How do you know that?"

"I can tell."

"Well, I am going to disappoint you but I do not have time for a relationship right now. I have one semester left. My days are full with my rotations, my thesis dissertation, oh and let's not forget my troublesome brother."

"Emma, Dylan is the best thing that's happened to you in a long time. You need to give him a chance."

"Sydney! Please! Can we talk about this some other time? I am really tired and I don't have the energy to argue with you."

"Fine!" she said aversely. "But this discussion is not over yet. How is Steve doing by the way?"

"Not good. I finally convinced my father to cut off his financial support. As long as he relied on him, nothing was going to change. He needs to stop being a troubled rich kid. I know he can do so much better if he would only try." I explained quickly. I was frustrated to see how nothing had changed after his accident. He was irresponsible and immature. He still thought he could fix everything with money and unfortunately my father continued to allow him.

"Wow! That's a big change. So, what is he going to do?"

"The last I heard he was staying in NYU dorms and looking for a job. He is still not talking to me."

"What did you expect? You're making him live like a broke college student."

"For his own good. He will thank me one day. He needs to grow up and take on some responsibility. He trashed a quarter million dollar car while he was high and walked away as if it was nothing. He could have killed someone, or himself. "

"Don't start grousing again or you'll lose your sleep. Get some rest. I'd like to see you soon. I miss you. Let's get together some time. Alright?"

"I miss you too. How about lunch next Tuesday?"

"Deal. Take care and promise that you'll tell me more about your hot boyfriend."

"He is not my boyfriend. Just a friend!"

"Whatever, Ems! Bye…" She said, with a whiff of sarcasm obvious in her voice.

"Bye Sydney." I muttered back and hung up. With my cell phone on my hand, I strolled back into the kitchen and put some water in the kettle to make some tea. While I waited for the water to boil, I started sorting my mail. Between the usual ads, grocery coupons and several bills, a gilded envelop with the most elegant handwriting caught my eyes. There was no return address and the stamp had yesterday's date on it. It was sent from Manhattan. I opened the envelope immediately and was surprised to see an invitation.

"Join me for opening night, La Bohéme,
Metropolitan Opera House on December 21st.
I will pick you up at 5:00pm. Please say yes. Dylan"

I stared at his neat handwriting in black ink for a long minute, contemplating what to do next. Should I say 'yes' or come up with an excuse? I was still ambivalent to going on a real date with Dylan. The more time I spent with him, the more I was drawn into his irresistible charm and it was getting harder to fight my feelings. Feelings… *Since when did I have feelings for Dylan?* Did it start when he showed up unannounced at the ER? Or my house? Or the day we met? One side of me wanted to run away from him, but the other side wanted to give in and embrace all the exciting feelings he offered. Oh, the amazing kisses, the mind blowing sex.

I picked up my phone and found his number. I typed "Yes" and hit send. My phone beeped right away.

"I promise, it will be an amazing night." He wrote back.

The day of our date arrived and after trying on five different dresses, I decided on a long, black satin gown with deep cleavage in front with an open back. I put on my high heel stiletto shoes and light makeup, except for lipstick. It was Russian Red, a gift from Sydney which I had never worn before, but today was the day to be bold. Even though I still couldn't admit it out loud, I certainly had feelings for this amazingly handsome man. I wanted to charm him as he charmed me. I was ready an hour early and impatiently sat by the fireplace, waiting for Dylan to come.

Dylan showed up fifteen minutes early again. I opened the door without waiting for him to ring my recently fixed door bell.

The instant he saw me standing in front of him, "Wow!" he exclaimed and furrowed his brows. His face looked too serious. It was like he was taking me in and undressing me with his intense gaze. I was struck, almost spellbound as I lost myself in his unblinking blue eyes. To ease the unspoken, heavy attraction building between us, I spun around like a little girl. If I didn't do something to break his intense gaze, I would have asked him to kiss me and take me right there.

"So, what you think? Better than my good old, bleached scrubs?" I asked jokingly after a deep breath.

"You look…" He swallowed hard. "Gorgeous! I don't even know what to say."

I blushed inadvertently and thought that he looked just as much, maybe even more beautiful in his black tuxedo. "I hope it's not too much." I said timidly.

"No, not at all. It's perfect." He answered and paused as he eyed me head to toe one more time. "You are beautiful in your scrubs, Emma, but in this gown you are breathtaking. I will need to be very careful tonight, maybe even hide you in our reserved box from admirers lurking around."

"We have a box? Those are so hard to get! How did you get one? Don't say a good friend owed you another favor." I muttered disbelievingly.

"I donate every year to the Metropolitan Opera and have season tickets for the company. It was time for me to finally use them." He said, and looked at me apologetically. "And also …I am sorry for being early again. I really tried to come here on time but time seems to stall when you stare at the clock, and I couldn't wait any longer. So here I am … early again."

"Isn't it a bit early for the show? I thought it didn't start until eight. What are we going to do for three hours?

"I have a surprise evening planned for you. Now…are you ready?" He extended his hand and clasped my fingers tightly. He didn't tell me where we were heading regardless of my begging, cajoling or whining. Only after we took a left turn onto 53rd street on Madison Avenue he did whisper "we are close". Then we came to a stop in front of the most visited museum in the United States, the world renowned: Museum of Modern Art.

"What are we doing here at MoMa on a Saturday? It is closed."

"I know!" He muttered smugly, as he pulled me out of the limo and led me toward the museum's entrance.

"So?" I asked again, a bit impatiently.

"I told you Emma. I have it all planned."

"But!" I tried to interfere, when he suddenly put his index finger gently on my lips and said, "Why don't you just relax and let go?" His eyes lit, wandered over my body, resting on my lips a bit too long. Then, he inhaled deeply, turned to Jeff and ordered. "Pick us up here in two hours."

We were greeted by an attractive lady, probably in her fifties, dressed in a pencil skirt and white blouse, looking very professional, in front of the museum. "Good Evening Mrs. Johnson," Dylan said, he shook her hand gently and introduced me.

"Good Evening, Mr. Hamilton and Ms. Collins. Welcome to the Museum of Modern Art," she replied, and turned to Dylan, speaking slowly and courteously. "It's such a pleasure to have you here tonight Mr. Hamilton. I'd like to express candidly how much we appreciate your contributions and donations to our museum. Although it wouldn't be enough to match your generosity, at least tonight, your special request, gives us an opportunity to return the favor just a little bit."

I was confused with what was happening around me. We slowly sauntered towards the elevator as Mrs. Johnson showed us the way. We were inside the museum on Saturday. There was absolute silence among the most amazing paintings by world renowned artists. Right in front of the elevator, Mrs. Johnson stopped and touched Dylan's arm, subtly. "Fifth floor. Room 21. It is all set up and ready for you Mr. Hamilton." she said with a big smile and waved us goodbye.

"Thank you so much for all your help!" Dylan said succinctly, nodded with his head and returned her smile.

"Is she really leaving us here, alone in the museum among these valuable paintings?"

"Yes!" He said with a grin and gave me the same look when I asked about our seating in the opera house.

"What is going on Dylan? What is ready? How did you arrange all of this?" I demanded him to tell me as the elevator ascended slowly to the fifth floor. He just kept his blazing eyes on me without uttering a word. His hands were on the small of my back, caressing my skin gently, sending shivers down my spine with his each contact.

Finally, the elevator dinged, announcing that we arrived. We turned the corner and suddenly I was speechless. In between priceless paintings, there was a neatly prepared table for two: Red and white checkered linens, matching napkins, a champagne bottle with two glasses and a wicker basket. All of these, set up right in front of the one of the most famous paintings of all time: Van Gogh's 'Starry Night'.

"How would you like to have a picnic with me, watching Starry Night?"

"Oh, my God Dylan, This is unbelievable! But...how?" I stuttered in disbelief.

"You wanted to visit the Gogh Museum in Amsterdam but we didn't have time. So, what you think?"

"What do I think...? I think you are amazing. Full of surprises."

"And that means... you like it?"

"Of course I like it! Having a picnic and drinking champagne in front of the most beautiful painting in the world. How could I not like it?"

"Then... shall we start? Would you like to look around first?"

"You already know my answer. Please tell me about the paintings, just like you did in Amsterdam."

We walked around, his hand on the small of my back, caressing me softly as we appreciated the amazing paintings; from 'Hope' by Gustav Klimt to 'Sleeping Gypsy' by Henri Rousseau. After my private and very informative personal tour, Dylan whispered in my ear. "Would you like another glass, or maybe something to eat? I packed us some cheese, crackers, grapes and your favorite sandwich."

"You know my favorite sandwich?"

"Peanut butter with honey and sliced bananas." He spat out surely.

"How do you know that?"

"I am a good researcher and I like to keep my sources secret."

"I should tell Sydney to stay out of my personal life."

"Oh, come on, take it easy on her. She was so excited that she got to help." He admitted with a sly grin.

His peerless blue eyes didn't leave mine for the rest of the night. He held my hand and brushed his lips over my fingers before he pushed my seat in. We sat at the table, talked and laughed for almost an hour.

"It is so easy to connect with this painting." Dylan said as he turned his gaze away from me for the first time, looking at 'Starry Night'. "I think that's why it's so popular. It is a scene that anybody can relate to, feel comfortable and at ease with. Swirling clouds in the night sky, a bright crescent moon... below the hills on the horizon, a small quiet town. At the center, a tall steeple of a church. It is such a serene scene that reminds me of peacefulness. Then the dark, biggest object in the painting, maybe a bush or a mountain, reminds me of isolation, loneliness. It evokes many different emotions at the same time."

"I don't even know how to describe how I feel. It's ... amazing. Thank you, Dylan. Thank you for bringing me here tonight."

"There is one more thing..." He said, and brought his phone out of his pocket. He started playing a song. I instantly remembered the tune; it was the one we danced to in Amsterdam. "Shall we?" He asked and extended his hand. I took it nervously. With a killer combination of Dylan, his intoxicating smell, his fathomless eyes and champagne, I was already feeling dizzy. My heart was throbbing so fast and I thought my legs were going to give way.

I wrapped my arms around his neck and rested my head on his shoulder. "Don't worry, I've got you." He said in my ear, probably sensing my dizziness as he moved slowly with the music.

"I am not worried. Not with you." I said back, looking at his eyes, his perfect lips only an inch away. The pull, the attraction, the intense air between us was ineffable. I bit the edge of my lower lip to restrain myself, but I couldn't resist him any longer. I leaned in and kissed him. It was everything I was scared of. Kissing him meant losing myself in him and I did. I closed my eyes and dove into the abyss as his lips moved softly over mine. Warm. Tender. Sensual.

I had no idea how long we kissed. As if it was just us, and everything else was an irrelevant. A nuisance detail in the background. "Emma..." He moaned abruptly. "We have to go. Jeff is probably downstairs waiting for us. But don't forget where we left off." He said playfully and pulled my hand.

We got in the limo, "To the Opera House, but tour around the block 'till eight," he said to Jeff.

As soon as we were in, he closed the partition. He pulled me on his lap and immediately we started kissing again. Our kiss was not tender or gentle as it was in the museum. It was full of passion and desire. I held my breath and broke away for a second to ask. "What about Jeff?"

"He can't hear or see a thing." Dylan answered. "We have twenty minutes."

I pulled up my gown up and straddled him. I could feel his definite bulge underneath me. "Let's see what we can do in twenty minutes." I winked and whispered in his ears boldly. His eyes grew big. Full of desire, promising me pleasure like no other.

"Are you sure about this Emma? I don't want this to be another night like in Amsterdam. I want you and I to be all in. Don't play with me."

"I am in."

"That means you and I..."

"Yes, I'd like to give this boyfriend, girlfriend thing a try."

And hearing my confirming words, he kissed me fiercely while he slid one hand under my gown and with the other, he lowered the straps of my dress, exposing my breasts. He took one into his mouth and teased me with a wet, velvet swipe of his tongue as he circled over the thin lace of my thong with his deft fingers where every nerve ending in my body merged. I gasped, tormented with his touch firing off my body, aching and trembling with the need between my thighs. I needed friction. I needed to feel him in me. I moved on his lap, up and down, slowly, almost instinctively.

"Not yet baby." He rasped. "Let me get you ready first. Then, you get to ride me." He smirked, denying me what I wanted so badly, making me squirm inside, all the while I was feeling his forceful hardness between my thighs.

He grabbed my hips and lifted me up as he pulled my thong aside, swiftly with one hand. He started kissing my inner thigh, slowly reaching my heat. He slid one finger in me first and then another, as he sucked my wetness, torturing me with his slow strokes at the same time.

"Dylan...Please." I said huskily, craving for more pressure. I was about to shudder as he dipped his fingers and swirled his tongue over and over again.

"Give in Emma. Enjoy it. I know you are close...I'd like to give you two orgasms before we park."

He increased the intensity of his strokes while he circled my bud with his thumb. I was inebriated with extreme pleasure. The intensity of ecstasy was building up every passing second as his tongue continued doing amazing things. I slowly climbed up, and with his last touch, I shuddered. Panting heavily, my body convulsed and I held on to his shoulders tightly to keep myself steady.

"This is the first one..." He kissed my lips. With a mischievous smile, he added "Now let's work on a second one where I can join in."

"Condom?" I mumbled, still trying to catch my breath.

"There is one in my wallet. Please don't think I was planning this."

"Don't worry. There is one in my clutch too." I grinned.

"Oh, you are so amazing." He pulled my face to his and kissed me hard, fervently. I pulled down his zipper and finally freed him of his boxer briefs. I took his rock hard length between my fingers, feeling elated for getting my turn to torture him with pleasure. I stroked him slowly, leisurely, grazed my fingers over, teasing him unmercifully and then lowered my head and licked his velvet tip with my tongue. He squirmed and groaned my name. "Emma."

I loosened his bow-tie, unbuttoned his white shirt and slid my other hand inside, feeling his chiseled abs under my palm. I wanted to slide my lips over his perfect masculine body and taste his skin. I grazed my fingers slowly over his chest following up with my lips, slowly descending to his navel and then took him in my mouth again.

"Oh, God, Emma. Stop this torture. We don't have time." He ripped open a condom and clasped his fingers over mine as I slowly put it over his length. "Come on. You get to ride me. Now!" He ordered as he gripped my hips, and lowered me on to him.

I grabbed his shoulders and began moving up and down, slowly first, then going in deeper, taking his length all in. "Oh, fuck. It feels so good. Ride me harder and faster baby." Dylan demanded. And I did, making him fill me completely.

"You feel amazing. I missed you so much." He whispered in my ear and claimed my lips again.

With every stroke, the pleasure was building higher and higher in me, and I knew I wasn't going to last long but I wanted to keep going, and stretch this pleasure as much as possible. He moved his hips with me while he put more pressure on me with his thumb. I was there, ready to shudder, coming down hard. His final touch with the flick of his finger threw me over the edge as I screamed his name, and he joined right after. Our hard breaths and moans filled the small area in the limo. He was panting as hard and fast as I was. He brushed his lips on mine, and was about to say something but he stopped, glared into my eyes instead.

Only a minute later, our limo came to a full stop, indicating our twenty minutes were over. Dylan took a deep breath and exhaled slowly, while he buttoned his shirt and tucked back in his pants. "I guess we should go." He said reluctantly.

I fixed his bow-tie, smiling broadly. Then I pulled the straps of my dress up and tidied my dress quickly, looking for my underwear.

"I'm keeping it. A reminder how great it feels when we are together for the rest of the night …" Dylan said playfully and put my thong in his pocket. He got out of the limo without giving me a chance to respond and extended his hand to help me get out.

I was speechless. I bet my cheeks flushed crimson red. He was making my head swirl and I was falling hard for him with every passing second.

CHAPTER 14
DYLAN

The last hour with Emma was like a dream. She agreed to give us a chance, and I was determined not to disappoint her. I couldn't fail... not with her. I loved her too damn much. Oh, God... I almost said it out loud twice but managed to hold it back. I didn't want to scare her again, coming off too strong, too demanding. If only she knew the thoughts in my mind, that I dreamed about her all the time. I wanted to spend every minute of my time with her, to wake up with her in my arms every morning, and to go to bed with her. God damn it. I was so in love with her that it hurt.

I had become a different person since I met her this summer. My company was no longer my priority. All I wanted was to be with Emma and now that I had her, it wasn't enough. I wanted her for myself and all the time. Never mind that she was about to become a doctor, worked sixty hours a week and could only spare me a few hours here and there. I was asking for the impossible. I was so desperate and helpless when it came to Emma.

Lost in my thoughts, I followed the young attendant taking us to our seats. I clasped Emma's hand tightly as I felt her panties in my pocket, reminding me of our intimate, mind-blowing moments a few minutes ago. We were alone in the reserved box in the center of the parterre level of the exquisite opera house. I kept the remaining eight tickets to myself since I didn't want anybody from work to mess up our special night.

Over the next two hours, while Emma watched the most talented opera singers in the world performing on stage, I watched her. My mind was occupied, completely elsewhere. All I could think about was finding a way to convince her to come to my apartment and stay with me for the night. I could still taste her in my mouth. Her jasmine smell was infused into my shirt and every breath I took made my head dizzy with pleasure. My body craved to make love to her, but holding her in my arms, caressing her soft, milky white skin and watching her fall asleep would be just as wonderful.

At the end of the opera, we waited outside for Jeff to pick us up. It was one of those moments where I was hoping she would say something, ask to stay in the city but she didn't. Her hand on my arm, she looked away without uttering a word.

"I know it's late but I wonder if you'd like to come to my place." I asked a bit hesitatingly.

"I would have loved to but I need to work on my dissertation. I was supposed to work on it today but you know … I preferred to spend it with a charming man." She said with a big smile. "Tonight was great Dylan. I enjoyed it so much."

"I understand." I said, hoping the disappointment in my voice wasn't too obvious. "As long as you promise me, I get to see you again soon."

"Yes. I promise." She agreed.

In the limo, she fell asleep on my shoulder before we even got to the Brooklyn Bridge. It felt so good to feel her soft hair touching my face as I inhaled her heavenly scent. Her soft, deep breathing was a soothing sound. I watched the New York skyline disappear as we drove towards her quiet, historical neighborhood. She opened her eyes when Jeff parked in front of her house.

"I am so sorry. I can't believe I slept the entire way." She said shyly.

"It was a beautiful sight watching you sleep so peacefully. I wish I could sleep like that."

"Why can't you?"

"Too much on my mind I guess." I said, without admitting the real reason. How my horrible past always hunted me down in my dreams and never left me alone. The only time I was able to sleep peacefully was the night she was in my arms in Amsterdam.

She unlocked her door and was about to step inside when she turned back and brushed her lips softly on mine. "Good night Dylan. Try to empty your mind tonight." She said, obviously ending the night.

I probably looked so hopeless and pensive that she turned back again. "Christmas Eve. I wonder…" She mumbled but then shook her head "Oh… never mind. You probably already have plans."

"Come on, Emma. What were you going to say?"

"I was going to ask if you'd like to join us for dinner on Christmas Eve. Sydney, my aunt and uncle, and maybe my brother Steve will be there. Unless you had plans with your family, of course."

"I'd love to." I managed to say. My voice cracked in astonishment. She wanted me to meet her family. I couldn't hide my enthusiasm. My face probably glowed with the excitement burning in me.

"Alright then, see you in three days …" She said, put a chaste kiss on my lips and closed the door.

On the day of Christmas Eve, in the late afternoon, I walked towards the house where Emma grew up, only a few blocks away from my apartment. I felt more nervous than I'd ever been in my life before. I was going to meet the family of the girl I loved and didn't know what to expect.

I rang the doorbell once and waited at the door, taking deep breaths to calm myself. A beautiful middle age lady with short blonde hair, dressed in a black pencil skirt and white shirt opened the door quickly. I could immediately see the resemblance. Sydney looked just like her mother.

"You must be the famous Dylan," she said with a big smile and invited me in. "I am so happy to finally meet you. We have been looking forward to it. I'm Helen. Emma's aunt."

"Nice to meet you, Mrs. Watson. I am very happy and honored to be here today."

"Oh please, call me Helen." She said and laughed. "You are as handsome and charming as I've been told."

I blushed as I stepped inside and could feel my cheeks burning. I then saw Sydney, pointing towards Emma, holding a drink in her hand. "Welcome Dylan. It was me of course, telling everyone all about you. They couldn't get a word out of my secretive cousin… Ms. 'I don't' want to talk about it' over there." Soon, a tall, grey haired man dressed in a colorful Christmas sweater joined the conversation.

"Oh, here is the man, the one sweeping our doctor off her feet. Nice to meet you, young fellow." He said and extended his hand.

"Nice to meet you too. Mr. Watson." I replied.

"You make us sound too old Dylan… Calling us Mrs. Watson, Mr. Watson. It's George and Helen. Alright?"

"Okay, George." I nodded and said hesitatingly.

"Now, tell us how you convinced our stubborn doctor Emma to be your girlfriend."

"Soon to be a doctor." Emma corrected him grinning. "George, Helen, and of course you too Sydney, please give him a break. He just got here. I am sure you will have your chance to interrogate him later, but let's get him a drink first." She winked.

"So, Dylan, what would you like? Wine, Beer, Scotch… or Eggnog maybe?" Helen asked.

"I am not so fond of eggnog. I'd go with red wine if you have a bottle open already. Otherwise, I can have a beer."

"Anything for our special guest…" Helen said, holding a glass of red wine in her hand. "Pinot Noir okay for you? We can open a Merlot or Cabernet if you prefer. You can also check the cellar yourself to find something you like."

"Pinot Noir sounds good." I said appreciative of her kindness.

"Here you go Dylan," Sydney poured me a glass and under the curious gazes of everybody around me, I reached for it and took a sip.

"Come, sit by me and tell us everything." Helen commented and then added, "Start with how you two met, what you do and where you work."

I inhaled deeply. My eyes met Emma's and she was smiling mischievously, as if she was telling me that I was in trouble and this interrogation would continue all night. But then, suddenly, she turned towards her aunt and said. "Come on auntie, I already told you all about it. We met during our Amsterdam city tour and then we found each other again by chance in New York."

I nodded eagerly, agreeing to her condensed version of our story, and grateful that she skipped the uncomfortable and unpleasant details, like how I came out of a brothel, totally stoned.

While I sat next to Helen quietly, I felt the power of her inquisitive eyes on me and I was compelled to continue where Emma left off. I answered her rather easy questions. "I work in an investment business. I started my own company with a good friend of mine after college. It's a hedge fund and asset management company called Phliant."

"You own Phliant!" Both Helen and George exclaimed at the same time.

"Part owner." I said without dwelling into more details. For the first time in my life, I didn't feel like talking about my company nor how we started with almost nothing and turned it into a huge successful business.

Helen raised her eyes and was about make a comment when Sydney interrupted. "It's time to eat. I don't want to listen to the usual boring Wall Street talk and then eat cold turkey. Can we start?"

"Aren't we going to wait for Steve?" I asked while I wondered what Helen was about the say. I was still curious about Helen's and George's earlier reaction.

"Unfortunately, my stubborn brother is still mad at me. He is not coming." Emma answered. "As a last minute decision, he decided to spend this Christmas with my father. My dear father is in London with his girlfriend who Steve hates. So… he is spending the Christmas with him just to piss me off." She sounded really upset. I sensed, although she told me that she didn't blame her father for leaving them, she was not very close with him either.

"I'm sure he will come around." Helen said, trying to calm her down. "Now, let's all go to the dining room and get started." She ordered and led us to a big room where a festively prepared table, adorned with elegant place settings, poinsettias, tall candles and awesome smelling food was waiting for us.

"I will carve the turkey." George said enthusiastically.

"I will bring the casserole." Helen added.

The next three hours passed quickly as we ate the delicious food, all homemade by Aunt Helen. We talked, laughed, drank wine and simply enjoyed ourselves. Emma's family, or at least the ones I met, were as amazing as her. Although they were so different, I understood why Emma was so fond of Sydney. They were like sisters and it was obvious how much they loved each other. Indeed, it was so easy to see how everybody in her family was so fond of each other. A pang of envy surrounded me and for the first time in maybe over twenty years, I wished I had a family like hers. The only person I was close to in my family was Rachel and she was the only one I wished was here with me tonight.

Emma, obviously aware of my sudden reticence, asked. "Are you alright Dylan?" Her eyes were quizzical.

"Yes, I'm fine." I answered succinctly.

"Why the pensive look then?"

"It's just… I just wish Rachel could have been with us tonight." I answered dejectedly. "She would have enjoyed being with you and your family as much as I have."

"I'd love to meet your sister." She replied. "Why don't you invite her over, it's not too late?"

"She is in Florence with her friends for the winter break but I definitely would like you to meet her when she comes back." I said, and I really meant it. The two important girls in my life: Rachel, my quiet, timid sister and Emma, the love of my life. I wanted them to know each other. I just knew that they would connect right away.

After dinner, the night continued with Sydney playing Sinatra songs on the piano. George asked Helen to dance with him and despite Emma's objections, he forced us to join them too. We flew to the moon and reached for the stars. We danced until we completely exhausted Sydney's song repertoire. When we finally sat down by the fireplace to rest our feet, Sydney brought out her childhood favorite board game: 'Hedbanz'. I was having so much fun that I felt like a little kid in a carnival. I didn't want to leave but it was getting close to midnight and I knew Emma was going to work on Christmas day. I wished a Merry Christmas to Helen, George and Sydney and then I took Emma's hand and asked her to follow me to the entrance of the house by the tall Christmas tree where I left my Chesterfield coat. I wanted to be alone with her for a few minutes before I left.

"You are not supposed to open it until morning but since I won't get to see you tomorrow, I guess it would be okay to open it now." I said, and took out the black Cartier box that I hid in my coat.

"Oh, Dylan, you shouldn't have!" Emma shook her head with disbelief.

"Read the card first." I said with a complacent grin.

She opened my card. I could see the gleam in her eyes and broadening smile on her face as she read it slowly. *"I wish I could give you time and make the days longer, but I can't. I hope you think of me every time you wear this watch."*

"Dylan, it's beautiful, but it's too much. I feel so bad. I was working all week and I couldn't get you anything."

"Nothing is too much for you Emma, and you gave me the greatest gift; this wonderful night. I don't remember enjoying a family dinner this much. But then... any day, any night, any event with you is wonderful." I said and placed a soft kiss on her lips.

Just the touch of her lips was enough to start the fire in me. It was impossible to control myself and my insurmountable feelings when I was this close to her. Slowly my lips trailed down her neck, I cupped her face with my hands and started kissing her more fiercely. I grabbed her thin waist and pulled her to myself. Lost in feelings, I broke away slowly and whispered in her ear. Almost imperceptible. "I love you".

Her gaze lingered on my eyes a second too long before she looked away, probably contemplating her response. Trying to look nonchalant, as if it wasn't a big deal for me to say those words, I put on my coat avoiding her eyes. I reached for the door. I grabbed my umbrella and was about to leave. Then suddenly, Emma pulled my arm and made me stop. She turned me around swiftly and held the collar of my coat as she pulled me to herself unexpectedly. Her hands on my face, caressing gently my day-old stubble with her finger tips, she kissed me again. It was a long, tender kiss. Although my heart longed to hear her say those words back, her kiss felt like she was trying to show me what she couldn't say in words. She loved me too.

During the days following that Christmas Eve, I could only see Emma a few minutes here and there. She was either working at the hospital or working on her dissertation and I, Dylan Hamilton, who couldn't stand waiting, spent my days waiting for Emma to call. I cancelled my meetings and cleared my days just to spend a few precious minutes with her that I stole during her breaks. Even on New Year's Eve, instead of partying with Max and guys from work as I would have done any other year, I spent the night at the hospital, chatting with nurses and Emma in between her patient visits. I managed to have a few minutes with her alone before midnight and I kissed her as the ball dropped and the clock showed twelve o'clock.

A new year... a promise of a new life for me. I wanted it to start with Emma in my arms, our lips sealed together, but I wanted more than a just a few hours that she could spare. I was fighting with an invisible enemy that I had no chance of beating: time. Emma didn't have time for me, for us, for our relationship. I understood it was her last year and she was about to graduate, become an MD and get her PhD at the same time. I couldn't expect her to spend less time at the hospital or at the university, but I had to do something.

Being away from her and not seeing her enough was too hard to endure. Without her, my days were dull, my life boring and unpleasant. So, I thought about my options and discerned that there was only one way we could spend more time together... we should live together. There was only one problem...How would I convince her to say yes?

CHAPTER 15
EMMA

I was in the lab again, discussing with Amy how to remove the skin from the anterior thoracic wall on the supine cadaver. We were working on our dissection and identification exercise for hours, going over transverse incisions on soft tissues versus sagittal incisions. With more clinics and labs added to my schedule, it seemed like I was living on campus almost all the time. In the last month, I didn't sleep at my house more than two days in row. Many nights, I either stayed at the university working on a lab assignment or I was at the hospital for my clinics. I was relieved a bit after my ER rotation was over but the hardest one, my surgical rotation, had just started and it was nothing like the others. Our attendings were more demanding, the hours were longer and since I was planning to specialize in neurosurgery, this rotation was far more important for me than any other. With my caffeine intake shooting through the roof, I was tired, exhausted and sleep deprived, but I wasn't complaining. The operating room was where I wanted to be. I wanted to be a surgeon. Five months away from my degree, I was willing to do anything, even if it meant having to sacrifice living a normal life.

A normal life... It felt unreal and unreachable. I forgot what was considered normal. I had been immersed in this crazy routine for so long that I forgot what it meant to have breakfast in the morning, dinner in the evening or eight hours of sleep at night. My meals either came out of a vending machine or I skipped the meal totally, settling for a granola bar when my stomach started churning. I missed having long, girly talks with Sydney, indulging in Sunday breakfasts at Aunt Helen's house, morning jogs in the park, watching silly chick-flicks with Amy at her dorm room... all distant memories. However, of all the things I missed, there was one that affected me more than anything else. Dylan. Since I had avoided having a relationship for years, this feeling, needing to have that certain person in your life, was all new to me. I couldn't explain the void in me when I wasn't with him. It felt like I needed Dylan more than I needed food.

I spent every bit of my free time with him: fifteen minute coffee breaks, half hour dinners, but it wasn't enough. I missed being in his arms, kissing him, savoring the taste of his lips. I wanted to be with him all the time, I just didn't know how. It wasn't easy to fit Dylan into my hectic life.

I was thinking about him again, wondering if I could see him today as Amy and I headed to the lavatory to clean up. I was about to leave the lab when my phone vibrated. Dylan's handsome face with a short, puzzling message blinked on the screen: "I made a great plan for us today and you are not allowed to say no."

Under Amy's curious eyes, I picked up my phone and called him. "Hi Dylan, what's up? What is this great plan of yours that I can't say no to?"

"Why don't you meet me outside and I'll tell you all about it?"

"What? You are here? I thought you had a board meeting today."

"I have better and far more important things to do than sit in meetings all day. I asked Max to attend on my behalf. It's time he moved his lazy ass and did something for the company."

"And you trust him…"

"No, not really, but Rose Donnelly will be in the meeting too. She won't let him screw up too much."

"Okay." I chuckled. "I'll be out in a minute. You can tell me all about these better and important things that you've planned for the day."

I got out of the old brick building and suddenly my eyes were dazzled by bright sun light. It was a beautiful sunny day in New York in the middle of a cold, chilly winter. After ten straight days of rain, it felt great to feel the warm and caressing rays of sun on my face. I saw Dylan waiting for me by the stairs, swirling an unlit cigarette between his thumb and index finger. He had this most charming smile on his face that made my heart skip a beat.

"I thought you quit smoking." I said as I approached him slowly, carrying my backpack on my shoulder. "Please tell me you are not going to light that."

"No, I won't." He replied, taking my backpack from my shoulder as he always did whenever he met me at the campus. "But, holding it in my hand and having the absolute willpower not to light it makes me feel stronger."

I shook my head and grinned. "Okay Mr. Strong Willpower, what do you have in mind that I am not allowed to say no to?" I wrapped my arm around his neck and looked deeply into his intense, mesmerizing eyes.

"Well, Dr. Collins. I know for a fact that you don't have any other lab or clinic today. You have already written four chapters of your dissertation and you have been working in the lab for three straight days, even on Valentine's Day…"

"Good detective work, but you know how sorry I was for not being with you on Valentine's Day…"

"You preferred a date with cadaver rather than with me …" He scowled.

"Dylan! Please… you know I had to be in the lab that day."

"I know, I know." He raised his hand and smiled. "That's why I am calling today your 'off day', and kidnapping you."

"Kidnapping…" I chuckled and put a chaste kiss on his lips. "Don't you think it is a bit too much?"

"No, it is not, and this…" He peered down and pointed to my phone in the front pocket of my backpack. "Needs to be off all day. In case of emergency, your close friends and family have my phone number. They know how to reach you."

"Oh, God. You really thought this through and planned everything, didn't you?"

"Yes, I did." He replied resolutely, and then swiftly powered off my phone and put it in my back pack.

"Alright! I see..." I pursed my lips and narrowed my eyes. "Now, can you at least tell me what we are going to do the rest of the day?"

"That… my darling. I won't tell you." He clasped my fingers and started walking. "You gotta wait and see it for yourself. Now… let's go!" He demanded and pulled me to the sidewalk where I saw his black limo. Jeff was waiting by the door in his well-tailored black suit.

"Take us to our next spot, Jeff!" He told him without telling where we were going, but obviously Jeff knew. He nodded courteously and started driving.

"You are serious!" I uttered. "You're not going to tell."

He lifted his brows and shook his head. "Nope…" He replied. He smiled mischievously as he slid his fingers up and down my arm softly.

Ten minutes later, Jeff stopped at the corner of 59th Street and 6th Avenue, at the south entrance of Central Park where all horse and carriage rides were waiting.

"We're here." He said and helped me get out of the car. "Our carriage is the red and white one. We can hop on it anytime…"

"You are kidding right. We live in New York, Dylan. Horse and carriage rides are for tourists."

"Have you ever been on one?" He asked as a matter-of-factly.

"No. But..."

"Me neither." He replied, furrowing his brows. Not allowing me to object any further, he tugged my hand gently to cross the street. "I've been living in this city for thirty years and I've seen people on carriage rides every day, but I've never wanted to do it until..." He faltered and I sensed a bit hesitation in his voice.

"Until?"

"Until you. You came into my life and I want to do it all...all the silly, cliché romantic stuff, starting with a carriage ride. Now, shall we?" He said and added a wink.

I nodded, smiling widely and noticed the big black tote on his other arm. A bottle of wine and two wine glasses were visible. "Alright. Let's do it." I finally acceded.

We got in the carriage and Dylan told our well-dressed, young driver to move. With Dylan's command, he pulled the reigns and our horse started to trot.

Like many other New Yorkers, I loved Central Park. It was our heaven amidst the crazy city. I always enjoyed the picturesque views and the serene atmosphere it provided during any season, however, wandering through Central Park in a carriage as I sat next to Dylan, cuddled under a soft blanket and sipping a delicious red wine was something else. It was an utterly rapturous experience. Each time Dylan turned towards me and smiled warmly, my heart throbbed like crazy. His hand wrapped over mine, his eyes lingered on my lips, but he didn't pull me to himself to kiss. Instead he wetted his lips with his tongue slowly and waited. The wonderful taste of his lips was so close but also so far at the same time. He was building the tension between us on purpose. It felt like a game of willpower to show who was more stubborn and strong. Who was going to break first and kiss the other?

And of course, I was the loser. I couldn't hold myself back any longer when he was touching me softly and gazing deeply into my eyes. I leaned in and kissed him fiercely. It was a kiss that showed how much I missed him. A kiss to show ...how I wanted him, how I was empty without him, and how much I loved him.

I broke away when our carriage stopped. "Well, this was nice." I admitted shyly.

"I knew you'd like it." He replied in a bit priggish tone.

"So what is next? " I asked impatiently.

He tucked his hands into his pocket and grinned. Once we were back in the limo, he pulled out two ice skates from the bag stashed under the seat. "We are going to the Rink at Rockefeller Center." He said smugly.

"Oh, no…I can't Dylan." I immediately rejected. "I don't know how to skate and I don't want to fall and break a bone."

"Don't worry. I won't let you fall." He assured. "I'll teach you how to skate and I bet you'll start skating without my help before we leave the ring today."

In less than ten minutes, we were by the Rink and Dylan was on his knees tying up my laces. "Now, let's hit the ice." He exclaimed happily. He held my hand and helped me get into the ring.

"Don't let me go." I begged him, hugging the wall almost instantly.

"Don't worry. I promise you will have fun! Now let's start with feeling your blades. Hold on to the wall and slide one leg back and forth." He said.

"Okay." I uttered and did as he told.

"Now, turn around and feel the opposite leg. See… You are doing great. Next thing you need to learn is to swizzle."

"Swizzle? What do you mean 'swizzle'?"

"Feel the edge of your blade. Using your inner thighs, push your skates apart and glide back together in. Like this."

I tried to copy him, however not a moment too soon, my butt was on the ice. "It is easy to tell, not so easy to do." I scolded him.

"Come on. Don't be discouraged. Falling is part of learning. Even the professional skaters fall down." He cheered me up without any teasing. "You just need to learn how to get up. Put one knee up front and transfer your weight over while you bring the other." He explained and did it himself first, then waited for me to copy him. "You did it Emma. You are a natural. I also want to show you how you stop and after that, let's start going around the ring." He said excitedly.

Surprisingly, I stayed on the ring for close to an hour with him. My first fifteen minutes on ice were horrible. I fell so many times and also made Dylan fall with me, but he didn't complain. Instead, each time I fell down, he encouraged me to get up and try some more. Slowly, I started to pick up the basics and soon started to skate without holding his hand. I even managed to stay on the ice without falling for twenty minutes. Just like he thought, I was having fun. I wished I was good enough to go fast and chase him around the ring.

My feet and legs got extremely tired at the end of the hour. Dylan, sensing my exhaustion, helped me get off the ice. Once I found a bench overlooking the ring and sat down, I asked him to skate a bit more without me and show me some of his moves. Lucky me… he did.

Dylan looked gorgeous no matter what he did but on ice, skating fast, turning the corners as if he was a hockey player, he was more charming and attractive than ever.

"How did you learn to skate like this?" I asked when he came out and changed into his shoes.

"My uncle, my mother's younger brother Dean, was a hockey player. He taught me how to skate when I was little."

"I am glad he did. It is so much fun to watch you on ice. Why didn't you skate professionally and become a hockey player like your uncle?"

He glared at me with his you-know-the-reason look.

"Your father didn't let you…" I mumbled, but Dylan only shrugged.

"I am hungry." He commented and skillfully changed the subject. "Let's go, eat something. I know a great place a few blocks away."

"I am so tired Dylan. I don't think I have any more energy to walk or dine outside."

"I've got a better idea then." He grinned and pulled his phone out of his jacket. "Pick us up in front of the plaza in fifteen minutes." He ordered. I assumed it was Jeff on the phone. He turned towards me and held my waist. "Jeff is just a block away, he should be here soon," he explained quickly. Together we walked to the sidewalk. He clasped my hands and rubbed them to make them warmer. We were waiting for Jeff to arrive when Dylan pointed to a street vendor across to street, selling chestnuts.

"Do you want some?" He asked. His eyes were sparkling like a child offered a candy.

"Sure!" I nodded.

He rushed across the street and came back with two brown bags filled with roasted chestnuts. "My favorite street food" He declared, then opened one chestnut up, peeled the shell deftly with his fingers and placed it between my lips.

"Mine too." I agreed, savoring the sweet taste of warm chestnut melting in my mouth. We sat on a bench on the busy side walk, watched New Yorkers passing by and almost ate both bags as we waited for Jeff.

When Jeff pulled up to the sidewalk, "Will you please tell me where we are going this time?" I asked with beseeching eyes.

"Alright!" He agreed, surprisingly without arguing. "Dinner and a movie at my place. We can order Chinese, Thai, Lebanese… or good old pizza. You get to pick." He said, gazing into my eyes, waiting nervously for my response.

"Sounds good." I replied, curious to see where he lived, and what his place looked like. He had impeccable taste for everything and I wondered if his apartment was as elegant and tasteful as his office was.

We arrived at the luxurious building on 5th and 77th in less than five minutes. The apartment doorman rushed to our limo to open our door immediately. With one hand on his back, the other extended to help me get out of the limo, he welcomed us courteously. Then, he asked if we needed his help with anything while we waited for the elevator. "Thanks Russell, nothing for now." Dylan declined him curtly. "I am going to order some take-out. Bring it upstairs when it arrives." He ordered in a solemn voice.

"Of course, sir." He replied. His voice cracked a bit. "I will bring it right up."

I knew Dylan was influential and powerful but it still surprised me to see how people seemed to be always on the edge around him; scared to say or do something wrong. Dylan with me and Dylan around other people were completely different and I was very much perplexed about a lot of things concerning him. He was kind and amiable but I had seen his brutal and rough side more than a few times. I couldn't ignore his infamous reputation either. It followed me everywhere. I got constant warnings about my relationship with Dylan, from Amy, the head nurse and Rosie, at the hospital. They all told me to be careful. However, I didn't know how to be careful with him. He was the most instantaneous, adventurous person I'd ever met. He was talented… he could draw a picture of me in less than thirty minutes. Sophisticated…he talked about art, literature or opera as if it was an everyday subject. Smart…he was a successful CEO but also a romantic… His charming smile was enough to befuddle me, I was dazed and felt at a loss in the depth of his blue eyes. I loved him but at the same time, this feeling burned me from the inside, it scared the hell out of me.

"I'm calling Jade Lotus. You're sure you're okay with Thai?" He said when we got of the elevator which opened into a big marble hallway. I confirmed with a nod and started checking out his apartment. The exquisite paintings on the wall, a one of a kind sculpture on his white piano… His place looked like an art gallery. I was hesitant to touch anything.

"Food should be here shortly." He said. "Would you like some wine while we wait?"

"Yes." I answered, my eyes still wandering around the room, taking it all in. I imagined Dylan's apartment to be more like a bachelor pad, less like this immaculate, tastefully furnished, wholesome place. It looked amazing.

I had my eyes on a Degas hanging in his library. I knew he loved art, but I didn't know he had such an impressive art collection. He was telling me how he purchased it at an auction in London when the doorbell rang. It was Russell at the door, with two large bags in his hand. Dylan quickly set the table overlooking Central Park. With a stunning view of Manhattan in front of us, we started eating. The food was delicious. Everything I tried tasted better than the last.

I was watching the twinkling lights of the New York skyline when Dylan opened another bottle of wine and poured some for himself. "This is one of my favorite reds. Do you want to try?" He asked.

"Yes, but just a little bit…" I replied. I was already tired and the wine was making me more relaxed and drowsy. I didn't want to fall asleep in his arms like I did last time.

"Emma…" He whispered softly. "You look tired. Why don't you relax and choose a movie while I put the plates in the sink. I have all the holiday classics, award winners, even some romantic comedies for you to choose from."

"Okay." I agreed, but felt guilty for not offering my help. It had been a long day and my muscles were aching after an hour on the ice. I was so out of shape. I made a mental note to restart my morning jogs again.

While Dylan was busy in the kitchen, I got up and checked his DVD collection. I was impressed by his taste again. There were as many foreign, documentary, and independent films as there were Hollywood movies. I picked one of my old time favorites and put it into the DVD player.

"So, what are we watching?" He asked curiously as he scooted in next to me.

"Wait and see …" I replied with a smirk, copying his response from earlier. I was curious to see his reaction when the opening scene of "The Good, the Bad and the Ugly" appeared on the big screen.

"A western, seriously…?" He squinted with a puzzled look on his face. "I would have thought you'd go for 'The Notebook', or a 'When Harry Met Sally' kind of movie."

"We can watch 'The Notebook' if you want." I teased him.

"Oh, no thank you. One time with my sister was enough." He shook his head. Then he put his arms around me and I rested my head on his chest.

Feeling the warmth of his skin and crackling wood sound coming from the nearby fireplace, the quiet and romantic atmosphere in his large suite, two glasses of wine and of course, being in Dylan's comforting arms… I was in such a relaxed state. My eyelids were laden with sleep. I rubbed my eyes but couldn't hide my yawn.

"Dylan…" I breathed deeply. "I'm sorry to end the night early but I don't think I can watch any longer. I can't keep my eyes open."

"Then don't. Sleep and stay here with me tonight…" He paused. "Actually, I would love for you to stay here with me all the time." He added in a serious tone.

I was startled. I wasn't sure if I heard him right. "You mean, like live here with you?"

"Yes. What if you lived here with me? I would see you more often. We wouldn't have to wait days to see each other. What do you think Emma? Will you move in with me?"

"Yes … Okay…" I stuttered, still not believing my ears.

"Okay?" He repeated, with a scrutinizing look. "Did you just agree to move in with me?"

"Yes, I think I did, but if you weren't serious …."

"No…" He interrupted me. "I just couldn't believe you said 'yes'. I prepared this long speech to convince you. I even rehearsed it a couple of times. It's… It's just… so wonderful." He hugged me tighter. His tongue slid across my lips softly and then he pulled me into a deep, fervent kiss as his hands slipped lower and rested on the small of my back.

"Dylan…" I whispered as I tried to catch my breath. "I was thinking about you before you showed up today. Actually, I think about you all time…" I admitted shyly. "I want to spend all my time with you. All my available time to be more correct." I added.

"You have no idea how happy I am right now. Oh, God! Emma… you mean everything to me."

It took him only a second before he kissed me again and slowly unbuttoned my shirt. His soft fingers dancing over my body made me forget my tiredness instantly. All my senses came to life with his touch and my body was ready to explode with expectation. His lips descended to my breast, and I shivered with the touch of his warm, velvet tongue. He took my shirt off and his deft fingers immediately knew what I was craving for. He unhooked my black lace bra slowly and freed my breasts. He caressed them softly with his knuckles first and then lowered his mouth and started kissing them again. He was too gentle, too soft while I wanted him to be his usual self.

"I won't break Dylan. Come on… you know what I like and how I like it." I smirked.

He squinted at me, and without saying anything back, he kissed my lips hard. His hands curved and cupped my breasts firmly, squeezing, giving me both pleasure and pain at the same time. He wasn't delicate anymore. His passion and desire for me were too obvious. I arched my head back and gave him full access, enjoying the sweet sensation building in me as his tongue circled over and over, giving me small and teasing bites. I gasped as he found and caressed all the delicate spots on my body. I was already wet, aching for some friction. I wanted him to be inside me so desperately but Dylan, gazing intently into my eyes, shook his head and gave me a mischievous smile.

"Dylan, please…" I begged.

Then suddenly, without uttering a word, he lifted me up and carried me to his bedroom in his arms. He placed me on his bed covered with red satin sheets and slowly undressed himself while he watched me squirm and breathe in and out wistfully.

Dylan always looked gorgeous naked but in his dimly lit bedroom with twinkling lights of the city in the background, he looked like a Greek god. His broad shoulders, hard chiseled abs, firm muscles… I wanted to adore every inch of him with my lips. I swept my fingers swiftly over his abs and stroked him while I lowered my lips, kissing him slowly.

His eyes closed, he took a deep breath. I was ready for him and I knew he was for me too, however, suddenly he made me stop. "Do you trust me?" He asked out of nowhere.

"Yes…" I mumbled, my body trembling with need.

Without any explanation, he went to his dressing room and came back holding a green fabric and a feather crop on his hand.

"Remember this?" He showed me the green foulard, still smiling. His blue eyes were piercing through me.

I nodded and bit my lips. It was my silk foulard that I left in Amsterdam. He turned me around slowly and covered my eyes with it. The touch of soft silk covering my eyes, and his musky scent infused to my foulard made my other senses more alive. I was nervous but my body was ablaze with excitement.

"Just let it go. Trust me, you will enjoy it …" He whispered softy in my ear.

My heart was beating so fast with all the anticipation. Not being able to see anything but feeling soft feather like touches sweeping my body, my breast, my inner thighs and my core made me squirm with pleasure and breathe faster.

"Dylan. Now! I need you now!" I screamed finally.

 Dylan, ignoring my begging, placed me on my knees and continued riding his feather crop over the small of my back.

"You look amazing. So hot. So sexy. Oh, Emma, I want you so much." He finally spoke. "Are you ready for me?"

"Yes. Hell, yes!" I answered him beseechingly.

Finally, with a sudden but amazingly pleasurable jolt, he was in me. He braced my body with his arms from behind, making me lean on his shoulders, arching my head back and kissing my neck lasciviously as he moved hard and fast. Feeling him in me, I felt full and complete like I'd never felt before. With his every move, every thrust, a delirium of joy passed through my body. We climaxed together and fell on the bed tangled in each other tightly. Dylan, still breathing heavily, looked deeply into my eyes and then spoke softly, caressing my cheek with his fingers.

"I love you so much Dr. Collins." He said, smiling.

"I love you too." I finally admitted it out loud.

I loved him more than I loved anybody in my life. Dylan made me not only reach the stars but also stay there. He was my ecstasy. I needed him so much. In his arms, I forgot everything. My problems, my difficult family, my never easing life. Dylan was my cure and I couldn't have enough of him.

CHAPTER 16
EMMA

I was in Dylan's limo, trying to get to the hospital and got stuck in the middle of the morning traffic again. Since I moved in with Dylan, I was late for almost everything. Every goodbye kiss turned into something more and I couldn't leave his apartment on time. My work and school life were getting more chaotic thanks to Dylan's sweet disturbance, however I wasn't complaining. I was happy. Extremely happy to be more correct. Living with Dylan was sheer bliss. He was everything I wanted and more.

This morning, after amazing sex and a well prepared breakfast, I again left his apartment fifteen minutes later than I was supposed to and Jeff ended up giving me a ride to the university for the third day in a row.

I was going over my notes, waiting impatiently for the light to turn green when my phone rang. I couldn't believe my eyes when I checked who was calling. It was Steve… my dear brother who hadn't been speaking to me for three months. "Oh, this can't be good!" I mumbled to myself, hesitating to answer. It was like I was cursed. Anytime something good happened to me, life threw me a curve ball without letting me enjoy myself a little. As if it had to balance all the good with the bad immediately.

"I hope you are not calling me because you are in trouble again…" I answered my phone edgily.

"Hello, sis, I missed you too." Steve replied, ignoring my snide remark.

"Hi Steve. It's good to hear your voice. I guess this means we are talking again."

"Yes! We are." He replied. His voice was genial and close. "I am really sorry Emma. I should have never said those things to you. I was out of line and see, I am calling to apologize!"

"You are apologizing. I can't believe my ears."

"You better believe it. I might have realized a bit too late, but you were right about me, dad… everything. I knew I had to change. I couldn't stand myself, what I've become. I've rejected dad's money and started working. Wall Street of all places."

"Don't tell me you're working for dad."

"No, of course not. I don't want to see his god damn face ever again."

"Hey… careful there. He is our dad."

"I don't care. After what he did to me in London, this past Christmas, I don't think I'll ever want to talk to him again."

"Why? What happened in London?"

"Dad's girlfriend… stupid bitch, Marlene!" I could hear him getting riled up on the phone as he said her name. "She was so drunk on New Year's Eve that she hit on me. She kissed me and then tried to… you know. I told dad what she did. Instead of believing me, he called me a drunk and a liar."

"Were you drunk?"

"Yes, I was drunk but I wasn't lying. She really came on to me."

"Why didn't you call me and tell me earlier?"

"I don't know. I guess I was ashamed of what happened."

"Did something happen between you and Marlene? Be honest with me Steve!"

"No, of course not… are you crazy? I hate her. I found her appalling even when I was drunk. She kissed me, that's all. I promise you Emma, and I swear on the precious memory of our mother that I'm not the wayward brother you don't know how to handle anymore. I stopped drinking. No more weed, coke or alcohol. I wanted you to hear what happened from me first. Dad will be in town soon and he wants to see you. I guess he heard that you have a boyfriend. He wants to meet him too."

"Oh, no…" I sighed grudgingly. "He knows about Dylan."

"I think he just knows you are in a relationship. I don't think Aunt Helen told him anything more than that."

"I hope not. I don't want him going around my back, doing all kinds of background checks. You know he has done that before." I complained.

"Kyle was a jerk. He was right to check on him, but I understand how you don't want to him to poke his nose into your relationship with Dylan. Call him and tell him that."

"Yeah. Well. We'll see about that. I don't like talking to him about my life in general, so I am not looking forward to our boyfriend talk. Actually… You know what…I would prefer if you met Dylan instead of dad."

"Well…I've already met him Emma." He said, baffling me completely.

"How? When?"

"He is my boss. I've been working at Phliant as an intern for over a month now. Dylan is great. Smart. Funny. I like him. Definitely a keeper." He told me all this very quickly and chuckled. I was about to ask about his working for Dylan but he didn't let me. He cut me off, "Hey…I gotta go Emma. I'm late for class. I'll catch up with you later." He rumbled.

"What? No… You can't just tell me all that and hang up." I grumbled hopelessly. But my words were useless. Steve had already hung up without giving me a chance to ask any questions.

Holding the phone in my hand, confused by all the things Steve said, I decided to call my father right away. He was in a meeting as always. So, I left a message with his secretary, asking him to call me back.

Later in the evening, instead of a call, I received an e-mail from him, inviting me for a Sunday brunch at 11 o'clock at Garden Terrace. I e-mailed him back, letting him know I was going to be there, but also planning to bring my boyfriend. He replied back shortly. "Looking forward to seeing you both there." Nothing else.

"Well, that's a first," I thought. He wasn't prying into my life or my relationship. I wondered if he was saving his usual intimidation for our face to face meeting.

I got back to the apartment late at night and I found Dylan in the bedroom, sitting on the bed, snoozing with his glasses on and a book on his lap. I approached him slowly and picked up the book from his lap. I took his glasses off and set them on the night stand. I was pulling the blanket over him when he opened his eyes, "Hello, gorgeous." He drawled sleepily.

"Sorry. Did I wake you up?"

"I was waiting for you. I guess I dozed off. Come here…" He said and then pulled me into a hard kiss immediately. I was on his lap, kissing him back with a desire I couldn't contain. I missed him so much. After a long day at the hospital, being in his arms, kissing him passionately felt so good. I wrapped my arms around his neck and straddled him. I could feel his growing bulge under me through his silk pajamas. He was as ready as I was. Full of passion and desire.

He moved his hand underneath my blouse trying to unclasp my bra, when I gripped his hand and shook my head. "First… you need to explain to me why you didn't tell me about Steve…"

"Oh, he finally called you…?" He smiled wickedly.

"Yes, my little evil brother called me and told me he works for you." I said in between my kisses. "And you didn't tell me…"

"It wasn't my place to tell." He cupped my face with his hand and deepened our kiss. "I wanted Steve to do earlier but I guess he wasn't ready to talk to you. You know he had his issues, but since he started working at Phliant, he's doing good, free of drugs and alcohol. He works twenty hours a week and goes to school every day, he even signed up at the gym. So… I think he is on the right track."

"You have no idea how happy I am to hear all this. When he called I was so scared to answer. I thought he was in trouble again. But what you're telling me… It's great!" I blurted out happily. "Oh, speaking of news. My father is in town and inviting us for a brunch. He wants to meet you…"

"Oh God… meeting your father. Should I be scared?"

"Nah… He is okay. You might even like each other. He is a Wall Street guy just like you."

"Oh, that worries me even more."

"You've got nothing to worry about. Just be your charming self. Helen and George love you. Sydney thinks you are the best thing that's ever happened to me. Steve told me you are amazing. I'm sure my dad will like you too." I said and kissed him passionately without giving him a chance to ask any more questions about my dad. Then slowly I started to move up and down on his lap. We were both naked in less than a minute, and I was riding him, the way we both liked. It was crazy how we were always ready for each other and couldn't get enough of one another. Dylan and I … it was one crazy, flaming hot combination.

Sunday morning, we left his apartment without our usual morning flirt or casual talk. I could sense that he was nervous and edgy, although I told him many times that he shouldn't be. We arrived at the Terrace a few minutes early and a young waitress took us to our table by the window, overlooking a beautiful garden where we could see colorful tulips in bloom. We were already enjoying our mimosas when my father showed up at eleven o'clock and asked the same young hostess at the reception for us. She pointed to our table and our eyes met across the dining hall instantly. At that fleeting second, I saw both Dylan's and my father's expression change dramatically. Dylan's face went ice cold, as if he saw a ghost. My father, on the other hand, instead of approaching our table, turned back and called someone on his phone. I had no idea what was going on.

"Your father is Charles Reed?" Dylan muttered after a long, deep breath.

"Yes. I thought you knew."

"No, I didn't!" Dylan's voice cracked. He narrowed his eyes, shaking his head worriedly.

"Didn't you have that detective on me? I thought he gave you all my personal information."

"After Max found you, I stopped Nolan's search. All I know about you are the things you shared with me. All this time, I knew you as Emma Collins, not Emma Reed."

"I am Emma Collins." I replied with a bit of reproach. "I took my mother's last name when I got accepted to Columbia. I didn't want my father's prestigious last name to undermine my own personal achievement."

"How about Steve? He is employed as Steve Collins."

"I don't know why or when he changed his last name. I guess it must be a recent change. My father and Steve are not getting along lately." I explained still trying to figure out why he was so upset. "Why is this so important to you or bothering you this much?"

"Because my darling." He drawled. "Your father, Chuck Reed, is my number one enemy. We have hated each other for years. He cannot be civil with me, even for a minute; therefore I avoid seeing him and I try not deal with him personally. In a minute, when he arrives at this table, you will get to see how much he hates me."

"Oh, God. Dylan. But why?"

But before he could explain 'why', my father reached our table. He wasn't looking at me. He didn't even attempt to give me a hug, a kiss on my cheek or show any affection to a daughter he hadn't seen in over five months. His cold eyes were fixed on Dylan. Dylan got off his chair courteously, extended his hand to my father, which he refused to shake. Then he greeted him in a chilly voice. "Hello, Chuck. This is a surprise for me too. Believe me... I wasn't expecting to see you."

"What the hell are you doing here Dylan?"

"Emma invited me to meet her father. I was expecting to meet Mr. Collins, not Chuck Reed."

My father turned towards me and almost yelled. "You are dating Dylan Hamilton."

"Yes, she is." Dylan answered him for me. "Actually it's more than just dating Chuck. We are in a serious relationship. We've been living together for over two months." He told him without giving me a chance to speak. His voice was harsh and gruff as if he was defying him.

"You are out of your god damn mind if you think I would let you have a relationship with my daughter." My father blurted out.

"You don't have any say in this Chuck. This is between Emma and I."

"She is my daughter, and you will do as I tell you. Stay away from her."

"That is not possible. I am in love with her."

"Dylan Hamilton does not love. He screws..."

"No. Not with Emma. I love her so much. It's different. I want to be with her forever. I want to marry her." He said so unexpectedly, then turned towards me and talked slowly. "Sorry baby... this wasn't how it was supposed to be. I was planning a romantic getaway after your graduation in May. I was going to propose to you there. It wasn't supposed to be like this... not like this at all." He shook his head vigorously. I could see the disappointment in his eyes.

"Marrying my daughter..." My father yelled at him. "Over my dead body!"

"You can not to tell me or Emma what to do."

"I am her father. It's my job to protect my daughter from assholes like you."

"Your job to protect your daughter..." Dylan repeated his words mockingly. "Where were you when she needed you; when she lost her mother? What kind of a father abandons his twelve year old daughter and four year old son after their mother dies. Yeah, you are definitely a role model!"

"You bastard!" He shook his head and made his hand into a fist. "I am going to make you pay for every fucking word..."

I was at a loss, caught in the middle of their quarrel. I didn't know what to do. With every insult they threw at each other, they were getting beyond control. I was scared one of them was going to hit the other, or do something worse.

Finally, I couldn't take it any longer. "Enough!" I screamed. "Dad...I'll come and see you in your office later. Dylan, shut up. Don't say another word. Call Jeff and let's go." I said and pulled him away. We left the restaurant in a hurry without looking back. I wanted to get away from my father's rage as soon as possible. I had never seen him like that before. He was unreasonable, boorish and vulgar. Whatever the problem he had with Dylan, it was obvious they weren't going to solve it while throwing insults at each other.

I held Dylan's hand and led him out of the restaurant. We were walking hastily to get out of the building and I saw the uncontrollable anger in Dylan's eyes and realized how much he was holding himself back in there. He was infuriated. "This is crazy. I am not going to let him ruin this Emma, I swear to God!" He yelled and punched the door opening to the parking lot angrily with his fist. The glass window shuttered in thousand pieces and glass cuts turned his hand into crimson red. Blood dripping from his fingers soaked his shirt, and made it look like he had a serious injury.

"I am sorry, Emma." He groaned. His voice was afflicted with his distress. His faced showed his agony. "I love you so god damn much. I didn't know what to do! How are you? Please tell me you are not mad at me." He implored.

"I am fine, Dylan. I'm not mad, just confused. I have no idea what that whole thing was about. Why do my boyfriend and my father seem to be mortal enemies?"

"I will explain everything. If you let me …" He begged.

"Not now, Dylan. We need to take care of your hand first." I cut him off.

"It is just a scratch…"

"It is more than a scratch. You hurt yourself pretty bad. You need stitches and all I have with me is a few Band-Aids." I held his hand and put pressure on the deep cut with a tissue, but I couldn't stop the bleeding. Blood dripping from his fingers stained my jeans and sweater too.

"I want to know what you think…" Dylan whispered gazing into my eyes in a very concerned face. "You are not going to listen to him, are you?" He said, his hands were shaking, his voice cracked.

"Let's get you fixed first. Once you calm down and we are back in the apartment, we'll talk about it."

"Okay…" He mumbled. His eyes were still full of worry.

As soon as Jeff arrived, we rushed him to the nearest ER and he ended up having five stitches. It was a deep wound as I suspected. On our way to the apartment, Dylan was unusually quiet, as if he was contemplating our upcoming discussion.

We got to the apartment and Russell greeted us with his usual warmth and courtesy. He glanced at our blood stained clothes and I could tell he wanted to ask what happened. However, Dylan ignored his attention and told him to call the elevator brusquely. And poor, old Russell just complied.

"We are okay, Russell, nothing to worry about." I said to him, before the elevator door closed.

"Would you like something to drink?" He asked when we were back in the apartment. He was still pensive.

"I don't know. Should I have a drink before I hear you out?"

"I guess it wouldn't hurt." He pursed his lips. He poured me some wine and got himself a neat scotch. "I am not sure where to start. It is not my favorite story to tell. I am scared you won't understand."

"I don't know why my father doesn't like you, but I am not going to hold it against you. You already know that I am not close with him. I won't let him meddle with my life or any of my personal relationships. On the other hand, I need to know the reason behind this strong animosity between you. So, just be straight, honest, and tell me nothing but the truth."

"Nothing but the truth…" He mumbled to himself and started talking. "It was four years ago. I was trying to acquire Ortuin Assets Management based in Hong Kong. It was my strategic move to get us into Asian market. We were expanding our business greatly and we didn't want to lose a perfect opportunity in the fast growing hedge fund market in Asia. It was a billion dollar deal for us. We heard there was another American investor interested in them but our offer was strong; reviewed and already approved by the board of directors. The final transfer of title and agreements were due upon our visit. Max and I arrived in Hong Kong to sign and finalize the deal with our attorneys. On the day of the agreement, Mr. Chiang, Ortun's CEO, did not show up to the meeting. We didn't understand what was going on. Our translators were at a loss as well. They were telling us bits and pieces of what they heard. Soon we found that Mr. Chiang received another offer at the last minute. Reed Capital Management sent an offer, ten percent higher than ours. We couldn't understand how it happened, how they came in higher than us. After a detailed investigation, we found a security breach in our office network and we realized one of our interns leaked our bid. We lost OAM to Reed Capital and lost our access to the Asia Market."

138

"And you thought my father paid off your intern and got the tip."

"I am sure that he did. I always knew Chuck Reed was a brutal businessman. What I didn't know is that he would go to that kind of level to win. Everything is fair in love and war, and Reed was at war with Phliant."

"But…what you have explained sounds like corporate espionage. Isn't it against the law? Why didn't you take legal action?"

"Because we didn't have any proof. The intern left no trace. His computer was clean and we had no paper or electronic trail to link them. Other than two eye witnesses who saw them having a meal together, we had nothing that would stand up in court. A few months later, he transferred to a college in Melbourne and we couldn't chase him any further. We ended up dropping the case. It was a lost cause anyway. It wouldn't have changed the fact that Reed acquired OAM."

"This explains why you hate him. You had a big loss. But why does he hate you? It seems like he was the big winner. My father always finds a way to pull through."

"I am getting there. I just wanted you to know how it all started."

"Okay…I'm listening."

"Two years ago, Max and I were working on another deal in Singapore. After losing OAM to Reed Capital, we were being extremely careful. But I knew Chuck. He didn't play fair, so we decided to change the rules of the game and play like he did." Dylan spoke slowly, and then looked deeply into my eyes as if he was gauging my response. "Do you remember Trisha, your father's girlfriend?" He asked hesitatingly.

"The one before Marlene. Yes, I remember her. I also remember that they had an ugly break up. My father never explained us what she did. But I heard she cost him a lot of money."

"Yes, she did. I was the reason for that."

"What do you mean?" I asked curiously.

"We didn't have anybody or any way to get to Chuck the way he did to us. So, Max and I made a plan. We knew that Trisha was Chuck's girl. We studied her for a month and knew everything about her. What she liked, she didn't like…What her weaknesses were. Our plan was to use her against Chuck. I wanted Max to carry on the plan, flirt with her and win her heart, but in order to do that he had to give up his wicked bachelor life and only date her. Of course, Max couldn't do it." He paused, took a big sip from his glass. "So I did. She was easy to fool. Since I studied her so well, she fell for me. She continued her relationship with Chuck as I told her to do. But she was coming to my apartment, spending her days in my bed after she left Chuck's."

"What? You... you were..." I stuttered. I couldn't believe what I was hearing.

"Yes Emma. I used your father's girlfriend for six months to get to your father. She was so in love with me that she was ready to do whatever I asked. She had access to all his files. She fed me all his business information. Now that we had the insider information, we closed all the deals when we were competing against Reed. We acquired an even more powerful company in Singapore for the Asia Market and we turned a record profit that year." He explained. His face was solemn, eyes not blinking. "Of course, Chuck found out about Trisha and me eventually, and we've become mortal enemies ever since."

"Oh, Dylan. How could you? What you did is..."

"I know, it is disgusting. Horrible. Immoral."

"Yes. All that...and more. I don't know what to say, or what to think?"

"That was old me Emma. I promise you, I've changed. You've changed me. Since I've met you, I've become a different person. Can you forgive me?"

"I am not the one to forgive. You used a girl to get to my father. I don't care how you made my father lose millions, but using a girl the way you did... it's unacceptable."

"Trisha wasn't a good girl Emma. She was using me as much as she used your father. She saw that I was a better catch, so she played an ugly, unethical game to get me. I am not proud of what I did but please believe me when I say, she wasn't in it for love, she was in it for money."

"I don't know what to believe any more."

"I know. You asked for nothing but truth. This is the truth. Please let me hold you?" He said and wrapped his hands over my waist. He leaned in, his face a few inches away, breathed in the side of my neck. His lips were close but not touching my skin.

I put my hands on his chest and pushed myself away from him since I knew the moment we kissed, I wouldn't be able to stay away.

I needed time to think and make up my mind about of all of this. "I think I should stay at Sydney's apartment tonight." I said after a long silent minute.

"No, I can't let you leave." Dylan rejected. "You won't come back."

"Dylan, please… "

"I'm scared Emma." He muttered and buried his face into my hair. He wrapped his arms tightly around me again and whispered in my ear. "I'm scared that I am going to lose you."

"I love you Dylan. I can't just turn off my feelings for you. But I need some time. Give me some time."

He crossed his arms over his chest and gazed deep into my eyes. When I opened the door to leave, "Please come back to me, Emma," he said and watched me get into the elevator with doleful eyes. Oh, God… What was I going to do?

CHAPTER 17
DYLAN

"Just give her some time…" I kept repeating to myself on my way to work after I got out of the gym. I couldn't sleep all night. Being alone in a cold bed and her absence in my arms was horrifying. My apartment felt like a strange place without her. It was so bothersome and uncomfortable that I couldn't stay inside. I rushed out of my apartment before dawn broke. I crossed the empty street and started my usual five mile jog around the park. I ran faster than my usual pace. I was out of breath and sweating like crazy by the time I completed my run but it wasn't enough to distract me. So I went to the gym next, worked out for another hour, took a shower and then called Jeff to pick me up. I was staring at the New York skyline through the tall windows in my office blankly, absorbed in deep thoughts when Max came in. With one look at me, he noticed my miserable mood. I was in anguish and my face obviously showed it.

"What the hell is wrong with you again?" Max growled.

I turned around and glared at him without saying anything. I was still on edge and felt like I was ready to punch someone in the face. If Max wasn't careful with what he said, he was going to be the unlucky victim of my burning rage.

"Come on, man. You look like shit." He commented bluntly. "What's up with your hand? I left you all fine and chirpy on Friday. Tell me what happened."

"Chuck Reed happened." I mumbled.

"I thought you guys didn't do face-to-face anymore. Is it the same old shit again?"

"No." I sighed deeply before I told him the disturbing news. "He is Emma's father."

"What? What are you talking about?"

"Just as I said… Chuck Reed is Emma's father. We had a very pleasant brunch yesterday." I said facetiously.

"You've got to be kidding me. How is that possible? She's *Dr. Collins.*"

"I guess she took her mother's last name when she got into Columbia. She doesn't talk much about her father and definitely does not act like the daughter of a billionaire. I've never suspected anything."

"No, I wouldn't have guessed Emma was that son of a bitch's daughter either." Max replied unbelievingly and shook his head. He looked as shocked as I was when I found out about Emma's father. "So… You met Chuck and had a fight. Is that why your hand is bandaged? Don't tell me you hit him, broke his nose or something?"

"If Emma didn't step in, I would have. The old bastard ordered me not to see his daughter ever again." I snorted. "Of course I got mad, punched a window, cut my hand, and then we went to the ER, and I got stitches. All that fun stuff."

"Oh, wow. Too much shit for one weekend. So…how is Emma? What does she think of all this?"

"I don't know. I told her everything when we got home…and then she left."

"What do you mean you told her everything? Did you tell her about Trisha?"

"Yes, even Trisha…"

"Oh, God. You're in trouble, man. Good luck!"

"Yeah…She said she needs some time to think." I muttered and started looking at the folder Max brought in. I had to distract myself and stop thinking about Emma…what she was doing or what she was going to do.

Max and I were going over Steve's ten year projection numbers for South America when Mrs. Donnelly called in. She spoke through the office intercom in an unusual panicky voice.

"Mr. Hamilton. There is somebody in the lobby and he demands to see you immediately. I told him you are in a meeting but he refused to listen."

"Who is he?"

"He didn't give me his name. He said something about your brunch on Sunday. He is a very unreasonable person and he is on his way." She said anxiously.

"Oh, shit!" I yelled at her inadvertently.

"I am sorry, Mr. Hamilton. I tried but he didn't listen."

"It is not your fault Rose…" I said and saw Chuck Reed's tall figure approaching my office behind the frosty glass door.

"What's going on Dylan?" Max asked, but before I could answer, Chuck entered my office.

"What are you doing here Chuck? Yesterday's meeting was unpleasant enough. It is seriously unhealthy for me to see your face two days in a row." I said.

"Believe me, I'd like to avoid seeing your god damn face for rest of my life and I am here to ensure that happens." He threw his usual insults at me immediately.

"If you are going to start up about my relationship with Emma again, don't bother. We've talked already…"

"And…"

"And I told her everything. She loves me and I love her. She just needs some time to think. But I trust that we'll get pass this. I was honest with her and that's what's most important."

"I am sure you missed a few details." He narrowed his eyes and couldn't hide the subtle twitch on his face.

"No… I told her about everything, even Trisha." I said, self-assured.

Hearing her name caused the effect I expected. He was irritated and pissed off. "I'm pretty sure you've skipped a few heated details. Like these…" He growled with a smirk on his face and threw a sealed yellow envelope on my desk. "I wanted to hand deliver it to you personally and make sure that you got it. If you don't remember the night, I bet these pictures and Max will refresh your memory. Wouldn't you Maximilian? You are the perfect friend. The perfect son. Always making your daddy proud! "

"What the hell you are talking about? What is in the envelope?" I asked angrily.

"It is proof showing what a fucked up person you are and the same goes for your dear friend Max. Emma needs to stay away from both of you, and I will do everything in my power to make that happen. Why don't you enjoy the nice photo album I prepared for you?" He said, mockingly. He was trying to intimidate me and I wasn't going to give him the satisfaction of showing that I was worried. I glared back at him and then turned to Max to see if he knew what the hell he was talking about. Max crossed his arms over his chest and shook his head.

"Go ahead open it…" Chuck snickered.

Max and I reached for the envelope at the same time and I let Max tear it open. He pulled a stack of photos out and the instant he grabbed the first picture, his eyes grew wide. Almost in shock, he started swearing and cursing, while Chuck smirked back and lifted his eyes, daring me to look. I took the stack of photos from Max's hands and checked them out quickly.

144

They were photos of me and Max at the Fleur-de-lis party from a year ago. Obviously they were taken secretly in the mansion, in one of the private rooms without our knowledge. The photos were very graphic, showing Max and I having sex with the same girl while she was blindfolded and handcuffed. We were wearing masks, but the tattoos on our arms were visible, giving us away. Neither Max, nor I denied our 'not so spotless' bachelor past. The business we were in, the wild parties, the call girls, it was all almost normal. Unfortunately, the way the photos were taken, it looked as if we were torturing her, while in reality it was nothing like that. It was consensual sex between Valerie, Manhattan's wealthiest and most famous nymphomaniac, and us. Valerie was every bachelor's dream in Manhattan. She was the female equivalent of Max, who also happened to be Max's impossible catch. He wanted to fuck her for years, but Valerie was a member of an invitation only club and she only hooked up with club members. No one else.

Last fall, after my sweet victory over Chuck and I turned a billion dollars in revenue, and Chuck found out about the game I played behind his back, I had a horrible confrontation with Trisha. I needed a night out to blow off some steam. I knew what we did was unethical and it bothered me in more ways than I thought it would. Wanting a way to put Trisha and my terrible fight with Chuck behind me, Max came up with one of his 'not so smart but supposed to be fun' ideas. He knew about Valerie's club and some of her connections. After some surreptitious meetings and many phone calls to some high up people in the Manhattan socialite, he got us in to an invite-only party that only certain people knew about. He didn't care what the party was about as long as he got to be with Valerie and he didn't even mind that I had to join them. At first, I wondered what he meant when he said I had to join them. A second after I saw Max's intense glare and insinuating smirk, I understood we were going to do it together; fulfill Valerie's fantasy, satisfy the most insatiable woman in Manhattan.

It was a cold, blistery night when we drove out of Manhattan, two hours north. We arrived at a huge mansion in the middle of nowhere, close to midnight. A tall blonde girl with a feathered masquerade mask greeted us at the door and invited us in. She was wearing only a thong and a boa hanging over her neck, covering her nipples slightly. She handed us our masks and told us to wait in the vestibule. It was my first time at a party like this. I was nervous and had no idea what to do.

A dark haired lady wearing nothing but a gold cloak and matching gold mask came out shortly and told us that our date was waiting for us. She offered us a red pill and explained that it was going to make the night, our first experience in the club, more satisfying and intense. A small red pill that all the guests took. It was supposed to be magical and all natural, better than ecstasy... or so we were told. Max didn't hesitate of course. He swallowed it immediately and assured me that we would be fine. I downed it with some whiskey after him and sure enough, the magic began in less than five minutes. Before I knew it, I was wearing a mask, and nothing else, with so many beautiful and naked girls around me, all eager to have sex. I was half-hallucinating, half-awake in a complete blissful state. For the rest of the night, I followed Max around the mansion without a clue what the hell I was doing.

Much later, I recalled being in a dark private room with black curtains and oil lamps. A group of people, all wearing masks, were watching us while Max and I had sex with Valerie and a couple other girls afterwards. There were awkward noises and whispers while an organ and a harp played in the background. The entire party was an orgy reminding me old, black and white paintings of Paul Avril. People were having sex everywhere... couples, girls, guys, groups, in every position imaginable, and only a few faces were recognizable since nearly everybody wore masks. It's strange how I remember bits and pieces of the party, like where I got to watch people, while I still don't have a clue who and what I did after Valerie. It was as if my memory of that night was erased. Since then, there have been times that I thought it never happened; that I imagined it all. However, looking at the photos in front of me, it was becoming clear that the awkward night indeed happened, and it was more fucked up than I thought, because the photos in my hand were getting worse.

I was shocked seeing the explicit and inglorious images of that night. The entire thing was obviously a set-up. Fleur-de-lis was an invitation only, very exclusive party. The pictures were probably taken on purpose by someone at the party, maybe by the host, to blackmail me and Max at some point. Unfortunately, even the people who got the invitation didn't know who was hosting the party. There was no way for me to figure out who did this to us and what they got out of it. However, at this point, it didn't matter. Chuck Reed got a hold of those pictures and he was glaring at me with a sly grin as if he won a big victory.

I stood by the tall bay window, worrisome and nervous. I was petrified, knowing my worst enemy, the father of the love of my life, who hated my guts, was going to use those pictures against me.

"How did you get these pictures?" I asked. My hands were shaking.

"Does it matter? It shows what kind of a person you really are."

"It was just one night and I was drugged."

"Drug or no drug…I don't care. This is who you are. I have seen you with other girls too and I know what you do to them. I don't want someone like you to be with my Emma. You are an asshole and she deserves better. You will stay away from my daughter!" He threatened me.

"You, son of a bitch!" I yelled back.

"You will stay away from her. This is my final warning." He shoved me against the wall and tried to punch me in the face. Reflexively, I moved my head to the side and instead of my face, his fist hit the wall. His knuckles opened up immediately and started bleeding. He was standing in front me, shaking his hand and glaring at me with disgust, getting ready to throw another punch. I could tell he wasn't going to miss this time. I clenched my hand, made it into a fist. I was about to hit him back when Max got in between us.

"Let it go…He's not worth it." He spat out.

I inhaled deeply to calm myself. After a couple deep breaths, "Get the hell out of my office," I told Chuck and pointed at the door. I threw all the photos into the trash right away.

"I guess you don't want to keep them, but don't worry, I have another set printed." He taunted me and paused to check his watch. "It should be delivered to Emma within an hour. Let's see if you still trust your relationship after she sees them." He said with a scornful face just before he left my office.

I collapsed on my chair, hearing his last words.

"What the fuck was that?" Max murmured. I stared at him blankly, speechless. My mind was busy contemplating the ramifications of what Chuck had just said. Last night's argument was bad enough and now with the photos, it was going to be much worse. The possibility of losing her terrified me. I had to find her and explain everything before she saw the photos. I checked my watch. It was close to her lunch break. I hurried out of my office, ignoring Max and his prattle. I hailed a taxi cab and handed him a hundred to hurry up. I promised another hundred if we arrived at Harlem in less than ten minutes, and after running three red lights …we did.

I couldn't wait for the elevator. I rushed to the stairs and climbed up four floors, two steps at a time. When I arrived at the surgery center check-in desk, I saw that one of the grumpy old nurses, 'Nurse Linda' was on duty. I was out of breath after climbing the stairs too quickly. Still panting, I approached her and asked for Emma without any pleasantries. "I need to see her right away!" I commented seriously.

"Wait here." She ordered. "I'll page her for you but you should know that she is very busy today. She might not be able to see you." Linda brushed me off. Her voice was cold and distant. She always gave me the feeling that she didn't like me much.

I sat on a chair in the waiting room that smelled of an acrid combination of bleach and Pine Sol that burned my nose each time I breathed in. Twenty minutes passed as I waited patiently, but no one showed up. Linda gave me an 'I told you so' look, but I didn't care. I had to see Emma, even if it meant I had to wait for her for hours. Twenty more oppressive and torturing minutes later, the door to the waiting room opened and I saw Emma coming out in her green scrubs. She stopped at Linda's desk first and asked for something. Linda handed her some paperwork and her mail in return. She held them under her arm and then slowly approached me. I could see the yellow manila envelope tucked between her pink patient folders.

"What are you doing here Dylan?" She asked tersely.

"I had to see you. You didn't call." I replied back.

"I told you I needed some time alone, and I had my clinic this morning, I didn't have time."

"I have to tell you something…" I muttered. My voice was hoarse, the words barely escaped.

"Okay…" She hesitated. "What do you want to tell me?" A piece of hair fell into her eyes. I wanted to brush it off her face but I held myself back. She looked so distant that I was sure she wasn't going to let me touch her.

"First, that yellow envelope in your hand. Please don't open it." I almost begged.

"Why?" She looked at me sideways.

148

"Because..." I stuttered. I didn't know how to tell her about the pictures... that night, and all the horrible things I had done. I was thinking of how to start the story when Linda interrupted, "Emma, you have a call on line one."

"Let me take this..." Emma walked back to the nurse's desk. I watched her carefully. She was serious, didn't say much on the phone, other than yes or no. She pulled the yellow envelope out of the stack as soon as she hung up the phone. She flipped it over and stared at it and then at me for a long second before she broke the seal.

Holding the envelope in her hand, without looking inside, she approached me quickly and then sat next to me. "What is in this envelope, Dylan?" She lifted her brows, narrowed her eyes, demanding me to answer.

I couldn't reply. I closed my eyes, and bowed my head. I rubbed my forehead with my fingers, trying to fight this terrible nightmare. I wanted to tell her it all, what happened that night, how it all happened, but the wavering expression in her face told me that she wouldn't understand.

"My father who never calls me at work called and asked if I received his package. What is so important in this thing that he called me personally and not his secretary?" She asked softly this time, looking deep into my eyes.

"There are pictures of me in there." I finally admitted.

She pulled the stack of photos out and started looking at them. Her face, expressionless at first, turned ice cold quickly. She looked at each picture less than a second and skipped to the next, and to the next, until she couldn't handle it anymore.

"Is this a sick joke?"

"Unfortunately not."

"Is this Max and ..."

"Yes, it's Max and me..." I finished her sentence, stutteringly.

"Oh, God. I can't look anymore. It's too much. Too disgusting. You are..."

"I know, I'm sorry Emma. I'm sorry you had to see these."

"Who are you Dylan? A member of some cult group, shooting your twisted version of an 'Eyes Wide Shut' movie?"

"No. No... It's nothing like that. Let me explain..."

"There isn't much you can explain Dylan. These pictures... I simply cannot..."

"Don't say it Emma!"

"I can't be with someone like this. The person in these pictures, I don't know who he is, but he is not the person I fell in love with. Bondage, masochism, group sex... It's too much."

"I am not into any of those things. It was one night, Emma. Only one night. I took a pill. I was high and I didn't know what I was doing. I am sorry. Please...Emma!" I begged desperately, collapsing onto her knees.

"How does it, you, taking a drug and not knowing what you did, make any of this better? You know how I loathe drugs. Drugs ruined Steve, ruined my family. I cannot be with someone who does drugs."

"I am not doing drugs. Not any more..."

"I don't believe you and I don't trust you, Dylan. I don't think I know you."

"You know me. You know everything about me."

"No, I don't think I do, not after seeing these pictures. I can't even wrap my mind around this concept. How could you torture someone while having sex?" She shook her head in disbelief.

"No, I wasn't torturing her. I promise you. She demanded it... Oh, God. I don't even remember."

"See, that's what I mean. You don't even remember what the hell you did. This picture .... It's just... I don't know, makes me sick!"

"I...I am sorry ...Please Emma. Please forgive me." I stuttered.

"Forgive? This is not about forgiving Dylan..." She shook her head. "I have to go. I need to scrub in for another surgery. I can't deal with this. Your life, your past... is too much for me to handle. I simply can't..." She said and left the waiting room without looking back.

Watching her disappear behind the door, in a cold, emotionless state as if what we had was nothing, was the final blow. All my strength left my body, my shoulders shook, my legs gave up and I fell onto my knees beside the coffee table in the waiting room. It felt like someone took a knife and carved out my heart. For the first time in my life, I cried. I cried without caring who was there, looking at me. I felt stupid, weak and incredibly foolish, but I couldn't stop my tears.

I called Emma every day for the next ten days. She never came home, she neither returned my calls, nor stopped by my office to talk. I stopped by the hospital, the university, even her house in

Brooklyn every day, but I couldn't find her anywhere. It was as if she disappeared into thin air. Emma was gone, or she simply didn't want me to find her.

Desperate to talk to her, I called Sydney. I told her how much I loved Emma and how sorry I was and added, that if I didn't hear from her soon, I was planning to hire a private detective. A few hours after my phone call to Sydney, I received a short email from Emma. It was devoid of any emotions, it just explained the fact that we could not be together, that I had to move on and stop looking for her.

After reading her bitter, glacial words, I couldn't breathe. I felt like my heart was ripped apart and stopped working. She was telling me that it was over. I was to go on with my life without her. I just didn't know how to do that.

CHAPTER 18
DYLAN

"Open your god damn door, Dylan!" Max yelled for the second time. He was outside, shouting loudly and banging on the door. The cracked dry wood of the old deck squeaked underneath his feet.

'How in the hell did he find me?' I groused inwardly. Only my personal assistant, Rose Donnelly, knew about the house, and that's only because she helped me with the purchase and all the associated tedious paperwork. Nobody else was supposed to know about it. Not even my sister, or at least that's what I hoped.

"Dylan! You idiot! I know you are there." He hollered inside from the open window this time. "Come open the door right now or I am breaking it, and I am fucking serious!" He admonished.

Max and his god damn mouth. He was rogue and crazy as usual and I knew if I didn't let him in, he would continue cursing and would make a fool of himself. I certainly didn't want to explain him to my neighbors. I had to let him in, although I wasn't ready to talk to him. Or anyone for that matter.

I left Manhattan six weeks ago, a week after I got that god-awful email from Emma. It was a befitting response from her, as always. Blunt, incisive and keen…just like the first time I met her. It was over between us. She was pretty damn clear about that. I couldn't blame her for ending it. My past ruined it for us. It was my fault, and knowing that it was my fault made it that much worse.

Now that she was gone, I was supposed to get on with my life, as if it was something easy to do. I wished I could just reboot and start over, but life wasn't easy and simple that way. I couldn't just continue from where I left off. I couldn't sleep. I couldn't go to work. I couldn't stay in my apartment, it was full of her memories. My bed, my sheets, my pillows…all smelled like jasmine, like her hair and her skin. My closet was still full of her clothes, which she didn't try to get back. Every corner of the apartment had a trace of Emma. Even the city reminded me of her. There was always a subtle, small thing that triggered a memory button in my brain. A street vendor selling chestnuts, a girl with earmuffs crossing the street, a violinist playing Offenbach in front of the subway… New York City was like memorabilia of Emma. Everything reminded me of her.

So, there was nothing I could do except to get away from the city, disappear and try to forget about her. 'How does forgetting work?' I wondered inwardly. Could you forget someone just by telling yourself you had to? Could you rewire your brain so that a familiar smell or an object would not remind you of them? Is it even possible to erase memories ingrained into your soul so profoundly? I was in a state of self-pity. Horrible images of my past kept coming back. My life had become one big nightmare, full of remorse, guilt and mistakes of a past I could not change. That's when I knew I had to leave and somehow, move on…

On a warm spring evening, I got out of the city on a whim, not knowing where to go. I drove towards Brooklyn instinctively at first, hoping I could see a glimpse of her, maybe cooking in her kitchen or eating soup, but her house looked deserted. No light. No noise. There was at least a week's worth of newspapers at her door step which confirmed that she wasn't staying at her house, just like Sydney said. Thinking of her unwittingly, wondering where she was and what she was doing at that moment, I kept on driving. I drove an hour on NY-27 East without a purpose, without a plan, while listening to a random radio station. I was about to pass West Hampton when the radio show host started talking about the best surfing towns in the USA. Montauk was in the top ten. I was only an hour away from one of the best surfing towns in America. Never mind that I had never surfed in my life, but all of a sudden, I decided to go there to fight with big waves, instead of my demons and nightmares.

I arrived in Montauk late at night. I was looking for a motel to stay at when I saw a flyer "beach front property, for sale by owner" on the window of a seafood restaurant. I called the owner right away and told him I wanted to buy the house. Aaron, the owner, replied back incredulously, asking if I had seen the house, not believing I was serious about buying it. I explained to him that I didn't see it but I didn't care what the house looked like. It was by the beach, furnished, and ready to live in. That was enough for me. Confused and befuddled, he agreed to show me the house right away. He told me to wait for him at the restaurant 'Bonefish Grill'. I found out soon enough that it belonged to his fiancé.

Aaron lived with Jane in the apartment above the restaurant. He came down after a few minutes while I was eating and talking to Jane, his shirt buttoned wrong and his hair all messed up. Aaron was a young, carefree guy in his twenties. Obviously, he wasn't expecting to meet someone interested in buying his house late on a Sunday night. He explained more about the house to me quickly... It was built in 1940 and belonged to his grandfather who passed away two years ago, it had been vacant ever since. He frankly admitted that I was the only one who showed any interest in buying it since he put the house up for sale a year ago. He even told me that we could negotiate the price after I saw the house. He warned me about some minor problems like a couple of broken windows, stained carpets and cracked wood, just in case I wasn't serious and wanted to back out. I told him I didn't mind a few broken things and he told me to follow him, shaking his head and smiling doubtfully.

We drove about ten minutes on Montauk Highway and arrived at a small, single story house with two bedrooms. The entire house was smaller than the living room of my penthouse. A shabby little place, obviously in need of a lot of work. There were no marble countertops or expensive hardwood floors. No big walk-in closets or a wine cellar. Nothing luxury. However, all the basics worked; plumbing, heating and appliances, and it had a great view of the beach. I could hear the waves crashing, the whooshing sound of the water. It was the perfect place for me. Quiet. Small. Isolated.

I wrote him a check for ten thousand dollars as a deposit and told him my personal assistant would handle the rest of the sale and the paperwork. Then I requested if I could stay in the house for the night. Aaron was shocked to see I was going through with it. He agreed eagerly and allowed me to stay the night.

The next day, I called Rose and told her that I was going to be out of town for a while. I gave her the full responsibility to represent me and make decisions on my behalf at work. I explained to her about the house, the purchase, and how I wanted to keep it a secret, and she did. Rose, my wonderful, humble assistant, took care of everything for me while I tried to nurse myself back to life without Emma. She didn't tell anyone about my whereabouts.

Things were going according to plan. I was having a calm, quiet life. I even found a little inner peace. I kept busy working in the house and fixing things by myself. I started with the broken windows and the cabinets were next. I even pulled the stained carpets out and purchased some hardwood. I laid them over the areas I cleared and then nailed them to the floor by hand. It was a slow and back breaking process. I did it for couple of hours and realized soon enough that it was too god damn hard to do it by hand. I rented a nail gun and a compressor from the local hardware store. After that, I completed the entire kitchen in a day and moved on to the living room. Thanks to all the work I did around the house, my days passed quickly. I didn't have time to sit idly, thinking about things and being miserable. By the time it was dark, I was completely exhausted. Working out in a gym was nothing compared to a day spent doing heavy labor. All the nailing, lifting, sanding and painting made my muscles hurt so bad that I would crash out on the sofa immediately after dinner, hardly making it to my bed. Once I put my head down, I fell asleep almost instantly. I wasn't haunted by the same horrible dreams and awful images every night. I was doing alright... surviving... at least until this morning. This morning I woke up to the usual quietness, which was unfortunately ruined by the loud yelling and banging on the door. Then I heard Max's voice with his usual profanities.

I opened the door slowly, showing my obvious discontent for seeing him. "Max! What are you doing here?"

"I should be the one asking you that question, you idiot!" He growled, standing only a couple of inches away from my face. "You are the one who disappeared without a word, or any explanation."

"I had my reasons, obviously. I had to get away from the city." I spoke slowly.

"I get that... but we could have done that together if you had just told me. Nobody knew where you were, or what happened to you. We have been partners for nine years, damn it! You cannot just bail on me like that..."

"Phliant is in great shape, Max. It is steady and stable. You have many smart people working for you. Jason, Ben, Adam... they are good kids, eager to make money. You also have Rose. She is good, meticulous, detail oriented... I told her everything she needed to know and she was supposed to take care of things in my absence. You really don't need me to run the company." I explained, trying to reason with him since he made me feel like I abandoned the company, which I literally built from scratch.

"The hell with Jason, Ben, Adam and Rose. I'm not talking about just work. I missed you man..." He admitted openly, completely catching me off guard with his unusual frankness. Max wasn't an emotional person, and this was the first time he was sort of sharing his feelings. He paused a minute, then he groused again, switching back to his usual vulgar attitude. "You're an asshole, you know…God damn it Dylan! We have been friends for twenty years. You can't just disappear on me like that. I thought you were dead or something."

"Stop exaggerating Max. I was fine. I just needed some time alone!" I said. I stepped out to the porch and sat on an old wooden chair. Max took the other chair across the table. Staring at the horizon, he pulled a cigarette out of its pack. He lit it with his original 1933 Gold Zippo, a precious $100,000 graduation gift from his grandfather, he then offered me one.

"You know I quit." I rejected it kindly.

"Yeah, I know, but I thought maybe you started again. You know, after… "

"After Emma you mean. No, actually I've been living healthier since I moved here. I am not smoking or drinking. No cigarettes, no hard liquor, no stress…I feel alright."

"You feel alright?! Are kidding me? Have you looked at yourself in the mirror? You look like fucking Bin Laden, living in this shit hole for a month."

"It is not a shit hole. It's a small, quiet place, right by the beach. I have good neighbors, clean air. No crazy traffic, no rude drivers, no car honks; and I'm close to great local food…" I kept on going.

"Whatever, Dylan…" He interrupted me. "Why didn't you call me? I've heard nothing from you for over a month. I was seriously worried about you. I talked to Rose. She didn't say a thing. She kept saying she didn't know. Then I called Rachel, then your mom. I even called Emma."

"You did what?" I exclaimed, and got really mad at him for butting into my private life.

"Calm down! It isn't like you think. I called Sydney, but Emma answered the phone instead. I didn't know she was staying with her. I was very surprised to talk to her. "

"What did she say? What did she sound like?" I asked. I couldn't help my curiosity. Any news about Emma was exciting but also unsettling.

"Not much… she didn't sound too good, either she was sick or dejected. All she said was that she hadn't heard from you for weeks and she didn't know where you were. That's when I really got worried and called Nolan two days ago and he figured out where you were hiding. Tell me what the hell are you doing here? In this stupid house…"

"Hey… Stop insulting my house. I happen to love this old place." I pushed my chair back and its legs lifted up a little. I turned my head to the ocean, enjoyed the beautiful view with waves crashing on the sand and sun glittering on the water in the horizon. It was a beautiful spring day and it looked more beautiful from my deck.

"I guess the view isn't so bad." Max finally smiled and spoke a bit calmer. "Do you have something to drink?"

"Yeah, coffee should be ready soon."

"I sure need some." He agreed and continued with his usual fuss. "I woke up so goddamn early to get here. I drove two hours in morning traffic just to check on you, you know."

I rolled my eyes and took a deep breath. After a month of quietness and solitude, Max's whining was unbearable. "You know Max, you didn't have to drive up here." I said. Then, without waiting for his next complaint, I went back inside. I grabbed the coffee pot, now full of freshly percolated coffee, and two mugs. I poured Max a cup of dark coffee, no cream, no sugar, in a chipped ceramic mug. "Here you go…this should wake you up. Looks like you need a kick." I teased him.

Max made a wry face after he took a sip. I handed him some cream and sugar, sensing he needed it. He took another sip after adding some and blurted out with a grimace "This coffee tastes like shit," and then asked, "Isn't there a place like Cafés Verlet or Lantana in this God forsaken town where we can get some good coffee?"

"No. There isn't one and it tastes fine to me." I chuckled and took a big bite of my leftover donut with my dark coffee. And suddenly, I realized how I got used to things in Montauk. Manhattan, with its luxurious, pampering lifestyle, expensive restaurants and fancy dinners felt so far away from me. It was strange to realize how I didn't miss any of it. My life was simpler in Montauk, everything from my coffee to my dinner. I got so used to this simple lifestyle that I didn't want to go back to the city again.

"So…you hired Nolan to find me, eh?" I asked, smiling.

"Damn right, I did," Max snickered back.

"I guess I should feel special."

"Don't be so smug! I was worried about you. Tell me what are you doing here? What have you been up to?"

"Not much actually. Fixing the house takes up most of my time. I get so tired after working all day, I basically just crash at night."

"Why in the hell you are fixing this house? It doesn't even have a decent deck to enjoy the beach. You want a house by the beach, call Shelly, my realtor, she'll fix you up with a great place in The Hamptons."

"I don't want a place in The Hamptons."

"The best beach front properties are there. I think there will be a great one up for sale soon, and it's next to my house. Grumpy old Donald Sherman, one of my father's old business associates, is selling his house. You should make an offer. We'd be neighbors. It would be awesome. You and me, taking on The Hamptons together, we could party like we used to."

I took a deep breath, "You don't get it Max." I said, trying to express my frustration with a scowl.

"What don't I get?"

"I don't want a million dollar mansion by the beach. I don't want to party, or take on The Hamptons, or Manhattan for that matter. I don't want to be part of New York's rich, hypocrite and arrogant socialites anymore."

"You are rich. Like it or not, those rich, hypocritical and arrogant people make up eighty percent of our clients. So, suck it up and deal with it. I need you back."

I took another big gulp of my coffee and shook my head. "I can't take it anymore. That life... The life in the city, all the bullshit things we have to do, the business parties with clients, the girls we hire for them, the lies we have to be a part of to win the account...it is disgusting. I can't be part of it anymore!"

"We do what we have to do. Everybody does it. It is part of the business. Plus, you weren't in it as much as you used to be since... you know... since Emma."

"Maybe. Still, the last couple months do not erase the sins of my past. It never should have been like this. We live and work in this corrupt world, full of hypocrisy and lies. Things that we used to do Max, they still haunt me. I came here to escape all that." I confided to him finally, the way I had never done before. "Our past ruined the one thing that was so precious and irreplaceable for me. I want out Max...and I mean it."

158

"What do you mean you want out?"

"I'm not coming back."

"You can't tell me that you are not coming back. What about the company?"

"Those young accountants we have, they are good. They haven't been spoiled with money and success like us yet. They are clean and honest. They'll take care of the business for you. I... I'd like to sell my share. Hopefully to you. That way you don't have to deal with an outsider."

"Fuck you, Dylan! You can't do that."

"Yes, I can."

"No. I can't let you ruin the business that we built so hard together. You need time, I get that. Take all the time you need, but don't rush into making irrational decisions. You are acting emotionally and not making any sense."

"I am not acting emotionally. I know what I want and do not want."

"I know what you want. You want Emma and all this 'getting out and selling your business crap' is because you can't have one girl, but guess what! None of this bullshit will bring her back. If you want her back, grow up and be the determined, strong willed, strong minded person you've always been. Do something. Instead of staying in this god damn house, living like a loser, come back and win her back."

"She was pretty damn clear Max. She doesn't want me or anything to do with me."

"Since when has Dylan Hamilton accepted 'no' for an answer?"

I couldn't reply. He was right. I've never accepted defeat or taken 'no' for answer, until Emma. With her, I was helpless. Defenseless. Yes, I wanted her more than anything else in my life; however, I wasn't ready to go back to the city yet.

Hours after Max left, I was still thinking about our conversation. Could I win her back? Did I still have a chance with her? I wasn't sure what to do. I was ambivalent about everything, work, company, my family, my future. So, instead of contemplating my painful life, I did what I'd been doing best for five weeks, I grabbed my sledgehammer and started knocking down old cabinets, and it felt so good!

CHAPTER 19
EMMA

I was sitting in the very back row of the big auditorium, pretending I was listening. Professor Bissette, a visiting scholar from France, started his seminar on principles of intradural spine surgery with a video compilation of his past surgeries. He was one of the most highly praised, esteemed neurosurgeons in Europe, also teaching at Faculte de Medecine Pierre et Marie Curie in Paris. Since he was extremely busy year round, he was very selective about the seminars he presented at. It was rumored that our dean, Professor Harris, was Professor Bissette's old college roommate and that he used his close ties to convince him to participate in our 'end of the year' seminar. It was a privilege to have him at our university, even if it was only for one day. Students, residents, and even faculty members filled up the auditorium half an hour before he arrived. Completely engaged with his presentation, I could see everyone around me taking notes. Everybody was excited to be part of this rare opportunity, listening to him attentively. Well, almost everybody, there was one exception: me.

I was staring blankly through the tall windows of the auditorium and scribbling circles in my notepad instead of paying attention. Amy, Sam, Chris…all my classmates were asking questions about his non-traditional surgery techniques. Even the most introverted, reserved person in our group, Adam, raised his hand and asked about the professor's approach to unruptured intracranial aneurysms. I, on the other hand, looked down and stayed quiet during the entire lecture.

I was at the end of this long, tiring journey. My life as a medical student was almost over. My dissertation was complete. I was done with my defense too, in spite of Kyle's, my ex-fiancé's, presence and many hard, challenging questions. I was nervous about Kyle attending my defense at first. I hated that he was selected to be part of my research committee, however, he was kind. More than kind, he was very helpful. He shared his past experiences with Doctor Reuben, the toughest professor in my committee, and helped me finish my experiments and present the results in the format Doctor Reuben liked. All my grades were posted. I earned a 3.88 GPA, which put me in the top ten in my class. Everybody was telling me that with my credentials, GPA and recommendations, I could get accepted to any residency program in the States.

So, as far as work and school were concerned, everything was going well. On the outside, my life seemed to be perfect, or so my friends thought. Maybe they were right. I was about to achieve what I had wanted for years. Soon, I would be Doctor Collins. Doctor Emma Collins... such an impressive, fascinating title in front of my name. Something I wanted since I was a kid, playing 'operation'. Considering the last ten years, pre-med, med school, PhD program and just a week away from graduation, I should have been feeling more excited, joyful. Then, why was I feeling so dejected and sad? *Why wasn't this, the most important success of my life giving me the satisfaction I desired for years?*

It was disheartening and demoralizing to realize, after longing for this day for years, I felt nothing. It was as if I lost all my emotions. After I told Dylan that it was over between us, my life continued as usual, however, nothing felt the same.

Ending our relationship was my decision. I listened to all of his messages on my phone. Some of them over and over again. He was sincere, open and honest, declaring his love for me, begging for me to forgive him. The problem was that there wasn't anything to forgive. He didn't cheat on me, or lie to me. He didn't do anything to me personally to forgive him for. From the beginning, he had been honest with me and told me what he felt for me, and what I meant for him. I was certain that I was the only woman in his life that he loved with such deep affection. My problem was neither about his feelings for me, nor about forgiving him for what he did. It was about him.

He was Dylan Hamilton. The infamous bachelor of Manhattan. I had heard enough about him to scare me off before I agreed to give him a chance, therefore I shouldn't have been surprised. However, my heart disagreed with my conscience from the first moment we met. He had such a compelling smile and charming manners. He was full of surprises, coming up with new unexpected romantic gestures all the time. My heart disobeyed my brain and convinced me that the Dylan I fell in love with was different than the Dylan people talked about. He wasn't the licentious man, living a life of debauchery, adultery and lechery that people talked about. He was a romantic, loving person with an incredible artistic talent. I shut my eyes to all the talk and rumors about him. Maybe love made me blind. Maybe, I was so infatuated that I couldn't see the obvious facts. However, ever since I saw those awful images in front of me, I couldn't let it go. Regardless of how much I loved him, or wanted to be with him, I couldn't deal with his past. The wicked images of him with all those girls kept coming back. All the stories I heard about him that I chose to ignore, now appeared as the ugly truth.

I had to break up with him, although my heart was fighting with my reasoning. I knew if I saw him again, I wouldn't be able to do it. I couldn't look into his eyes and tell him that it was over. So, I took the easy way out and sent him one last email. Short, concise. I told him that we couldn't be together and I didn't want to see him again. However, my harsh, blunt words didn't reflect my true feelings. I was still madly in love with him. He was the only one I opened my heart to, the only one I truly loved. I never felt such a deep affection to anyone else before, not even for Kyle. Trying to continue my life without Dylan was like living without fresh air. I had to remind myself to take deep breaths. Every day was a fight, and I had to survive.

After not seeing him for over a month, loneliness settled in and became my norm. I felt numb. The wound stopped bleeding. I wouldn't say that I was healed, but at least it scabbed over. I still had to force myself not to think about him. I avoided everything that would bring sweet, painful memories. However, as I listened to Professor Bissette talking in his thick French accent, I fell into another reverie, thinking about Dylan unwittingly again.

I was wondering where he was and what he was doing when I heard Amy jabbering next to me. "Earth to Emma…answer me Emma. Do you hear me?"

I was caught off guard while I was daydreaming, about things I promised myself I wouldn't think about, "What?" I muttered dolefully.

"You haven't heard a word I said. Did you? What's going on with you, Emma?"

"Sorry, I spaced out for a second." I said, evading the questions I was asked almost every day lately, as if they didn't know …*What's the matter with you Emma?* "What were you saying?" I asked her, feigning interest.

"We are going to Quills for a drink. Are you coming with us?" She asked. Chris and Jackson joined us too as we walked out of the auditorium.

"No. I can't. I am very tired. I think I'd like to go home, take a long bath and sleep." I said, coming up with my usual excuse to ditch the group and be alone. I was living an automated life, like a robot since I broke up with Dylan. School, work, clinics and my research. Nothing else, and I wanted to keep it that way.

"Oh, come on! Emma! This is our last week. We will end up working in different parts of the country soon. Let's enjoy our final days together a little." She insisted.

I was dragging my feet, coming up with more excuses when Kyle showed up and stood right next to us unexpectedly. "You have to come." He chimed in. "We still haven't celebrated your successful defense yet. You were amazing."

"I was just another doctorate student, trying to graduate. I wouldn't call that amazing." I replied.

"You have no idea what you have accomplished, Emma. Dr. Reuben, Dr. Howard and Dr. McKenzie, they all told me that your research and defense was one of the best they had seen in years. You deserve a celebration."

"Thank you Kyle!" Amy exclaimed. "I've been telling her the same thing for days, but she doesn't listen. She's put her walls up again and it's hard to get through," she added.

"I have not..." I tried to object.

"I haven't seen you smiling, doing anything fun since..." She paused, probably wondering if she should say his name, and then muttered quietly. "Since Dylan."

Hearing his name out loud had the same effect even after six weeks. My grin turned into a frown immediately. I bit my lips, evading my eyes from Kyle's intense glare.

"Come on Emma. Just one drink." Kyle insisted and put his hand on my arm. His unexpected closeness bothered me. He was acting unusually friendly. I didn't want to go drinking and certainly not with Kyle, but I couldn't reject him in front of all the other students. I felt compelled to acquiesce.

Outside, the weather was warm. It was a glorious, beautiful evening; the sky was dappled with white clouds and had many shades of color; from amethyst to amber to dark blue, giving the tall skyscrapers a colorful glow. It was a typical New York moment with vivid displays, lit windows on tall buildings, busy streets, long lines of cars waiting in the traffic and people standing on sidewalks, impatiently waiting to cross the street. The 'City that never sleeps' was its usual self, lively and vibrant as ever. However, I felt lonely and despondent amidst its liveliness. I wanted take a cab and rush back to Sydney's apartment where I'd been staying for the last couple of weeks. I couldn't stand to be alone in my house in Brooklyn. Although Dylan had been there only a few times, it still brought back memories I wanted to suppress. Living with Sydney was my only escape; she was the only one who could quell my continuous bickering with myself and self-doubt. *Did I do the right thing?*

I walked quietly and slowly next to Amy following Kyle, Chris and Jackson. Kyle turned his head and smiled a few times, checking on me unnecessarily. Then he stopped and waited for me and Amy to catch up with him. For the rest of the way, he walked next to me, making me more uncomfortable.

We arrived at the Quills Brewery in less than five minutes. A block away from the medical center, it was a favorite hang-out spot for many med students after school. Since it was Friday night, they had live music, and the place was packed. We managed to find a tall table at the back corner. Amy and I took the only available bar stools. Jackson, Chris and Kyle hung around the table. A young waitress, Claire, soon showed up to take our orders. Jackson, Chris and Amy ordered their favorite beer, 'Blondie', a locally brewed pale ale, and Kyle asked for a dark lager. He turned to me and started telling me why their lagers tasted better and then asked if I wanted to try.

"No. I just want some water," I said tersely, cutting him short. The words came out harsher than I'd planned. I didn't want him to buy me a drink, but I wasn't upset about that. His chit-chat about lagers and ales reminded me of Dylan and our first day in Amsterdam. I hated when some silly little thing brought up memories I tried to bury. I scowled inevitably, closed my eyes and rested my chin on the back of my hand.

"Emma, Are you alright?" Kyle asked.

"Yes, I am fine." I said, still agitated. "I'm just not in the mood for a beer." I yelled to be heard. The place was so loud that it was impossible to have a normal conversation, for which I was grateful. I didn't want to talk to Kyle. I was already resenting my decision to join them.

By the time everybody finished their first drink, the band took a break and the uncomfortable silence in the air became more obvious.

"What's your plan after graduation?" Amy asked, trying to get me to talk and soften the heaviness in the air.

"I am not sure yet." I shrugged. I didn't want to talk about my plans in front of Kyle.

"You should apply for Mayo Clinic. We can do our residency there together," Amy said.

"Did you get accepted?" I asked.

"Not officially, but I've had a phone interview with the director of surgical residency and he said I have a good chance to be accepted."

"They say that Mayo has a reputation as a great place to be a patient, but not a good place to do surgical residency. They have a very controlled environment without much trauma experience. Don't expect it to be like a Grey's Anatomy episode. You will get to watch a lot, but you'll be lucky if they let you scrub in once in a while." Chris commented instantly.

Chris enjoyed picking on Amy. They were famous for their constant arguments and their opposing views on everything. Chris never missed an opportunity to tease her. Sometimes to the point where it annoyed Amy a lot and drove her crazy, which made him enjoy it more. Everybody knew that he had a crush on her. Everybody, except Amy.

"I totally disagree." Amy objected immediately. "You work with the best, you learn from the best. Mayo Clinic has the best surgeons in the States and the best residency program," she carried on. "You are just jealous because you can't charm your way in using your wicked smile as you always do. Maybe your smile has lost its magical power."

"Oh, stop it Amy. I am not jealous at all." Chris replied with a sly grin. "I think my smile still has a lot of power. Let's see if it works," he said, turned to Amy and smiled his famous crooked smile and winked. Amy frowned even more. "Nuh-uh… It doesn't work with uptight, frigid girls. I guess there's no way to charm you Amy. You are one impossible girl." He said laughing.

Amy flicked Chris's forehead with her finger teasingly. "Ha-ha, very funny." She snorted. "If you were a bit more like Doctor Stevens, you might have a chance. He is such a gentleman and also so charming. I would have loved to go on a date with him. I wonder what he looked like at our age."

I smiled and nodded showing my agreement; Doctor Stevens was every girl's dream at school. He was a successful surgeon, charismatic, handsome and happily married for forty years. He had two daughters, a son and ten grandchildren. He was the perfect dream husband for every med school girl.

"If I knew you were into salt and pepper hair, and a walking stick, I would have died my hair and carried a cane with me." Chris said after he tilted his head sideways and sipped his beer.

Amy shook her head, folded her arms over her chest, "Oh, shut up, Chris!" she chided him and asked Jackson, trying to change the subject, "How about you, Jack?"

"My top three choices were Johns Hopkins, MGH and UCSF." Jackson replied. "They are also the hardest ones to get accepted to since they get the highest numbers of applicants. I think I'm more likely to be matched with UC Davis, still a great hospital. I definitely wish I had Emma's GPA and references. I am sure she can get in wherever she applies." He sighed heavily.

"If I apply…" I mumbled to myself, but luckily nobody heart me. I didn't want to talk about my plans after school just yet.

After fifteen minutes of long, boring arguments about the best residency programs, Jackson left our table and joined a group of girls doing tequila shots. Soon he was laughing loudly and clicking his shot glass with a tall blonde girl. Chris, craving for a cigarette stepped outside. Amy also left to find a quiet place to take a phone call, which left Kyle and me alone at the table.

Kyle didn't talk much during our discussion about the residency programs since he was doing his at Columbia. Other than a few comments, he sat there and looked at me stealthily, not making much eye contact. However, now that we were alone, he scooted up next to me, standing disturbingly close. Eyeing me openly, he grabbed a strand of my hair and was about to tuck it behind my ear when I pushed his hand away abruptly.

"Emma!" He whispered, glaring at me as he sipped his drink. He had three beers already and had just switched to hard liquor, whiskey.

"What?" I answered, feeling annoyed. I couldn't hide my grimace.

"Come on, Emma. Don't I at least deserve a tiny smile?" He said, his voice was slurred and he looked more than tipsy, clearly inebriated. "You should smile all the time. You have the most beautiful smile Emma. Actually, not just your smile, everything about you is beautiful." He kept on complimenting me although I didn't want to listen to it.

"You are obviously drunk Kyle. Maybe you should stop drinking."

"Maybe a bit tipsy, but I am not drunk. I needed to drink to have the courage to talk to you, which I've been trying to do for weeks. You, Emma, are the most beautiful and amazing girl I know."

"Please don't talk to me like that." I replied.

"Why? I am just stating the truth. You are gorgeous." He muttered, and then tried to close the distance between us. "I've missed you Emma. I've missed you a lot," he whispered.

"Why? Freshman girls weren't enough anymore?"

"Insult me all you want. I deserve all of it. I was an idiot and I made a big mistake. I am begging for a second chance. Don't you remember how great we were together?"

"Actually Kyle, we weren't great together. I was just another score for you. When a new girl showed up admiring you, falling for your fake charm, you couldn't stop yourself. You can't love anyone Kyle, because you love yourself more than anyone else."

"No. I loved you Emma. I still do. I was so stupid not to realize it sooner, but after seeing you with that son of a bitch, I knew it. It was always you." He said, breathing in deeply, as if he was savoring my closeness and my scent; his face was now an inch away.

"Kyle, what we had… it wasn't love. I didn't love you. It was just stupid affection." I said, knowing what true love felt like. However, he was too drunk. I doubted he heard or understood what I said. He kept on staring at me. His eyes were feral, like a wild animal. Unfortunately, I sensed his intentions too late. Suddenly, he pulled me to him and tried to kiss me. I was able to dodge his abrupt, unwelcome move and pushed him back.

"Get a hold of yourself, Kyle! I already told you I don't feel anything for you. I don't even like you."

"You don't like me?" He looked up with a devious grin. "But of course! You dig billionaire playboys who like to fuck every female in town."

"You are an asshole!" I burst out. "Stay the hell away from me." I shouted at him, grabbed my purse and quickly rushed to the door. After all he had done, I couldn't believe he had the nerve to talk to me like that. I was frustrated, mad and all his insulting words about Dylan brought back a flood of emotions I couldn't control. My eyes welled up. The tears I was holding in for weeks seeped down my face unrestrained. I opened the heavy metal door and threw myself out. I needed fresh air to recompose myself, however just then, I bumped into someone. I lifted my head up and saw that it was Sydney.

"What are you doing here?" I said, surprised, trying to hide my tears.

"I called Amy to help me with something and she mentioned that you were coming here to have a drink. I wouldn't miss the night you finally cracked out of your shell and decided have a little fun." She said. She then made me turn towards her and look into her eyes. "From the looks of it, you are not having fun. What the hell happened?"

"Kyle…" I stuttered and looked away.

"That asshole. What did he do?"

"It doesn't matter. I just want to get out of here."

"Only after I tell him what he deserves to hear." She attempted to push the door open and go in the bar. "Somebody should kick his arrogant ass and teach him a lesson."

I stopped her before she reached the door. "Forget about Kyle. He's not worth it Sydney. Let's go. I am serious. He is not the reason I am sad."

"Okay, but you need to tell me what's going on with you. Also, let's get Amy too. She sounded like she wasn't having much fun either."

"It's Chris. He likes to push her buttons. He's been picking on her all night. He should just come out and admit how much he likes her, instead of acting like a high school kid."

"Men. They never grow up!" Sydney said, shaking her head and grabbed my arm.

Amy, Sydney and I walked to the nearest coffee shop. On the way, I was quiet, wondering how I should break the news. When we finally sat down by the window at Stonehenge Coffee House, "I need to tell you something," I said, after I took a sip from my chai latte. "Actually, I am glad both of you are here. I didn't want to have this conversation twice."

"What are you talking about?" Amy asked.

"Yes, Emma. What's going on?" Sydney repeated.

"I decided what I am going to do for next year." I said. "I know you are both going to be against it, but I want you to understand, this is my life and my decision. So, please try not to be judgmental."

"You are making me nervous." Sydney muttered. "Just be straight and tell us what you are up to."

"I signed up with MSF. I leave New York in a month." I finally broke the news. 'To leave or not to leave. My hardest choice in life!' I thought inwardly. My ambivalence and indecision had been bothering me for weeks. I felt relieved that I finally decided. Whether it was a good decision or not, I didn't know, time would tell.

Amy glared at me with a shocked expression. "What the hell is MSF?" Sydney asked, confused.

"Médecins Sans Frontières." Amy spoke before me. "Also known as 'Doctors without Borders'. But how is it possible? I thought they only accepted doctors with a minimum two years of experience."

"Yes, that's usually true, but they are short staffed. Since I have done MD/PhD, they counted my additional years in research as field experience. I think they will send me to Syria first, to assist more experienced doctors. They are in urgent need of surgeons after this never-ending civil war."

"You can't do that Emma. You can't leave us and go off to Syria, of all places. Is it even safe to go there?"

"It is not easy for me either Syd, however I have to go. Doctors are well-protected. Don't worry, I will be safe."

"I can't believe this. Is this because you feel lost and overwhelmed with emotions after Dylan? It is, isn't it?"

"Maybe… I don't know. I just know that I have to leave the country for a while, use my degree and be helpful. There are a lot of children out there needing help."

"You don't have to go so far away to help. You can help here too. Actually, I was going to talk to you about that before you dropped this 'I'm leaving town for a godforsaken country for an unknown amount of time' bomb."

"What is it?" I asked curiously.

"I signed you up for a fundraising event. It's for St. Mark's Children's Research Hospital. It's the night of your graduation. Dinner starts at seven and there will be a live auction."

"I didn't make any plans for the night after the graduation ceremony. I don't mind attending a fundraising event benefitting a research hospital."

"Yeah, but there is more to it than just attending. Don't object right away, hear me out first." Sydney said hesitatingly, she pursed her lips and narrowed her eyes as if she was trying to gauge my reaction. "Amy and I were helping Brie Kemper, the event chair. She asked for our support for something a bit unusual. She is looking for volunteers to participate in date auction. She needed about ten bachelorettes to auction off to raise money for the hospital and she was short one…"

"Oh, no… Amy, Sydney! You didn't."

"Sorry Emma. We did. We signed you up too. It is for a great cause. You get to have a dinner date, and generally retired doctors or faculty members attend this event. It won't be so bad. Last year I got to have dinner with Professor Gardner and he was very kind." Amy explained.

"I am doing it too Emma. So is Amy." Sydney chimed in.

"I can't believe you two. I know Brie Kemper. I will call her and explain that I can't do it."

"But Emma, it is too late. They already have all the girls' names for the live auction printed in the catalog."

"You knew about this and agreed to include me … when?"

"Last week when we had a meeting with Brie. I thought it would cheer you up. It's kind of fun. I promise you that you will enjoy it. " Sydney said, smiling, batting her eyes, faking an innocent look.

I shook my head, grimacing. I knew there was no point in arguing with her – she had that look on her face. I finally consented to her unreasonable request. Knowing I had less than a month in the States, I decided not to fight the unnecessary fights. I just let it go.

CHAPTER 20
DYLAN

The sky was cloudless and the water was shining clear blue under the bright, warm, almost summer sun. The beaches in Montauk were getting more crowded as summer approached, especially on the weekends, and today was one of those days. There were little kids running around, some making sand castles, some playing in shallow water. Girls in their 'latest fashion' bikinis were lying under the sun and guys were playing beach volleyball, showing off their fit bodies. I didn't feel like joining the crowd, however, I didn't want to waste such a warm, beautiful day indoors either. Although I still had a ton of work in the house, I took Copper out and we ran together on the beach. I agreed to take care of Jane's one-year-old golden retriever, Copper, while Jane and Aaron were away for the weekend. As people raided the beaches of Long Island, from The Hamptons to Montauk, many locals like Aaron and Jane left town to avoid the rude and disrespectful city folk. I didn't blame them. The more I stayed in Montauk, the more I found New Yorkers annoying.

"Come on Copper! Fetch it!" I shouted and threw a twig up high after I ended my jog and slowed to a walk on the sandy beach, barefoot, in my swim trunks. The twig landed close to the front porch of my neighbor's house. Copper, all jumpy and excited, brought the twig back to me. "Good boy!" I said and petted his bright golden fur. I tried to throw it further away, hoping it could occupy him a bit longer. But no, he ran and fetched it back again quickly. Copper, still a puppy, had more energy than I could handle. When I agreed to dog-sit, I didn't think it could make me this exhausted, however, after running an hour and then playing fetch for another half, I was completely beat.

"I am going to swim a bit and enjoy the water, Copper. You be a good boy and wait for me here." I told him and tied his leash to the front post of my wooden deck. I poured some cold water into his bowl. Copper looked at me with his sad little face wanting to play more, but he sat down after my second command and finally understood that play time was over.

Feeling a bit guilty for leaving him alone, I rushed to the beach and threw myself into the cool, soothing water. It was warmer than the first time I tried it, back when I first moved into the beach house almost two months ago. After a couple strokes, I realized I was too exhausted to swim and fight with the waves. I turned around and noticed someone standing at my front porch, checking out my house. His back turned towards the beach, I didn't notice who he was. In a dark blue suit, he was too over dressed for a local, and too business like for a weekend vacationer.

Wondering about this unusual trespasser, I got out of the water and dried my body with my towel as I walked towards my house. The tall blonde guy with side-combed hair and a typical Wall Street look, was now petting Copper.

"Hey, there...what are you doing?" I asked casually.

"I guess it is true. You are indeed living like a hippie." He said as he turned around and took his Raybans off.

"Steve!" I exclaimed utterly surprised. "It's good to see you. What brings you here?"

"Max told me where you were hiding. I didn't believe him at first. Mighty Dylan Hamilton, living in a ramshackle house, nailing and buffing floors. I wanted to see it myself."

I dabbed beneath my sunglasses with my towel and smiled broadly. "Hard labor gives you a different kind of satisfaction. I like seeing all that work and sweat turn into something nice." I said, and climbed the wooden stairs which needed staining and refinishing. 'I should work on the stairs next' I thought inwardly, and added it to my never ending to do list. Steve followed me into the house and stood on the deck, glancing towards the horizon. "Great view." He whistled.

"Yep!" I nodded, and opened the door with my hideaway key, stashed underneath the flower pot. "Would you like to see the house?"

"Sure." Steve nodded. "Everybody at work is curious about you, wondering what you've been up to for the last two months."

"Well, see it for yourself." I said and gave him a quick tour pointing out the work I'd done around the house. Our tour of my two bedroom beach house ended rather quickly. I opened the fridge and took a bottle of Stella for myself. I handed him a bottle too.

"Thanks, but I'm still not drinking." He rejected kindly.

"Good job Steve!" I praised him and patted his back, impressed that he kept his promise to stay away from alcohol. "Tell me, why are you dressed like this?"

"Max hired me full-time for the summer. I am working on weekends too. I had a meeting with a customer. We've been short-handed since our CEO abandoned us." He said with an insinuating grin.

"I didn't abandon you guys! Think of it like a long-term leave of absence."

"I heard otherwise. Max shared your possible plans of selling your share. Phliant is not the same without you, Dylan. You should come back."

"Is that why you are here?" I narrowed my eyes and took a sip from my beer. "To convince me to come back?"

"Well, yes. Kinda…"

"Did Max put you up to this? If he did, he is wasting your time, so you know."

"He told me the same thing when I told him I wanted to see you and ask you to come back."

"Oh, I see. Why didn't you listen to him then?"

"Because, I am not here to ask you to come back just for Phliant. I am asking you to come back for Emma as well." He enunciated carefully.

"Emma…" I exclaimed. Her name had that same inevitable effect. "Is there something wrong with her? Tell me, is she alright?!" I gasped nervously.

"Yes, she is doing…" He paused a second. "I don't know how she is doing. I guess she is doing okay. At least for the time being, but I might not be able to tell you the same next month."

"Why? What do you mean?"

"Emma is leaving town in three weeks. She has signed up with 'Doctors without Borders'. Since she is fluent in French, she is being sent to Syria to assist the French medical team in Aleppo."

"No! Why? Why is she doing this?"

"Why do you think? She hasn't been the same since you two broke up. I only got to see her a few times when I visited Aunt Helen and I can tell you honestly that she is a mess. She is not herself. She looks lifeless. Sydney told me a bit about her and how she's been doing these last two months. It isn't good. She does nothing but study and work. She never goes out or does anything for fun, not even with Sydney or me. She doesn't even eat properly. I'm worried about her."

"You know that Emma broke up with me, Steve. Not the other way around. I tried to talk to her many times and it was useless. Your sister is a determined, stubborn girl. She made her mind up about us and there is no way to change it."

"You've got to try again. You are the only one who can convince her not to go."

I chuckled. "You're giving too much credit to a guy who she doesn't want to talk to or see."

"That's all an act Dylan. It's her defense mechanism for something she can't deal with, but I know her. She loves you and this … her life without you… is suffocating her. She just has too much pride to admit it."

"What do you expect me to do?"

"Talk to her. Get her to spend some time with you."

"But how?"

"Her graduation ceremony is next Saturday. After that, she is attending a fundraiser event for a children's research hospital. It is like a year-end gala for med students."

"You want me to ask her out to a gala full of doctors. She would never agree to that."

"I know! Just listen…" He shushed me with his hand and explained. "You should attend the gala as an anonymous donor. Sydney has put Emma's name down for the date auction. Emma objected but the catalogs were already printed, so she couldn't withdraw her name. If you attend the gala …"

"I could participate in the auction and win her as my date."

"Yes!"

"And once I take her on a date, I could talk to her and convince her not to go." I mumbled to myself. "I can't believe she is doing this to herself. She shouldn't go to Syria."

"My thoughts exactly…" Steve uttered.

Inevitably, I found myself thinking and dreaming about Emma, her soft lips, her emerald green eyes. I realized how much I missed her and how silly I was, pretending I was okay without her. It gave me a sudden chill. "I will do my best to convince her Steve," I promised hesitatingly. I wanted to help Steve and convince her not to leave, but I wanted more than that. I wanted to win her back. Her trust. Her respect. Her love.

"Alright then, you have a week to get ready. You'll need a tux, a good shave and a haircut too." He uttered jokingly. "You won't pass for a wealthy philanthropist in this shape."

"I guess you are right." I nodded and ran my hands through my disheveled, sandy hair. It had gotten too long and almost touched my shoulders. Even I couldn't recognize myself in the mirror anymore. With my long hair, tanned skin and bearded face, I looked nothing like the Wall Street guy who left Manhattan two months ago.

The following week couldn't pass any slower. I was excited and nervous at the same time. Saturday morning came and I left Montauk early in the morning to drive to Manhattan. After being away for two months, the noise and the crowd in the city overwhelmed me. For the first time in my life, I felt like a stranger in the city where I was born and raised.

I arrived at my apartment and greeted Russell curtly. At first he didn't recognize me. After squinting at me for a few long seconds, he hurried to open the door. "Mr. Hamilton. It is you. It is so good to see you sir…" He said cheerfully in shock. "You look…"

"Don't bother Russell. I know I look like an ax murderer…"

"No. No… Not at all, sir! You look different but also relaxed. The beard suits you in my opinion."

I rubbed my chin and smiled. "Thanks Russell. You are too nice, but I think I will be better off without it."

"You look handsome either way, sir." He complimented. He was courteous and kind as he had always been.

As soon as I got into my apartment, I called Peter, Max's sixty year old barber. I asked him to come to my apartment and give me a proper shave and a decent haircut. I supposed Max had warned him about how I looked, however he still looked really shocked when he saw me.

"You can grow a mean beard Mr. Hamilton." He commented, shaking his head, disapproving my look.

"I know. You have an hour to fix me up, Peter. I trust you can do it. Let's get going." I said smiling. He pulled the chair out for me and started trimming my beard with scissors before using his famous sharp blade.

My legs were restless, I couldn't sit still. "Stop fidgeting." Peter chided me in his usual gruff voice, "You will get a nasty cut. You don't want to wear a Band-Aid to match your tux, do you?" He warned me after I moved my legs up and down again. I was nervous and also in hurry. I wanted to catch Emma's graduation ceremony and watch her walk proudly to the stage be announced as a doctor of medicine. However, I didn't want her to see me before dinner. I was planning to make myself invisible until the fundraiser.

I arrived at the commencement area long after the ceremony started. I glanced quickly at the graduates already seated, listening to the valedictorian. Moving quietly towards the back, I ducked my head and put on a hat to avoid being recognized by any familiar faces. I tried to find a seat without disturbing anyone and I was able to find one in the last row. As with any another ceremony, it was long, boring, and full of so-called impressive speeches by many faculty members. I wasn't interested in listening, I was busy searching for Emma in the large group of students.

I finally located her at the end of the ceremony when she got up to walk to the stage to be hooded. She looked stunningly beautiful in her Columbia blue gown with three velvet stripes on the sleeves, her green hood and cap with gold tassel dangling on the side. When her name was announced, she approached the dais and shook the hands of the professors who were lined up to congratulate each graduating student. She smiled as she took the symbolic scroll tied with a red ribbon from the dean's hand. However, she couldn't hide the sad look on her face. I wanted to run to her, hold her in my arms, kiss her delicate lips and erase that sad look. The Emma I remembered always smiled, and when she smiled her eyes shined, reflecting her inner beauty. Glancing at her misty green eyes, I understood what Steve meant when he visited me last week. Emma wasn't herself. She was smiling, waving her hand and acting happy. That look in her eyes, however, was telling me something else. I had to find a way to reach her, take her out of the deep abyss where she was stuck and make her see that she was making a wrong decision.

I left the ceremony after Emma's turn to walk. I wasted time in my apartment until the evening, thinking about what to say and how to convince her to stay. I rehearsed my words in my mind again and again. After wandering around the house idly and nervously for hours, I couldn't stand the anticipation any further. I called Jeff and got out of my apartment. I was one of the small group of guests who arrived early at the Marriott Marquis. I was wandering around the ballroom, checking out silent auction items when I heard a familiar voice calling my name.

"Well! Look who is here. Mr. Dylan Hamilton! Also known as anonymous donor and bidder number 15. What are you doing here so early?"

"Sydney!" I turned around and exclaimed. "It's wonderful to see you."

"Steve warned me about how you looked but I see that you are as handsome and charming as ever."

"Well, thank you." I smiled happily and placed a chaste kiss on her cheek. "I had some help this afternoon. One of Max's old friends got me back into shape."

"I'm glad he did. A lot depends on you Dylan. I need you to look your best, but you shouldn't be here this early, wandering around. Come on, hurry up, let's go!" She grabbed my arm and pulled me towards the back of the ballroom.

"Why?" I asked curiously, walking swiftly by her side, her hands in the crook of my arm.

"I don't want Emma to see you until the auction starts."

"Sydney, this whole thing, is this some kind of scheme you are planning?"

"Not a scheme… a well thought plan." She objected, smiling mischievously. "I made this plan before she dropped her "I'm leaving town to volunteer in Syria" bomb. Now, you are more critical than ever. Since you are the reason she is doing this crazy suicide mission, you need to help us reverse it."

"Why do you think I am the reason?"

"God dammit Dylan. Are you really asking?" She snickered, looking annoyed. "She is obviously still in love with you and can't get over you. So, she is going on this crazy thing to forget about you. Amy and I made this plan so that she would talk to you and see her mistake."

"So, it was you who sent Steve to talk to me."

"Of course! Do you think that scatterbrained brat could have planned all this?"

"Unbelievable! You girls are more sneaky and dangerous than I thought. How did you know I would agree?""

She looked at me with insinuating eyes. She had her 'I know you better than you know yourself' look dialed in. "Okay fine!" I smiled. "I guess I was a sure thing. How did you convince Emma?"

"Well, that part wasn't easy. She gave Amy and me such a hard time for getting her involved. We had to lie to her and say it was too late to withdraw her name."

"Oh, that's mean, but good!" I said approvingly. "So, tell me, how does this date auction thing work? Is it like any other auction? Are there many people participating?"

"Yes, it is just like any other auction. Auctioneer will start the bid at one thousand dollars. Highest bidder will win the date. Usually quite a bit of people participate. The date auction is the most popular event at this fundraiser. Most of the participants are retired doctors. Some academicians participate for the fun of it, but they never win the date, they always get outbid. There are some attorneys, Wall Street guys like you. I hope you came with your checkbook and enough money in your bank account, because you need to do whatever it takes to win her date, understood?"

"Of course Sydney! For a date with Emma... sky is the limit."

"Awesome!" Sydney smiled. "Now let's hide you. For dinner, you will sit at table 112 with Dr. and Mrs. Abbott, Dr. and Mrs. Saccone, and Dr. and Dr. Kelly"

"Who are these people?"

"You will meet them soon, be nice!" She warned me with her eyes and rushed to deal with another event crisis.

I found my table and chuckled quietly when I took my seat. The average age for the guests at my table was about seventy and just like Sydney mentioned, four of them were retired doctors attending the gala to have a fun night and support a good cause. Despite not having anything in common with them, our conversation during dinner was more interesting and entertaining than I thought it would be.

The soft jazz music accompanying our dinner ended when a tall, middle-aged, brunette lady took the stage and announced the date-auction was about to start. One by one all the volunteers came up to the stage and the audience burst into loud cheering, whistling and clapping. The first girl on the stage was a short, skinny girl with glasses. She was laughing and waving to her friends. The next was a red head with a lot of freckles followed by a blonde wearing braces. Sydney, Amy and Emma were the last ones to come.

I wasn't sure what to expect from the date auction when Steve told me about it last week. All I cared about was finding an opportunity to be with Emma, however, I didn't expect a lineup of attractive, smart girls with college degrees. Most of them were doctors doing their residencies in various New York City hospitals. They weren't tall, super skinny runway models with fake smiles. All the girls looked kind, congenial and modest; many of them seemed to be very shy and uncomfortable on the stage. It was obvious that they were there to raise money for the hospital and contribute towards this good cause.

The auction started with Linda, a senior year med student from Mount Sinai School of Medicine and continued on to Nora, a resident at Columbia Medical. I watched the bidding from the back of the room. I hid my face with my fedora as much as possible while I patiently waited for Emma's turn. With every new bid, the auctioneer was making an effort to raise the price a bit higher. His enthusiasm, fast and loud speech was creating friendly competition and an entertaining atmosphere.

"You cleaned up nice, Dylan!" Steve said as he walked over and stood next to me while I was glancing at Emma furtively.

I took a sip of my wine. "You don't look too bad yourself either Steve!" I said. I turned around and shook his hand, smiling broadly. "Are you going to bid?"

"Oh, yes! I promised Sydney I'd be here. I guess Amy was worried nobody would bid for her. She didn't want to be the bargain-date of the night, but she doesn't know Chris is participating in the auction."

"Who is Chris?"

"Chris Martin… I'm surprised you don't know him. He's Emma's classmate. I find his jokes annoying but the girls seem to like him. Sydney told me that he's had a big crush on Amy for a year, but he doesn't do anything about it other than give her a hard time. Now it's my turn to give him a hard time." He said grinning stealthily, cocking his brows.

When the bidding for Amy started, I stepped back and watched Steve raise the bid a thousand dollars every time Chris lifted up his paddle. When it reached ten thousand, Steve let Chris win. Amy looked relieved and there was a big smile on her face.

Whether it was planned or simply my luck, which made me additionally nervous, Emma was the last girl called onto the stage. She looked timid and hesitant when the auctioneer asked her to step out and introduce herself. She held the microphone, her hands quivering, obviously showing her nervousness and reluctance in participating. The auctioneer thanked her and started the bid at one thousand dollars.

An old man in a designer tux to my left raised his paddle immediately. "One thousand from bidder number 8," announced the auctioneer." A young, sharp but cocky looking guy at the other end of the room bid next. He looked familiar for some reason, it seemed like I'd seen him somewhere before. "Two thousand from bidder number 23," came the announcement right away.

"Who is that old fellow, number 8? That cocky looking guy over there, number 23?" I asked Steve while I let the two men run the bid up to ten thousand. I watched them closely and stayed quiet, evaluating my competition.

"I believe number 8 is Dr. Tucker from Harlem Hospital. I know Emma worked with him during her clinical rotations there. She used to tell us what a great teacher he was and how much she enjoyed assisting him. He is a nice guy, probably participating in the auction to make Emma feel more comfortable. Number 23 though, you need to watch out for him. His name is Kyle, second year resident at Columbia. He shouldn't even be here. Emma is probably furious and upset now, seeing him at the auction. Did she never talk to you about him?"

"No, she didn't. Why? "

"He is Emma's ex-fiancé. Also, he's an asshole. Let's leave it at that."

"What the fuck are you talking about? Emma was engaged to that smug guy!" I blurted out. "You need to tell me more."

"Not now, Dylan." He cut me off. "You need lift up your damn paddle, man. Come on… I can tell Emma is getting nervous because Kyle is the highest bidder!"

So was I… I had been waiting for the right moment to join the bidding and for Emma to see me, however, now that I knew her ex was one of the bidders, I was furious. Without waiting any further, I lifted my paddle up. "Twenty-thousand dollars," I said loudly.

The auctioneer who was running the bids up to now turned towards me, looking surprised. "We have twenty-thousand dollars from bidder number 15!" He announced.

I lowered my paddle slowly. Now, with my face visible, I turned to see Emma's reaction and our eyes instantly met from across the crowded ballroom. Finally, I was able to look at her without hiding my face. In her strapless red gown that wrapped her body tightly and accentuated her luscious curves, she looked incredibly beautiful. With all the noise and mumbling going on around me, I couldn't hear her. I saw her lips move and utter my name in complete bewilderment. She took a step forward with her eyes wide open, looking at me with disorientation, probably wondering what the hell I was doing there. Her lips didn't curve up into a big smile, it was more like a faint grin. I also sensed some relief in her eyes.

With my unexpected participation and the big jump in the bid, all eyes turned towards me, even Kyle's. I assumed he knew who I was and my intentions. His frenzied look told me that we were at war. He wasn't going to give up easily, and I didn't care. I was patient and determined.

"Twenty-five!" He turned towards me and narrowed his eyes as if he was sizing me up.

"Thirty!" I said, ignoring his intimidating glare. Instead, I looked at Emma and tried to tell her that I wanted to be with her more than anything, without using words.

"Forty-thousand dollars!" He drawled. He couldn't hide his frustration.

"Fifty!" I lifted my paddle up again and shrugged.

"One hundred thousand!" He yelled out frantically, daring me with his cocked eyebrow.

"What the fuck!" I mumbled to myself, only Steve could hear. "One hundred fifty!" I increased again without waiting for the auctioneer to repeat his bid. Afterwards, I turned to Steve and asked, "Who the hell is this guy? What's the deal with him? I thought he was just a doctor."

"He might be 'just a doctor', but his father is Eric Milton."

"Eric Milton? As in 'Milton Pharmaceutical'?"

"Yes that one…"

"Shit! Eric Milton is a billionaire and his two sons are…" I mumbled.

"Eric yes…but not his son. Kyle is a jerk who uses his daddy's money to get what he wants. He is playing you."

And suddenly it dawned on me how I knew him. Max mentioned the Milton brothers to me before, and how they were frequent members of the gentleman's club. They were also at that god damn Fleur-de-lis party Max forced me to attend which ruined my life.

I was about to tell Steve about Kyle when I heard him suddenly yell, "Two hundred thousand!" And the auctioneer repeated Kyle's bid.

The auditorium was dead silent. Everybody around me were whispering and waiting for my next move. I didn't have the patience. I was tired of playing into Kyle's hand. I could feel that the bidding war between us was making Emma very uncomfortable. The pressure and climate of the room was too much for her. She was taking deep breaths, playing with her fingers. She puckered her lips and drifted her eyes away from me. Feeling Sydney's, Amy's, and the entire ballroom's eyes on me, I decided to end Kyle's game. "Fuck this!" I said to Steve and shouted "One million dollars!"

The auctioneer was speechless at first. He repeated my bid, enunciating the number slowly. Kyle was exasperated. He threw down his paddle and walked towards me angrily. "One million once... one million twice ..." The auctioneer repeated excitedly one last time. "The date with Dr. Emma Collins... SOLD at one million dollars to bidder number fifteen! Mr. Dylan Hamilton!" he remarked and closed the auction. The auditorium nearly exploded with applause and cheers. Everybody in the audience was congratulating me and thanking me for my contribution while my eyes were searching for only one person: Emma.

CHAPTER 21
EMMA

I couldn't believe it when I heard his voice through the crowd. It was the same powerful tone: self-confident and asserting. At first, I thought my mind was playing a wicked game on me, but then I saw him. Tall, handsome, charismatic, looking staid and solemn in his black tux, black bow-tie and well groomed hair... His bright, blue eyes were so mesmerizing that for a second I forgot where I was and what I was doing. I found myself in a reverie where Dylan and I were alone. I was in his arms, caressing his face with the tip of my fingers, tracing his sharp features. God, I missed him so much. Kissing his sweet lips, savoring his musky scent. All the dangerous, tantalizing memories came back to me almost instantly. I was completely absorbed, enjoying my daydream when Kyle's snappish voice disrupted my digressing thoughts and brought me back to reality. Kyle, the arrogant bastard who couldn't leave me alone, looked confused, bewildered and furious.

I was the one who should have been furious, not him. I couldn't believe he had the audacity to be here, participating in the auction. I gave him a nasty stink-eye, though I couldn't stop him from bidding. I certainly had no intention of going on a date with Kyle, but I was worried he would win and I would be forced to comply. I was getting more concerned with every passing minute. Then, I heard Dylan's voice and there he was, standing right in front of me, smiling his dazzling smile. Suddenly, I felt relieved. Seeing Dylan, knowing undoubtedly that he would do anything for me, that he could outbid anyone, was comforting, but also terrifying. I just got my life on track. Whether it was heading in the right direction or not, I didn't want to think about it. I made a decision and was planning to stick with it. However, going on a date with Dylan would certainly make things go off the rails again. I was afraid that after spending a few hours with him I would lose all my willpower to stay away, and I'd change my mind.

Dylan, the one person who could turn my life upside down was just a few feet away, looking at me adoringly. His eyes were promising me everything I'd missed in the last two months. No, I couldn't let it happen. Nothing had changed and I had to be strong.

With every bid, the air in the room became more intense and stressful. My dear teacher, Professor Tucker, who was there only to support me, was pushed out of the auction quickly as Kyle and Dylan got into an aggressive bidding war. It was more like an ego-driven, conspicuously aggressive pissing contest, which I hated being a part of. I couldn't do anything other than stay calm and watch Dylan and Kyle make outrageous bids that had never been reached before. I was embarrassed and frustrated. When the auctioneer lifted his gavel and announced that Dylan had won the date for one million dollars, I didn't know what to do, say, or what to feel. Was I relieved that I didn't have to go on the date with Kyle? Or was I feeling humiliated for being a million dollar date, as if I was some object being auctioned off at Sotheby's Auction House? Or did I feel happy to spend some time with Dylan before I left the city? Maybe I felt a little bit of everything.

As if she heard my inner thoughts, "You can just wipe that sulky expression right off your face, the million dollars isn't for you, it's for the hospital." Sydney said, while I watched the crowd scatter around the ballroom now that the auction had ended.

"I know, but still, it is a ridiculous amount of money! I can't believe he did that." I grimaced.

"Dylan is just being generous for a good cause. He donates to different charities every year. This happens to be one of them. Just leave it at that Emma. Stop over-analyzing and enjoy your date." She scolded me.

I rolled my eyes and couldn't help but make a face. She was just being typical Sydney; carefree, easy going, the ultimate insouciant.

I clambered down the stairs and approached Dylan and Steve nervously, while Amy and Sydney accompanied me. I was contemplating what to say to Dylan when I saw Kyle walking towards him rampantly.

"What are you still doing here Kyle?" I asked, implying that he wasn't welcome. He ignored my comment, stood a few feet away from Dylan, glaring at him insidiously, ready to do something stupid.

"You can't buy Emma like you buy your whores for your customers." He inveighed.

"Watch your language." Dylan rebuffed. "This is a fundraiser. Nobody is buying anybody."

"Who do you think you are fooling? Everybody knows what you do with your money Dylan. You are a sick bastard, a lecherous man who uses women!"

"You don't get to talk to me like that. I know who you are Kyle Milton and all the sick things you and your brother like to do. You are quite famous according to my friend, Max Donavon. So get the hell out of here, before I tell Emma who you really are."

Kyle gazed over at me and then back to Dylan with total frustration, "Fuck you!" He blurted out. He turned his hands into fists and was about to hit Dylan when Dylan, with his quick grip, clasped Kyle's hands behind his back dexterously. "You don't want to make a scene here." He narrowed his eyes and admonished him while still keeping calm.

"You can't tell me what I will or will not do. You asshole!"

"Yes I can. I won't let you bother her anymore. Just get out of here," Dylan said calmly and pushed him towards the exit. He was still holding his hands clasped in the back, and Kyle squirmed to free himself from Dylan's strong grasp, looking totally irritated, but he couldn't.

"You two deserve each other. She's as fucked up as you are!" He spewed his anger in despair again. On any other day I would have let his insolent, vulgar remark go. Not this time. I was so enraged that abruptly, out of nowhere, I slapped his face. He certainly didn't see it coming and he just looked at me, utterly mad. He was about to speak, when Dylan shook his head and spoke calmly.

"Don't even think about it!" His eyes were throwing daggers at him. Kyle, obviously scared, finally shut up and bowed his head down. Steve and Dylan dragged him out of the ballroom and Steve stayed outside to make sure Kyle left the hotel.

Dylan returned back quickly. "I'm sorry you had to see all that. I didn't expect that."

"Why are you apologizing? He is the jerk, not you. I can't believe he had the face to be here. Kyle, he is my …" I tried to explain.

He cocked his head to side, his eyes full of affection, his lips curved into a charming smile. "Let's not talk about him anymore," he cut me off as he closed the distance between us quickly.

And now that we were finally alone, he caressed my hands first and then touched my face with his back of his fingers. "Emma!" He whispered my name which sounded like a magic word opening the doors of heaven coming out of his mouth.

He tilted my chin up. His arms wrapped around my waist, his face an inch away, I breathed in his intoxicating smell. It was so damn hard to resist him while all my body was craving for him.

"I missed you so much". He spoke very softly.

"Dylan! Please don't!"

"No. Emma. You do not get to reject me tonight. You cannot deny me this. We have to talk. Please!"

"Alright. Let's talk!" I said and pushed myself away. Around him, I felt like a little firefly attracted to bright light. It was so hard to resist him, to break away from his attraction.

"I don't want to talk to you here. I want to take you somewhere. Somewhere special where we can be alone."

"I am so tired Dylan. I don't think I can go anywhere else tonight!" I declined.

"Tomorrow morning then. I'll pick you up."

"Dylan...I ..." I muttered, trying to object again.

He pressed his index finger to my lips. "You owe me one date Dr. Emma Collins! One date!" He smiled.

I grinned and shook my head. "Yes, I do."

"So, what do you say? Tomorrow morning I will pick you up early, let's say around eight and we will have our date." Dylan asked with beseeching eyes.

"Is it possible to say no to you?"

"I guess not..." He smiled mischievously.

"Okay, then. I'll see you tomorrow morning. You need to pick me up from Sydney's apartment."

"Yes!" He nodded with a knowing smile. I'm sure Sydney had something to do with tonight and Dylan's presence. My dear friend was meddling with my life again, but this time I wasn't mad at her. I was grateful that she did.

The next morning I woke up early, got dressed and fiddled around the apartment to occupy myself to suppress my excitement. Dylan arrived right at eight in his black Maserati Quattroporte. I was surprised to see him driving his car, instead of picking me up with Jeff and the limo.

"So, where are we heading, Dylan?" I asked, without hiding my curiosity when we got into the car and started driving towards Queensboro Bridge.

"To my place... where I have been staying for the last two months." He spoke blithely and held my hand over the stick shift, gazing at me occasionally as he drove leisurely. His eyes sparkled every time he smiled. Other than talking about the weather and answering my trivial questions about work, he was unusually quiet.

At every city sign we passed, I asked him if we were there yet, but he just kept smiling and driving along.

"You are as bad as my five year old cousin, Emma!" He joked after my fifth attempt of guessing where we were going.

"It's your fault. If you'd have told me already, I wouldn't have to keep bothering you." I said, pouting.

He turned slightly towards me while holding the steering wheel with one hand and my hand with the other. "I even missed your complaints." He said, and placed a soft kiss on the back of my hand.

Quivering inwardly with his touch, I bit my lips and stayed quiet for the rest of the ride. At the end of our three-hour drive, I saw the sign for the city of Montauk and said, "This should be it because after this, it's the Atlantic Ocean."

"Yes, we are close. Just a few minutes left." He replied.

In less than five minutes, we stopped in front of a small, single story house with yellow clapboards, overlooking a long beautiful beach, stretching into the horizon.

"Here we are!" Dylan exclaimed excitedly. He parked the car on the driveway and rushed around quickly to open my door. As soon as I was out of the car, a golden retriever greeted us happily, shaking his tail, and a cute couple appeared right after.

"Welcome back Dylan! You are right on time," the young girl said. "You must be Emma! I'm Jane and this is my fiancé Aaron." She added. Then she turned to Dylan. "Everything is all set and ready for you. We even got you a new coffee pot. I can't believe you were still using that piece of junk." She explained.

"Thank you, Jane and Aaron for all your help. I owe you guys a big one!"

"Oh, it's nothing compared to all you have done for us since you moved up here." Aaron replied.

"Also, one last thing…can Copper stay with us for a little while?" asked Dylan. "We can bring him to you in an hour or so?"

"Sure. Copper will be so happy. I think he likes you more than us. Aaron is so jealous." Jane chuckled.

I looked at Jane and Aaron and then at Dylan for an explanation. Before I could ask any questions, the cute couple left.

"Come on Dylan… You've got to tell me now. Who are they? What were they doing here? What is ready?"

"This house used to belong to Aaron's grandfather who passed away two years ago. Jane is Aaron's fiancé and has a little restaurant in town. When I am too tired to cook I eat at her place. We became very good friends since I bought the house and moved to Montauk. I dog-sit Copper when they go out of town." He explained very quickly. "Now... shall we?" He took my hand and pulled me towards the open front door.

It was a cute, little, cozy house which reminded me of my grandparent's house in Rhode Island. It had such a familiar charm to it that all of sudden, I felt I was ten years old, playing tag with Steve while my mother chased us around. My eyes welled up and I couldn't help but let a tiny tear seep down my cheek.

"Emma, what's wrong?" Dylan asked worriedly.

"It's nothing... this house. It's so beautiful, so peaceful. It reminds me of my childhood days at my nana's house. I can't believe you were living here for the last two months. I never thought you would be..." I replied stutteringly.

"You thought I could never live in a house without a doorman, an elevator or expensive furniture..."

"No, I didn't mean it like that." I looked at him apologetically.

"It's okay Emma. I understand. Believe me, a lot has changed for me in the last couple of months." He said, without explaining further what he meant.

"Would you mind giving me a quick tour?"

"I'd love to... but later. Now, come with me. Food is ready!" He held my hand and walked me outside. On his wooden deck overlooking the beach, a table for two was set up; a yellow table cloth, wicker place mats, daisy pattern plates, wine glasses filled with orange juice, and a glazed Bundt cake with fresh fruits placed neatly on it.

"Dylan!" I cried completely surprised. "Oh. My. God. This is amazing. What a beautiful view..." I pointed at the table. "How did you organize all this?"

"This is courtesy of Jane and Aaron, your welcome gift. Jane is an awesome cook. She prepared us her breakfast special. Would you like to start with your crêpes?"

"Yes! I'd love to!" I uttered happily. And in the next few hours as we enjoyed the delicious food Jane had prepared, we talked about his life in Montauk, how he found the house coincidentally at his first night in Montauk and how he rebuilt the house, piece by piece.

After brunch, we took Copper out for a walk on the beach. It was such a soothing feeling to walk on the soft sandy beach, barefoot, as the warm sun caressed my body. We spent hours at the beach, watched blue horizon, walked hand in hand, and played fetch with Copper. Being with Dylan always made me feel excited and elated but this time I also felt at ease and tranquil... Something that I hadn't felt for a long time.

Neither during our brunch nor during our walk did Dylan bring up any of the unpleasant subjects lingering in the back of my mind; our breakup, his gruesome past, my plans for next year. We talked about Copper, his quiet life in Montauk, art, music, and completely avoided conversation about our future. We enjoyed a day at the beach like two lovers united after a long separation, who were happy to be back together.

"Let's go back and I'll show you all the work I've done around the house!" He said after we dropped Copper off at Jane's beach house.

"Sure. I'd love to see it." I said.

Back in the house, he proudly showed the cabinets and the hardwood floors he installed in the kitchen and the living room, and then the tiles for his bathroom. I was heading towards his bedroom, when he stopped walking and hesitated.

"You don't want me to go in there?" I asked, wondering why he didn't want me to see his room.

"No, it's not that." He said, and stood in front of the door, cocking his head to the side, folding his arms over his chest, making me more curious.

"Come on Dylan. What are you hiding in there?" I asked playfully.

He bit his lips, and squinted at me as if he was still thinking. Then he stepped aside and let me in. There, by the window overlooking the ocean, stood an easel and a tall canvas covered with a white cloth.

"Dylan! You started painting again?" I asked, utterly surprised.

He nodded shyly and smiled.

"I'd like to see it."

"It's not finished yet! I still have some final touches to do." He replied, still ambivalent to showing me his painting.

"Please show me!" I asked again, begging this time.

He removed the cloth slowly and I was completely shocked when I saw the oil painting. It was me, standing on the deck of this beach house, holding the wooden rail; my body turned towards the ocean, my face turned towards the house, looking at him, smiling. I was holding a bouquet of flowers, a jasmine branch in the middle of it.

"But how... how did you paint it? It looks so real."

"I imagined you standing there looking at me for days, maybe weeks. I painted your face out of memory but seeing you today, standing here, I realize that I didn't do your beauty justice. You are much more beautiful in person."

"Oh, Dylan! This is...the painting...it's amazing. You are amazing. I don't know what to say." I mumbled. My heart was beating as if it was about to come out of its cage. After spending a wonderful day with him, I couldn't fight with my emotions any longer. I trotted towards him quickly and wrapped my arms around his neck. My lips found his almost instantaneously. I kissed him softly and delicately, savoring every second of it, as if it was our last kiss. As our lips moved in unison with an unstoppable passion, I realized how much I missed him and how my life was so empty without him. I wanted to be with him again so desperately. My desire for him was too much and succumbing to that desire was inevitable.

As if Dylan read my mind, he lifted me up without breaking the kiss and straddled my legs around his hips. I felt his growing bulge over my skirt as I caressed his rippled abs, strong tattooed arms and his muscular chest with my palm. His breathing quickened as I explored every inch of his body hungrily. I craved for his touch for weeks and now that all the emotions that were sealed and locked inside us finally erupted, we couldn't stop the avalanche of lust.

I kissed him fiercely, explored his mouth with my tongue and he returned my kiss with equal abandon. His hands and my hands tangled, I started unbuttoning his shirt with trembling fingers. A deep sigh escaped his lips as I slipped his shirt from his shoulders, admired his chiseled body once more with my avid gaze, and brushed his naked skin with the tip of my fingers. I trailed kisses down his chest and judging by his restless body, I knew we wanted the same thing, and we wanted it right away. His eyes wide and feral with unfulfilled desire, his hands reached to the bottom of my pale pink t-shirt and with a gentle tug, he pulled it over my head. He tossed it over near his shirt lying on the ground and revealed my breasts, covered slightly with my pink lace bra.

I threw my head back, rested it on the window, giving his mouth better access as his lips trailed down to my neck and my breast while he held the small of my back with one hand and unclasped my bra with the other. Once my bra dropped right next to our clothes, he bent down and sucked one nipple first while he brushed his thumb over the other. Then he moved his mouth to the next, making me breathe hard and moan. Every time he twirled my already hardened nipples between his fingers and sucked them, a pleasure jolted through my body, my legs almost gave out.

Sensing my dizziness, he scooped me up in his arms and placed me on his bed. His hand moved to my leg, slipped under my skirt slowly, trailing soft touches along my thigh towards my already-drenched core. He pulled my skirt down and pressed his nose against me, nudging the small wisp of my lacy panties. Feeling his finger first, then his tongue inside me, I gasped soft moans, and breathy whimpers. His soft velvet tongue was relentless, flicking, circling, licking me, sucking my core into his mouth while he stroked me with one finger and then with two, in and out slowly, as I quivered in pleasure. I couldn't stifle my moans any longer, pulling his face toward me, raking my hands through his disheveled hair, I screamed his name. The pressure built up inside me where all the nerve endings in my body merged. I was at the edge of a precipice, freefalling as he took me into a wonderland of ecstasy. With the final flick of his tongue and one last stroke with his deft long fingers, I reached my climax and came down from the clouds as my body arched and then stilled.

Still panting heavily, I gazed eagerly at his bright blue eyes. I wetted my lips with the tip of my tongue and then bit them trying to suppress my hunger for him. I reached for his jeans, unbuckled his belt and unzipped his fly. I freed him of his boxers quickly. I took his long length between my fingers and I stroked him slowly. I licked it and placed a soft kiss on his pink tip, but he stopped me before I could taste more of him. "It has been a while, Emma. It will be quick. I want to be in you when I come," he whispered in my ear.

And quickly he pulled my hips to him and made me sit on his lap, as he rested his back on the wall. He entered me slowly at first, my eyes wide open, gazing into his maddening eyes. Then he moved his hips back and then plunged forward, hard and fast. I pushed against him equally, forcing him to go deeper. His salacious gaze lingered on my lips and his hands cupped my face and quickly he slipped his tongue into my mouth as we moved together in unison. I felt him deep inside me and oh god, it felt so good.

I wanted the pleasure to last longer but as the sensation built inside me, "I'm going to come," I moaned into his mouth.

"Hold on baby! I'm almost there!" He said.

"I can't. Dylan…" I whimpered as my body shivered reaching my climax.

"Oh. God." He cried. "You feel so good!" I felt his body buckle as he arched his head back and pushed in me one more time. Then he stilled. My name escaped his mouth.

He held me tightly, my face buried to his chest as his breathing slowed. He looked a bit pensive, but the tenderness in his eyes told me what he couldn't say in words.

"Would you like to watch the sunset?" He asked, after a few long, comforting and quiet minutes laying in his arms.

"Yes! I'd love to…" I replied.

"I'll grab the left-overs and a bottle of wine. Meet me on the deck in five minutes." He said, smiling. He put on his jeans and shirt quickly and disappeared into the kitchen.

I went outside a few minutes later with messed up hair and smudged makeup. I had put on one of his dress shirts instead of my white blouse. "It looks so much better on you!" He commented, as soon as he saw me standing by the door.

"I wanted something more comfortable!" I giggled.

"Come here, baby! Eat something." He uttered softly and placed one of Jane's bite-size quiches in my mouth. He then handed me a glass of wine and sipped on his. "To you… Dr. Collins! To your success!" He toasted, but his eyes were misty, something was bothering him. After such an amazing day, I felt that we were at that point, we had to talk about what was lingering in the back of our minds… us.

"I don't care about my success Dylan. I thought that the day I had my degree would be the happiest day of my life, but it wasn't."

"Why wasn't it?" He asked, his eyes were intense, demanding.

"Because of you. You weren't there with me!" I confessed, I couldn't hide my feelings any longer. I felt empty without him.

"I was there. I watched you from the back." He wrapped his arms around me and nuzzled his lips to my neck, taking deep breaths. "I saw the sad look on your face when you walked to the stage. I wanted to hold you in my arms and erase that sad look."

"Oh, Dylan… Life lost its meaning without you."

"Why didn't you call me?"

"I was scared. I was scared of your past but more so... I was scared of my feelings that I couldn't control."

"I love you Emma!" He whispered in my ear. "I love you so damn much! I can't breathe without you."

"Dylan ..." I tried to interrupt him.

"No, just listen." He said. "I prepared this long speech for you. But today was so perfect, I didn't want to ruin it. Now that finally I have the courage to speak... I forgot it. I forget everything when I am with you Emma. When you are in my arms, the world stops spinning, as if it is only you and me left standing."

"Oh, Dylan. I feel the same."

"Then don't go Emma. Don't leave me."

"It's too late Dylan. I have to go. I already signed up. I can't quit now."

"Then I'll come with you."

"It is safe there for doctors but not for civilians like you."

Then suddenly, he was on his knee, holding a black velvet box in his hand. "I don't want to go there as a civilian. I'd like to be a volunteer in the field like you, to support you, to support my wife. Of course that's if you say 'yes'. Marry me Emma. I know this is not the most romantic proposal, but you haven't given me much choice. When I learned you were leaving the country in two weeks, I couldn't wait any longer. So what do you say, Emma. Will you marry me?"

"Dylan. It's not that easy. What about your work? What about my father? He won't leave you alone. He will make your life miserable."

"I don't care what Chuck Reed thinks of me or wants to do to me. I'm not scared of him because I know that I am not that person anymore. Ever since I saw you in front of that church in Amsterdam, something inside me has changed. I don't care about the business, the profits that don't bring me happiness. I hated my life before I met you, I just couldn't admit it. Now I know. I cannot go back to that life anymore. I've already told Max that I want to sell my shares and get out of the business. I am not going back to Manhattan. I want to live here. With you! Go wherever you go. When we are together, the world becomes this wonderful place and nothing else, no one else matters. Tell me you feel the same. Tell me you love me too."

"Yes, I feel the same. Yes, I love you." I admitted, crying.

"So…will you marry me?"

"Yes, I will marry you!" I exclaimed.

Hearing my confirming words, he slid the diamond ring on my finger and lifted me up. He spun me around, laughing and screaming happily. Now that we were together, life had meaning again.

ACKNOWLEDGEMENTS

I would like to thank…

my beloved husband, who encouraged me to indulge in the fantasy of writing. Thank you for your patience and understanding,

my good friend, Rachel Clerico, for her meticulous editing and great feedback,

my good friend Tom – a first time romance book reader- for his great comments and edits,

my funny, crazy, *'bestest'* girlfriends in the world, without their support and inspiration, I could not have published this book.